June's Diner

Peter Martinuzzi

PublishAmerica
Baltimore

© 2009 by Peter Martinuzzi.
All rights reserved. No part of this book may be reproduced, stored in a retrieval system or transmitted in any form or by any means without the prior written permission of the publishers, except by a reviewer who may quote brief passages in a review to be printed in a newspaper, magazine or journal.

First printing

All characters in this book are fictitious, and any resemblance to real persons, living or dead, is coincidental.

PublishAmerica has allowed this work to remain exactly as the author intended, verbatim, without editorial input.

ISBN: 1-60836-199-3
PUBLISHED BY PUBLISHAMERICA, LLLP
www.publishamerica.com
Baltimore

Printed in the United States of America

For Janice

1

Summer Vacation

Life is too long. The diner was 12 years old when June Turner became aware of serious signs of age. She wiped the Formica counter and noticed the sheen was gone in front of each stool. "Shit," she said. "This diner's a piece of crap. I should sue the manufacturer." Years of plates, bowls, spills and scouring pads had worn a permanent scar at each station. The pattern of wear marks revealed the use of too much adhesive during construction she thought. It sure wasn't from a high volume of customers, which June openly discouraged.

By design, it was a slow summer Saturday. The new semester hadn't started at Southwestern Community College and it was between government holidays so there was no tourist traffic to chance by either. June had only recently returned from her annual summer vacation. She closed down every year after graduation. With the college kids gone, business ground to a halt and New Mexico was just too hot to hang around with nothing to do. She had the means and the desire so June chose a different exotic location every year and left town for a full month. Every year she returned as soulless and empty as she left, vowing she wouldn't bother again the next year.

Only one customer remained from the dinner service. It was Bert and it said so on the right side of his company shirt. He was a truck driver who always stopped by the diner when it was open even though it was well out of his way on the weekly route to Albuquerque. June knew why he was really there and enjoyed the company. She bent over to fill a napkin dispenser and felt his eyes on her. "Stop looking down my dress, Bert," she said. "You know Paul will be here any minute. I'll have you arrested."

"If you don't want me lookin' you shouldn't be wearin' that low cut waitress uniform," Bert said. "You own the place. Wear a turtleneck and quit with the push-up bras."

"You know these perfect breasts are all mine," June said. "Besides, if I don't wear a uniform here, it doesn't feel any different at home. Never mind the grease and dirt." A sedan pulled around the 18-wheeler in the dirt lot and skidded to a dusty stop in the spot nearest the entrance. On the driver's side door was a magnetic logo for Southwestern Community College. The block letters encircled a meaningless crest with a confused eagle clutching parchment and a quill pen in its talons. Beneath that tired symbol was the designation Campus Security. "See? I told you Paul would be here."

Paul waltzed in off-duty but still in uniform, nodded to the man at the counter, and took his usual seat at the corner booth. June hadn't seen him in over a month and she knew he was trying to play it cool. It was over a decade since his failed courting of her and he still held the torch like an adolescent puppy love crush. June walked over with his cup of coffee. It was black, caffeinated, no cream and certainly no sugar. She laid a menu down which he'd memorized years ago and waited for him to notice the new logo. "Arrest this pervert, Paul."

"She catch you staring again, Bert?" Paul said. He made a show of examining the menu as if it were the label on a bottle of fine wine. "Hey, what's with the new menu? You spend a month in France and we have to start eating quiche and escargot?"

"Relax, it's just a new cover photo. Same old crap on the inside and on the grill," said June. "And don't forget, I'm still serving up literature and philosophy on a weekly basis. Same charge, your mortal souls."

"Very funny," he said. Then to June's amusement, Paul rose from his chair and approached Bert. "You have the right to remain silent," he said and pulled out his flashlight to shine it in Bert's eyes. Bert put his wrists together and stared at the ceiling waiting to be cuffed and printed.

"You two are in a silly mood," June said.

"Yea, well, we're glad to see you," Bert said. "It's been, what? A month? How was France anyway?"

"Great!" she shouted. "You're lucky I came back at all."

"Really?" the men said together.

"No, of course not. It sucked, just as bad as the last 11 trips. One more piece of the earth I'm glad I don't live."

"Oh, come on, June," Paul said. "It can't have been that bad. Summer time in the south of France. Suave Lotharios. Topless beaches. You got any tan lines to show us?"

"Maybe later." She returned to her work behind the counter. "So. You want a burger? Fries, the usual?" she said to Paul. When he nodded she turned to the grill to prepare it and proceeded to tell them about her trip. She had decided on the south of France for a break from the relative routine of famous author's cities and nothing more. June Turner didn't go to Europe to see the old cathedrals or taste the exotic foods. She knew in the course of her stay she might do those things but she had no itinerary. It's no vacation to substitute one schedule for another. The point, both men knew was to be anywhere and do anything besides opening and closing the diner. Said another way, she was there in order to not be at home. She traveled alone because she was always alone, even amidst all the people she knew. It feels natural for her to explore on her own. There's not a single person she knows with the free time, money or interest to share her travel whims. She explained all of this background by way of introduction, the same speech she'd given the two men the previous summer. The men settled in like children waiting to hear their grandpa's old war stories. They didn't want to ask questions for fear of breaking the train of thought and June appreciated their attention.

The first impression was from the start of the trip and consisted of June Turner lying topless on a pebbly beach not knowing what time it was. She'd just had a brief and cold dip in the Mediterranean and spread out her oversized beach towel. She purposely failed to dry herself, instead, she squeezed her thick, sandy brown hair, put on her wide-brimmed straw hat, and lowered herself onto the towel. The pebbles crunched under her as she wriggled into a comfortable recline to let the sun dry and warm her. Her men friends had little trouble imagining the scene but she went on to describe it anyway. The beach was a semi-circle only a couple hundred yards in circumference with hills on all sides. Part of her started to calculate the degrees of arc, then got bored and she reminded herself she was on vacation. Besides, she had taught English, not math.

The taste of a warm croissant with real butter was still in her mouth. In one corner, by a back molar, was the tangy sting of some champagne and orange juice. Her rationalization for drinking at sunrise was that it must still be night back home. She couldn't recall what exact time that made it back in New Mexico, but after the days of flights and connections she felt she deserved a celebration drink, whatever the local time. Do they do Daylight Saving Time in Europe? Anyway, she had the beach to herself and no reason to be shy or apologize for being topless and slightly tipsy.

Lying back with her eyes closed she thought the water should be warmer in the summer. The pictures on the brochure looked positively dreamy. On the ad for the apartment were the mandatory blue, blue skies, blue water, and even a blue boat in the water. All of these were contrasted directly with the complementary orange buildings, clinging to the hillside. They helped confirm her plan. Her modus operandi was to always rent a room or house and act like a local. It forced her to really get to know a place when she vacationed. It was the Cote d'Azure after all. Her French isn't confident but she knows it translates to something to do with purple and blue slopes with vineyards. Names in America are boring and egocentric, always named for some person or tribe. She loved to say the name "Villefranche sur Mer." It was probably the reason she chose the cramped apartment over the more popular resorts up the coast. She'd feel more like a local than a tourist. For the 1000th time she wished she'd learned any other language as well as she learned English, just to teach it to her ungrateful undergrads. The foliage there was just in the way, a deep forest green, trees and shrubs she couldn't identify with her knowledge of botany limited to the Southwest juniper, cactus, and aloe with which she was raised. Skeptical as she is, June Turner was hardly one to be fooled by advertising, it's just that she thought the water should be more suitable for leisurely bathing.

Paul just nodded at her rambling monologue. Bert sipped his

coffee and picked a blank spot on the wall, above the grill and tried to imagine the scene, spread out like a movie. Both of the men stared at her behind when she turned to flip Paul's burger and dunk the fries in oil.

There was a boat cruising off the bay a mile or more from shore. Even at that distance the diesel engines made a considerable buzzing racket, probably amplified by the rocky cliffs. The noise was focused on the beach. June figured the owner would bristle at the enormous ship being called a boat. Why do they name boats after women? And why do the owners insist on referring to them in the second person as if the vessel were an easily offended sorority girl?

Determined to nap on the champagne she kept her eyes closed. There was an intriguing odor floating down the cliff. It was roughly like coffee but also smelled a bit musky, like a man she knows. It wasn't an offensive sweaty smell like men in a gym, but more the way an old afghan strikes you when you pull it down from Grandma's attic. She surmised that the water must be warmer than the land at this early hour for the wind to be moving the scent over her in that direction.

"And after that it was all downhill," June said. The men hadn't said a word. Burt stared at her rear again when she plated the burger and fries. Paul stared at her lips when she spoke and sipped her coffee. "Oh, I got around to all the landmarks, visited the museums, vineyards, tried some new foods, all that bullshit. It was good to get away, but I'm just as glad to be back."

"How old are you," Bert said. "Thirty, thirty-five?" June nodded by way of avoiding the question. "You're young, ya gotta learn to relax. Forgive me for sayin' so, Miss June, but could it be you just been thinkin' this one to death?" said Burt. She gave him a scowl. "Well, you know. Just go and be there, stop worrying about all the smells, and boats and water temperature. At least you weren't driving back and forth along I-40 the entire summer."

"Well, screw you Bert," June said. "It was my vacation, I'll tell you if it changed my life or not."

"Take it easy, June," Paul said. "I don't think he means to judge you, it's just that you seem to come back each summer from these dream vacations in a bad mood. It's a wonder you keep going on them. You get more complaints than memories. And most people would kill for that freedom."

"I'm so glad you're here to give me my psychoanalysis for free. I can save my money for more vacations," said June.

She served him his burger and fries at the booth, then returned to her work station and sat heavily back down on a stool by the stove. "I know I've got nothing to complain about. I don't have any financial worries, I can travel the world or not. But let's not get started on the meaning of life." Suddenly restless, June got up from her stool, scraped the grill clean of Paul's hamburger remains and turned off the fry oil. She refilled Burt's coffee, knowing he'd want an excuse to stay as long as possible. He could also use the caffeine for the late drive to Albuquerque. She watched Paul finish his burger in 4 large bites. She sensed the old familiar tension there as he lingered over the fries. What they had couldn't exactly be called a relationship. It amounted to a single formal date, but she knew Paul still held out hope. She'd never been so cruel to tell him to shove off.

"Don't you get lonely on a long trip like that?" Paul said looking out the window.

"You know I've been to China. That was twice as far."

Paul shifted his gaze back to June across the width of the diner. "No, I mean for a companion. You know, someone to take your picture or tell you you've got mustard on your lip."

"Yea," said Bert. "How come you always gotta go alone? Maybe what you need is a man in yer life."

"Oh, please fellas. What men I have let in my life have been complete disasters. And don't start in about some corny Electra complex. My dad and I were fine. He just died, like all good men do."

"There musta been one man that was special," Bert said.

Paul warmed to the direction this gentle line of badgering was going. He got up with the remainder of his dinner and took a seat at the counter. "Tell us, June. When are you going to settle down, get married and have a minivan load of kids?"

"I see where you're heading. Just back off, there, pal. The only man I ever felt treated me decent was my old college professor. I'm not going to call him up and ask him for a date."

"What I meant was, how about going back to teaching?" Paul said. When June frowned he went on. "Yea, I get it. Not exactly a change of scenery. Well, you've said yourself you're ready for a change, you don't want to go back to your old job, you don't want a man or kids, you've got to try something. Hell, why not just go back to Homecoming and show 'em all they didn't beat you? You were a graduate before you were a teacher."

June rolled her eyes as if to say nothing could be more useless than living in the past. Particularly, living in a past she was happy to leave. Visiting it would be torture, she could hardly imagine celebrating it. "What you need is a little misfortune," Bert said.

"Did you say 'misfortune?' You can't go around using big words like that, Bert. It ruins people's idea of what a trucker is," June said.

"Well, I can't speak for every big rig jockey, but I listen to a lot of books on tape. Nothing helps pass the highway miles better than a thick novel on 12 discs. You inspired me. I've done your Russians, your Romanticists. But you're avoiding my point. You got things a little too easy here, I think. You gotta take a risk and do something different. If you keep doin' what you've always done, you'll keep gettin' what you always got."

June let out an exasperated snort. She threw her dirty dishrag at Bert and it landed on his head, covering his eyes. He left it there while he took another sip of coffee. "You know I'm right," he said speaking through the cloth. "Don't make me double dog dare you."

June Turner let out a chuckle. "Get a load of this. I'm being schooled by a truck driving philosopher and a Romeo rent-a-cop. Yea, what the hell. It can't be worse than France," she said. "But you're wrong you know. I've already had my share of misfortune. And those people you want me to mingle with are the source." June poured herself a cup of coffee and raised it to the men. "Here's to new beginnings in old places. Cheers."

2

The Diner's Club

The kids were fighting again and June was the referee by default. It was the kind of fight where nobody really gets hurt. In fact, it was the kind of fight that one might choose to enter. Besides they weren't kids, they were adults ranging in age from 18 to 28. This group was the Diner's Club, having another spirited discussion of a topic that probably came up in someone's Literature 101 class. School was back in session, both literally and figuratively. The two women, Danny and Courtney, were arguing over which was worse, Greed or Avarice. As the only upperclassman, Paul was trying to settle the other fight before it escalated to shouting. If June was the referee, it was his unofficial role to be moderator and if necessary, get the group back on track. Josh and Will couldn't decide on whether there was some connection between the Seven Deadly Sins and the Signs of the Zodiac. Without the full lists, they were getting nowhere. June couldn't help but overhear every word. They were the only table left on a late Saturday night.

The Diner's Club always congregated in the corner booth. The five members rarely ate anything that could be called a meal. They sat there not because it's been reserved but because it's the only table in this classic diner where all of them will fit. It also has the best view of both the road out of town, the gravel parking lot and the woods beyond. Sitting in this booth allows them the practical perspective of not only seeing who's coming into the diner but who is leaving or coming to this small southwestern college town. It also allows the luxury of letting one imagine what lies in the woods. It's a good place to stare when a member of the club is wrestling with a particularly knotty subject. June serves the coffee and soft drinks.

What better topic for a warm Saturday night than the Seven Deadly Sins? The members were bogged down on the exact contents of the list. As June poured out the refreshment she also dispensed knowledge. It was a Diner's Club motif that Paul would enlist the retired teacher to assist in the matter of disagreements. She was sometimes the tiebreaker when members could not or would not agree to disagree. With respect out of proportion when addressing a career waitress, Paul begged across the room. "Excuse us, June. What are the Seven Deadly Sins?"

She looked up from a stain on the counter and gave a theatrical sigh. "What have you lame brains got so far?"

Josh, a freshman read the list off the back of a napkin. "We've got six: Anger, Avarice, Envy, Gluttony, Greed, and Wrath."

"I'll give you two points for managing to list what you've got in alphabetical order, but you need some serious help. First off, you've only got 4. Avarice and Greed are the same thing, also listed sometimes as covetousness. I'll bet you all a donut Will came up with that pairing. Wrath and Anger are the same, too. You'll have to expand your vocabulary, Will, or you'll never get off the farm."

Paul took credit for the redundancy and June, being a woman of her word, brought over a variety plate full of donuts. Paul was the oldest of the group and since he'd been there from the beginning, the Diner's Club's unofficial master of ceremonies. He also knew June the best and wasn't shy about asking for help in these otherwise awkward situations. "Just give us the list and we can get on with our sophomoric discussion of which is worst, thank you very much," Paul said, stuffing a homemade glazed into his mouth.

June was having a flashback to her teaching days and knew she shouldn't spoon-feed the apes. Otherwise they'd never come up with an original idea. "Look, I'll give you Lust. How could you overlook Lust? Your perverted little bodies are riddled with it. And Pride, which by the way is the worst, since it makes all of the other sins possible." The group let out a groan. She ignored their protest, knowing they'd still have plenty to discuss. "The seventh you'll have to come up with on your own but I'll give you a clue: You're all guilty of it."

She knew this accusation was not true for all of the Club members but she enjoyed playing with their heads. Accusing them, even falsely, would make them examine their own lives and prolong the delightful agony of coming up with the last sin on the list.

June figured Paul would be the one most likely to come up with it. He was an adult learner and the oldest by 10 years. Entering college as a freshman in one's late twenties isn't something done lightly, but by choice. It's a conscious effort of will. Had he started straight from high school he would not have been such a good student. She knew he was also paying his own way and wanted to get every penny out of his tuition costs. Working as a rent-a-cop for the school also showed him the underbelly of academia and had given him a perspective few other students have regarding the value of an education. It was also where he first saw June back in her former life as an associate professor. He'd been in love with her since their first meeting. Paul got up to freshen his coffee and June met him half way with the pot. She filled it without making eye contact and turned around to resume her place behind the counter knowing Paul would follow her every step. "Hey, thanks a lot," he said with all the casual sarcasm he could muster. "Your generosity is only exceeded by your good looks." When he returned to the table, Will politely stood to let Paul have the inside seat.

"Okay, that's six," Will said. "Anger, Envy, Gluttony, Greed, Lust, and Pride. C'mon guys, this is worse than the Seven Dwarves."

Will was 19 and the picture of a stocky farm boy. June knew from overheard conversations that he was the first of his family to ever attend college and was determined to lead a life away from farming and all things agricultural. He did well in high school but had neither the interest nor the means to attend anywhere other than the local college. Any degree for him would be a step in the right direction, away from the smell of cows at four in the morning. His work ethic was so firmly ingrained that attending college was like a vacation. He almost felt guilty for feeling clean since he started the semester. June knew she'd judged him unfairly by assuming he'd committed any of the Seven Deadly Sins. He was an eager member of the Diner's Club but neither well-read nor aggressive with his few opinions.

"Wait a minute," Josh said. "How is Gluttony different from Greed?" Courtney lifted a french fry to Josh's mouth and pushed it in when he opened out of reflex.

"Gluttony is all about food, honey," she said. "I think Greed is the unhealthy desire for material things."

"That also separates it from Lust," Danny said, "which is too much sexual desire."

"They're all three about desire," Will said. "Maybe we could lump them all together. Unhealthy or excessive desire for food, material goods or sex, all really boil down to unhealthy urges."

"Okay, so we've got Desire, Anger, Envy and Pride. That was easy," Danny said. "Revising two thousand years of theology can be fun!"

Danny is actually Danielle. She's 18 and won't tell anyone a thing about herself, including the fact that her real name is Danielle. June sees a bit of herself in Danny and understands the need for discretion. She knows Danny's not attempting to be mysterious or elusive. Danny just has no clue who she is yet, something June struggles with to this day. Danny is also painfully aware of this fact. She didn't fit in with any of the cliques in high school and has decided she'll try just about anything to get some meaning. She knew her first step towards self-discovery would be to get out of the house. She wears unflattering clothing from the bargain racks for two reasons. The first reason is, like June, she's rather attractive but knows she doesn't want to be accepted based on her looks. Second, the low cost clothing makes her life easier. She can get from snooze alarm to class in 8 minutes. Will has yet to notice her. Paul is glad she's not a sorority girl and that she never misses a Saturday meeting of the Club. June sees more than a little of herself in Danny but mostly appreciates that she actually dines at the diner and tips a respectable 15%.

Of all the Diner's Club members, June has the most trouble identifying in any way with Josh and Courtney, who are dating and have been since the beginning of time. They went to the same high school and planned to attend a prestigious university together. Unfortunately, Josh is a tad thick. While Courtney was accepted early in the application season, he never had a chance. Out of love, or the teen equivalent, she lowered her sights and agreed to attend the community college to be with her man. She doesn't see this as a waste of her prodigious mental talent, since all libraries have access to the same books. She could probably get a degree through the mail and be perfectly happy in life. She could work or not, she just wants to be with Josh. For Courtney life has been easy, not because she comes from a life of privilege but rather because she knows herself. At twice Courtney's age, June knows she can't begin to approach that level of self-awareness.

Josh is in line to take over the lucrative family furniture business and will only extend himself as far as needed to graduate. To June, his casual affluence is maddening. Aside from the Diner, for which she paid a price higher than gold, she's scraped for every penny her entire life. She knows he only agrees to come to Diner's Club meetings with Courtney because it's the closest thing to an actual date he's likely to get in this small town. Fraternities are for pompous losers and the parties only remind him of the dreaded time he's spent at his parents' country club gatherings. For Josh life has been easy, mostly because he comes from a life of privilege but also because he doesn't ask anything of himself. His life and career path have been predetermined by station and he really doesn't mind since he knows it can be a life of leisure.

"Sloth!" Paul said. The table had been silent since June brought the last round of coffee, sodas, and a sandwich for Danny. Paul raised the napkin from in front of Josh and read, "Anger, Envy, Gluttony, Greed, Lust, Pride and Sloth. Now do we all agree with June that Pride is the worst one or what?"

3

Paul's New Job

Paul Romero floundered after high school. His passion for learning didn't come until much later after a chance encounter with a certain associate professor. College was out of the question, and only partly due to a complete lack of funds. He couldn't fathom answering the question, "What's your major?" In high school he was proud to be voted, Most Likely to Live With His Parents, and fulfilled the prophecy. Better in his opinion to take a temporary job he hated than to start down a career path he loathed, stuck for life. Besides, after his high school years flipping burgers, he landed a cushy job at Southwestern Community College. True, it wasn't quite as glamorous as "County Sheriff," but "Rent-a-Cop" rolls off the tongue as pleasantly as "Toledo."

He'd been on the job about a month. Part of his responsibility was to tour each and every building on the quadrangle each and every shift. He was starting to learn the faculty names by testing all the door handles on all the offices. Should one be ajar, he'd call in and report it before securing the room. This diligence would generate an e-mail to the lax party in firm but gentle tones to secure their belongings from theft in the future. Never mind that the doors into the buildings are locked on a timer with weekends, holidays and leap years all taken into account.

Paul started with the administration building, the smallest on the quad. On the second floor he noted the meeting room had already been restored to its original pristine condition. Something had gone wrong with the buffet table at the faculty meeting a week before. The rumors seemed so fantastic, he couldn't entirely believe them. The popular version was that one of the teachers had been cut badly. Cleaning crews stayed late that night, working the fruit punch, chocolate cake, and blood out of the carpet. Satisfied that all was back to normal, he exited the back door and continued on his nightly rounds. "Officer 203 to Base," he said into his walkie-talkie. "Building 3 secure."

A cursory lap around the exterior of the English building revealed only two cars in the parking lot at the late hour of 10pm. This detail was not unusual on a weeknight. But it was Friday and he was sure one of the cars was the classic convertible of the Dean whom he knew does not teach in any discipline, let alone the English department. The other car he recognized as one of the new professor's but he hadn't yet matched the names to the vehicles.

What caught his attention on entering the building for his ground floor walk-through was the distant, rhythmic sound of squeaking furniture matched by soft exhalations of breath. Someone was having sex on the first floor of the English building.

New at his job, Paul was determined to do a thorough search of the premises. He started at the same end he always does. First was Roger Steadman's door, the Chief of the English Department. Secure. The next and the next, were all locked tightly. Coming to the end of the hallway where the new teachers were sequestered he saw a door ajar, and a narrow 4 inch shaft of light piercing the otherwise dark hallway. He caught himself holding his breath as the squeaking and breathing increased in both speed and intensity.

Paul stood across the hallway in the shadows to peek in and make sure this act was consensual. The first thing he could see was a porcelain breast jutting up from a blouse which appeared torn open rather than casually removed. The lacy bra was still fastened but pulled aside at the ample cup. Inching forward and leaning ever so slightly, he could see the lady's hand. There was a fresh, inch-long wound near her thumb held closed with bright, blue stitches. Still in the ripped sleeve of the blouse, she was holding the edge of the desk for stability rather than making any move at resistance. Fortunately, her face was looking away. Paul decided he'd interrupted a pair of lovers working out some stress and eased back to leave. That's when June happened to turn her head away from her lover to the open door. They made eye contact and she reached over with her free hand to cover her bare breast. The significance of this coy gesture was not lost on Paul considering the fact that she was a first year teacher having sex on her own office desk. Her eyes narrowed giving Paul the clear indication that this was to be their secret. A slight nod let him know she was in complete control and should the discovery of this event be made public there would be a scandal. Paul put the rest together himself. He nodded in reply, raised a hand in understanding and backed away into the shadows of the hallway. Upon exiting the building, he made sure to secure the door with his thumb on the latch to keep it from making any noise.

"Building 4 secure," he reported to Base on his way to Building 5.

4

Bedtime Story

Roger Steadman was trying to get his daughter Emma to sleep. He'd already helped her find her favorite night shirt. She'd had her snack, brushed her sandy brown hair and was tucked in mummy style. The goodnight kiss on the forehead was not enough. Now she wanted a story. One of Roger's stories. At age twelve he thinks she's too old for this sort of thing. Plus, he isn't particularly proud of the stories he's written and not just because none have ever been published. The stories are a mix of sophomoric science fiction, nihilistic rambling about life, and trite little ditties based on juvenile puns. His best writing was technical critical analysis of the classics and it secured him a comfortable place in the department of English at the college. He was long ago salaried, tenured and darn it all, a success by any definition of the word. Why his wife would leave just because he hadn't yet written the next Great American Novel was beyond even his formidable analytical powers. His daughter's insistence that he tell bedtimes stories underlines these two facts. One, his wife is gone since she used to do the bedtime chores. Two, he's a marginal success in his chosen profession, a critic who can't write well himself.

Still, he loves his adopted daughter as his own and can't help but spoil her. Certainly his ex-wife was no longer taxing his considerable capacity for love and affection. "Please, please, pleeeeease tell me one of your stories."

Emma is a pretty typical preteen. As she grows older she needs less and less sleep, but also lacks the ability to keep herself entertained. Growing up the only child in the house of a divorced college professor may be somewhat stagnant, but it's all she's ever known. She's not so intelligent to be described as precocious and if pressed would have to admit she doesn't understand the underlying themes of her father's stories. She just likes his voice and the way he smells, sort of like coffee and a bit musky, although she doesn't know what that word means.

"Alright, but let's make it one of the short ones, huh?" said Roger. "I have midterm papers to grade and another long day tomorrow."

"Let's do the one about the flood," said Emma.

"Didn't I just say one of the short ones?" This exchange was part of the game. Emma knew each story got longer and more detailed with each telling. Her not so subtle stalling technique was not missed by Roger. "Okay, okay, the one about the flood. Once upon a time there was a community on stilts, living fifty feet above a flat and dry plain," Roger said. He knew the interruptions were coming and he took them in stride and usually in the same order.

"How long ago was it?" Emma said.

"It doesn't matter. Could have been last year, 100 years ago or 100 years from now, or a thousand. The point is, they're an isolated people, in a small colony and they live on stilts, like a tree house for adults but without the tree. It's a fairy tale, okay? Go with it."

"Okay, but where is it? Utah?" Emma played her role to perfection at this juncture, knowing the answer. Roger acknowledged her contribution and pressed on.

Vertigo

 The Commune was on a distant planet in a faraway, undiscovered solar system. Utah is a good place to imagine but take out the mountains and iron down the eastern plains to a uniform sandy brown. Looking from any of the protective railings surrounding the elevated city the view was the same. Standing on the balcony of the Ruling Counsel, one might imagine the ground sloped a few degrees from left to right. The two suns crossed the sky in that direction and what breeze there was during the dry season hummed in that direction as well. Most importantly, the Flood came from the left. The elders say it's always been that way and they learned it from their elders. The young ones will teach this simple fact to theirs.

 Hanging from every possible point on the city are enormous hooks, baskets and nets specifically designed to catch what the Flood will give. In this way the community has lived and flourished after a fashion, believing they are the only ones on their world. With the water comes building materials for whatever repairs might be needed to keep the city safe and viable. Food is harvested in the form of floating vegetation and swimming animals of seemingly infinite variety. It seems every Flood brings a bounty requiring only a minimal amount of effort on the part of the inhabitants of this world.

 There are mishaps from time to time and the Counsel has been elected in a feeble attempt to right what wrongs they may, prepare for and avert unseen dangers, and console any unfortunate victims. At least having a body of relative experts on the Flood makes the rest of the inhabitants feel as though they have some control over their lives and even some meaning. A lucky or good fisher might receive accolades for his haul and the benefit of higher social standing being able to share his excess.

Deaths of natural causes are dealt with between cycles of the Flood. The reasons for this are a matter of pure pragmatism. The ground can only be turned when the water has softened the soil and passed. Also, the Counsel are too busy with their own harvests during Flood times to arrange a proper burial ceremony. Only once has a body been lost to the Flood. Any rumors of foul play were quickly dismissed by one and all as preposterous. In such a happy world the thought of harming another was never known. Equally unlikely was the possibility of suicide, for everyone here enjoyed the fruits of his own labor during both dry season and wet. Any unhappiness was as unthinkable as the notion of intentional harm amongst brothers and sisters.

A single dissenter was known by one and all, a vigorous man by the name of Rufus. As the only red-haired man of his generation he was physically different for sure, and stood a full head in height above the other men. His actions were as bewildering as his physical attributes. He never chose a life partner, let alone had offspring. As long as anyone could remember he'd been stock piling dry goods with each Flood. By conservative estimate he had collected enough to last through 10 seasons or more, should the Flood ever fail. Yet it never had. As long as any elder could ever recall, the Flood had always come and it always delivered more than could be harvested. Even those who had skipped the harvest for two or three cycles for various reasons, had always been able to recover with relative ease. Broken hooks, torn nets, or just simple bad luck, had never been enough to cause the demise of a single blood line. Indeed, charity amongst bloodlines was rare. More often gifts were given but were not needed.

More mystifying than his miserly lifestyle, Rufus had built himself a vessel. At first those living on his downstream side of the community merely thought he'd run out of space for storage. But then they saw him testing its buoyancy and refining its design. He'd placed more or less cargo, fore or aft, let the vessel float away downstream tethered by a thin line, then hauled it in for more experiments.

After one flood, curiosity got the better of a few neighbors and they approached Rufus to solve the mystery. "An admirable harvest as always, Rufus. Need any help putting it up?"

"No, thank you," said Rufus. He spoke plainly with no animosity and continued his work without looking.

"Mind if we ask what you're building?"

"No," said Rufus. "I don't mind you asking. It's a vessel to carry me and my supplies." He continued to load the boat with steady determination.

"Carry you to where?"

"I don't know, that's why I have to go," he said.

The on-lookers were astonished. "But you have all you need right here. We're happy to share our food, clothing, and shelter. There are women who would like your company."

Rufus remained unmoved. "The one thing I can't get here are answers. I need to know if we are alone on this world."

"But you may be injured or worse. No one has ever come back from the Flood waters. Aren't you frightened?"

Rufus looked up from his work to address the crowd directly. "I know my fate if I stay here. Out there is the unknown, the one thing we all lack. I must seek the answer no matter the risk. In either case you have to admit, the result will be astonishing. If there are other people, think of the possibilities. If we are alone, think what that means."

With the next coming of the Flood and a complete absence of fanfare or explanation, Rufus lowered his vessel and himself and drifted off downstream. Speculation abounded as to his true motives for such a peculiar action. The insecure took offense. They inferred he meant to suggest they were too scared, stupid or complacent to do such a glorious thing for themselves. Those who felt a small sense of kinship or had wonder in their lives about what might be over the horizon admired his adventurous spirit. They understood his life was likely in the balance. The rest just wrote him off as insane, and therefore his actions made no reflection on their lives whatsoever.

A few people lingered on the safety railing to watch him drift away. The vessel with its cargo covered a considerable area and from the height of the tower was visible for hours as the only thing on the horizon. Some children waved but if Rufus saw them he didn't respond, he only stared straight ahead as his vessel rotated slowly in the current.

Thankfully, there was the harvest to attend. When the tide fell, there was something to occupy both hand and mind. They left his corner room untouched, partly out of respect, partly not knowing whether he'd return, but mostly because the space was now excess. There had never been a vacancy that wasn't immediately filled by family and friends.

Rufus had prepared so well for his journey he realized he had nothing to do. In fact, he may have prepared too well for he now realized he'd made a gross miscalculation. While on the city all of his hard work was done solely to leave. He took what he thought he would need as a man alone, taking from the Flood all he could carry. Now he realized he not only had all he needed for the foreseeable future, but the same riches of the Flood for which he'd waited so patiently time and time again were a single arm's length away. A hook, a net, and some rope, and he could have left the city years ago when the vessel was first constructed.

He made his slow drift, rotating in relation to the city, sometimes to the right, at other times to the left. After a time he slept. When he awoke the city was much smaller but still visible as a small mushroom on the flat horizon. In all other directions was water, broken only by the rare floating plants or ripples he recognized as the movements of fish.

When the city was no longer in view, Rufus lost his sense of speed, but also his sense of rotation. With no acceleration to feel his direction, his vessel became an island, as still on the Flood as the city had been for him on its vast plain. He ate his fill when hungry and restocked the boat to keep himself busy. Still he floated, the Flood providing all he needed when supplies ran low.

By the number of times he ate and slept, Rufus surmised that he'd been utterly alone for over 300 days. He had no way of knowing but he was in fact, nearly correct. It was at this time that he saw something on the water he'd not seen before and prepared to throw his hook and retrieve it. As he watched it, the object moved slowly over the course of a day to his right, then again to his left. For a long time the two drifted together, then Rufus realized it was not the object moving, but rather his vessel was slowly revolving again. The sense of any fixed point was immediately nauseating to him and he spent the next two days emptying the contents of his stomach and sleeping.

When he awoke the object was closer, much larger and appeared to be floating on top of the Flood rather than in it. Then he had a sickening feeling worse than any nausea. In less than two days he realized, he would be floating past the city he'd left so long ago.

It was a matter as simple as breathing in and out to throw a hook through his old net, halt the motion of his vessel and climb back to his old room. No one disturbed him as he cut away his vessel and let it drift with its cargo for another lap. No one bothered him as he retreated to his room and lay down. Speculation was more ferocious than ever since he gave no audience to his people. The insecure felt vindicated having not bothered to take such a silly risk only to end up back home. The admiring were all the more curious to see what he'd seen and go where he'd been, and know they could likely return safe as well. The rest just wrote him off as insane, therefore his actions made no reflection on their lives whatsoever.

Rufus was left undisturbed through the remainder of the Flood, with most assuming he had plenty to tide himself over. It wasn't until preparations for the following Flood that his room was entered. The invading party wished to offer encouragement or help, whichever was needed to set his nets and hooks. Inside were Rufus' partly mummified remains, his red hair looking as lively as it ever did in life. He had taken to his bed after the previous Flood and allowed himself to die.

The Counsel decision was to allow the release of Rufus back to his vessel. The Commune's usual protocol of burial during the dry season seemed somehow inappropriate. With the next Flood it was a simple enough matter to draw in his pyre, still laden with it's cargo from the previous cycle. Rufus was placed in it and set adrift forever to cycle the planet, never resting in his search, never returning to the city.

5

Homecoming

Never one to shrink from a dare, June attended the annual alumni gathering. Her expectation was that it would be a complete and total bore. She'd be able to report to Paul that she'd not only made the effort, but that she'd been right. As an activity with the potential to shake up her life, visiting the past wasn't the answer.

Her choice of outfit was a simple, white cotton, peasant skirt and blouse she'd picked up in France. She regarded herself in the mirror from the front and sides and determined it was dressy enough for the occasion, but wouldn't make her look like she was trying too hard to impress. Plus, it would help her stay cool on her walk and throughout the length of the tedious event. June took special pains to make sure the day felt different from the countless days she dressed up for her classes as an assistant professor. She always tried to pick the perfect outfit, nothing too risque, serious but feminine, and she knew she failed in the end. Even on days when she struck the proper balance of academic and approachable, she'd end up late due to some unusual circumstance. She left her house on foot a full hour early for the 15 minute walk. She roamed the neighborhood in order to approach from a different route than the one she took during her brief and useless stint as a teacher.

There was no sense in driving the few blocks from her house to the campus. She knew there wouldn't be any parking anyway.

In her own mind, June was certainly not there as a faculty member, especially given the way she was encouraged to resign her post. One could even argue she had no reason to be there as an alumnus, but she'd never been officially banned from campus. It was more like an amicable divorce. Plus, she had the degree. As Homecoming gatherings went, she recalled it was invariably a letdown. She'd gone in years past as both a student and once as a faculty member and recalled only a tedious haze of ennui. It was always well-attended but in the end, just plain dull. The reason wasn't so much that there weren't plenty of alumni out there from this small college, it was more the fact that the young college had little history in the first place. Not to mention the painfully obvious fact that it never had a football team. That glaring omission from the weekend festivities made the Dean's speech the highlight of the celebration.

There were plenty of groups to reminisce on an annual basis. While no single year's worth of attending alumni would ever fill a dinner table, the accumulated mass of say, the Glee Club or the Astronomy Club made a fine audience for the Dean. They all met in the center of the quadrangle. Besides the Dean's mansion's absurd expanse of Kentucky Bluegrass, it was the only space of green for miles around. A tent was erected every year since the solitary scrub oak on the quad cast only enough shade for an overheated Security Guard. A small buffet of finger foods was provided by the trustees, but it was unmemorable by design. The annual giant bowl of fruit punch was an inside joke as was the inclusion of pineapple wedges. Nothing could be more out of place in New Mexico in October than pineapple, but there it was year after year. Those who didn't know the reason for its appearance began to accept it as much as the heat. Maybe it was a favorite of the Dean's. Thankfully, there was nothing too heavy to carry in one hand and certainly nothing with sauce that could spot a dress or suit coat.

June arrived at the time she knew there would be enough people milling about that she wouldn't stand out. But she was kidding herself. June doesn't mingle well and her choice of dress, while conservative in cut always draws attention. Despite the heat most attendees were wearing navy and black. Her choice of white, while practical, set her apart. Not to mention the perfect distraction of her formidable figure. June waltzed up from the far end of the quadrangle by the lone oak tree and gave Paul a courteous nod. Her point was made. The rest of the congregation appeared to be attending a funeral. They all wore navy and black as a nod to the formality of the occasion but were completely out of sync with the southwestern weather, architecture and time day. June was a desert flower by contrast.

June saw some old acquaintances by the buffet, and decided to make for the shade, get a drink to occupy her hands and pretend she remembered them. She recognized some of the faculty but none of the alumni. There was only one person she felt would be worth her time, her old professor and mentor, Roger Steadman. They'd been as close as colleagues could have been during her brief stint as a teacher. She remembered his dislike for these events and figured he would make a good ally to heckle the Dean. It was unlike Roger to be late and he certainly wouldn't miss the Dean's speech for fear there might be retribution.

Sure enough, with time to spare Roger arrived with his daughter hand in hand, walking from the far side of the quadrangle. She noticed he'd already removed his sport jacket in what for him was a significant act of defiance. He probably thought it would allow him stand out in the crowd and his ex-wife would then know he was more bold than she ever learned. Besides, it was a warm if unhurried walk, and he had good reason to take off his coat. June knew Roger and his demons well enough to supply his inner dialogue. It was not a cool Boston Homecoming. Oh, you don't have to remind me of that fact, his ex-wife would scream in his head. There should be towering old growth maples and oaks, leaves turning colors, a football game to cheer. But no, he's perfectly happy as a second-rate teacher at an unknown school. Roger's outward appearance gave no indication these were the thoughts on his mind, but it amused June to recall the messy divorce. The way he blossomed into such a wonderful single father was sweet enough revenge upon his nasty ex-wife Sharon, who didn't know what she was really missing. Yes, Roger appeared supremely content holding the cool small hand of his daughter. Emma couldn't have looked more carefree the way she skipped more than walked and her single ponytail bobbed in a circle.

Seeing Roger and his daughter, June decided there were too many ironies at play for her not to approach. Although June was unaware, this year was the first occasion Emma had ever attended dressed as a little lady. In her pristine white dress, Emma looked like a true princess among commoners. Emma stood out as the only underage person in attendance. June stood out because she always does.

Emma headed straight for the buffet while Roger got sidetracked with a colleague who insisted on talking shop. He let her go, knowing every other professor and attendee knew who she was and Emma would be safe. He'd arrived on time to hear the noon address by his boss and wondered how late it would be this year. If he were the type to gamble he'd start a pool with the lowest odds being 25 minutes late.

At 12:22pm a shiny convertible pulled up onto the lawn directly behind the tent where a podium and small amplifier had been staged. At his wife's insistence, Charles "please, call me Chuck" had arrived fashionably late in order to make a more significant entrance. She waited for him to exit his door with a flourish and attend to her door in front of the crowd. He waved to only one member of the crowd but failed to make eye contact on his way to the microphone. ~~Susan~~ [Sharon] made for the side of the tent where she could remain aloof from the others, a significant presence, yet remain in orbit around the center of this small universe, her husband, the Dean.

Needing no introduction, he launched directly into the same speech he gave every year as a formality. Sharon was more impressed with his performance than anyone, even Charles himself. She spied her ex-husband Roger and shot him a look that said in one glance his failure to wear his coat reinforced the obvious fact that she was right to leave him 12 years ago. Roger couldn't help but feel the old sting all over again.

Charles started with the usual banter, a comment on the weather, a joke about the imaginary football team, then went on to thank the alumni, benefactors, sponsors, his Almighty God, and his tireless wife for putting up with him. ~~Susan~~ [Sharon] blushed on cue with her chin dropped to show she'd been listening.

"Welcome, one and all," Charles said. From there on Roger's brain was a blank. He was sure the Dean hadn't noticed him let alone his bold suitcoat doffing. Thankfully, for everyone in attendance, the drone of a low-flying crop duster began growing and much of the remainder of the speech was lost.

All the adults but one had ignored Emma since the Dean started his annual address. Only June saw the trouble Emma was having balancing her limp plate of hors d'oeuvres on one arm while trying to save her tipping fruit punch. The plate got the worst of it and Emma managed to avoid spoiling her dress. Nonetheless the waste of food and fear of criticism from a yard full of adults caused her to begin a silent pout. June sidled over seeing her chance to make a connection. She dropped into a crouch and silently helped Emma clean the mess, hiding it under the skirt of the table. The pouting ceased without a word and the next thing June said brought out a big playful smile from Emma.

Roger forgot about his ex-wife and the Dean. From his place at the left side of the crowd he was able to see the entire interaction take place between June and Emma. As a man he could hardly have missed June's dress any longer, particularly the way it clung to her hips when she crouched to talk to his daughter. While the rest of the audience looked from the Dean to the airplane and back again, this woman had tended to his daughter. She managed the task not in a strictly clinical way, but her disposal of the mess had a certain efficiency. Even Sharon was capable of disposal. But it was the next gesture, one of genuine tenderness that his ex-wife could never have managed. June made Emma smile, then took her by the hand to walk out from the shade of the tent and looked for the plane. They ended up on Roger's side but with their backs to him, eyes raised to the crop duster.

The plane made two tighter circles around the quadrangle, this time at lower altitude and so close one could make out the grinning face of the young pilot. To say the trailing sign was easily legible was an understatement. In large block letters it read, "I ♥ you June." After the final circle the plane came frighteningly low, directly over the tent and podium. It came so low the crowd instinctively ducked as it passed. All except June and Emma, that is, who stood holding hands in their nearly matching dresses and Roger who stared not at the plane, but at these two women. With the crowd bent to avoid the noise and wind, Roger had the image they were bowing to a queen and her princess.

June had to admit, at 30 minutes into the proceedings, she was wrong about Homecoming. It may not have been a revelation, but it wasn't a bore.

6

Crop Dusting

On a sweltering Saturday in October, Marvin was doing laps around the college quadrangle in the crop duster. He was trailing a sign that said "I ♥ you June." He didn't know who June was but that didn't matter. Will said a friend of his did know June and would pay him $100 to make 3 laps around the quad during Homecoming ceremonies. The friend had the connections to fix any fines the underage flyer might incur.

Marvin is a modern Renaissance man. He doesn't think of himself in that way. He didn't set out to be one or to impress people with his skills. The things he's learned have come to him easily. He likes being skilled as an end in itself and views his competence to be both necessary and enjoyable. Marvin can fix anything on the farm and he has. He can safely pilot every motorized vehicle including the crop duster. Marvin is fourteen and Will's younger brother.

He likes farming and the idea of making an independent living directly off the land. He's as smart as Will and does most of his recreational reading over the slower winter months of the school year. Summer days are so busy he's usually too tired to read. The school year presents an easier set of demands and barely keeps his interest. Marvin once read about a boy almost his age who sailed around the world by himself. He'd never seen a body of water larger than a reservoir, let alone an ocean. Still, he likens farming to the idea of traveling around the world using only the wind. Marvin aspires to the notion of never going to a supermarket.

On his 3rd pass he looked down onto the crowd and was surprised to see every face turned up to him. The faces all blended into a single sea of flesh tones perched on navy and black. Only two women stood out for their white dresses. Really it was one woman and a girl he thought he new from school. He decided to make an extra pass to get a closer look. He was fourteen after all.

The way they were dressed he figured they must be mother and daughter. They looked similar not only because of the dresses but because they had the same brown hair, and the same confident pose when he flew a mere fifty feet above their heads. Other guests of the party ducked instinctively while they both stood tall. He flattered himself by thinking they wished they were with him rather than stuck on the ground at a stuffy college fund-raiser or whatever it was.

Marvin tipped a wing to his patron after the fourth pass. At the opposite end of the quad from the woman and girl, a security guard was standing casually with his arms folded, leaning against the only tree for miles around. The young pilot decided the 4th pass would be free. No extra charge. He dipped his other wing and sailed over the horizon of low buildings and was gone.

7

Comfortable Cruelty

Those in attendance at Homecoming had to admit it was the most memorable in years. Even though the trailing message was confusing, it was a nice touch by the Dean. Shouldn't it have read something like, "Welcome Alumni" or "Southwestern Community College Homecoming"?

Not one to miss a beat, the Dean said something about the future of education, then mouthed some words to make like the microphone had cut off, and walked from the podium to the shade of the tent and the gracious arms of his wife Sharon. There was a smattering of applause, 1/3 of the crowd dispersed immediately and the rest continued to mingle, delighted that the speech was cut short.

June and Emma turned around when the plane was out of sight and found themselves face to face with Roger. "Thanks for the message," said June.

"Huh?" was all he could reply. His eyes were following the plane and his mind was replaying the scene with June and Emma at the buffet.

"Yea, dad, that was cool " Emma said, still holding June's hand.

"Yes, it was Emma. Now can you think of a word that would be more descriptive?"

"Um, let's say it was interesting."

Roger frowned, then saw she was playing with him. "Yes, it was interesting, but I liked 'cool' better. Now you're just stalling."

"Okay, let's see. It was unprecedented and memorable." Roger nodded his approval.

"Always teaching, huh Professor Steadman?" June said.

"Yes, Ms. Turner, as a matter of fact, it's about the only thing I think I do very well. So, what brings you here? Besides Homecoming, of course. I mean, it's been what, 12 years?" He shifted his coat from his left arm to his right and immediately regretted his lack of skill at small talk. After just instructing his daughter he'd come back with the most obvious question of the day.

"I'm here to stamp out disease and pestilence. If the opportunity should arise, I'll be fighting for Truth, Beauty, and the American Way."

Roger chuckled and said, "You practiced that little speech, didn't you?"

"Guilty."

"Well, I must say, you're as good as Emma at avoiding a direct question. What's the real reason? I mean…" and he stopped. Roger realized he was starting to sound defensive and accusatory all at once.

"I'm here on a dare, if you must know. See, I was complaining about my summer vacation to one of my regulars at the Diner. He said I needed to shake things up, whatever that means, or quit whining. Coming back to the College is about the last thing I wanted to do, so he dared me to come to Homecoming. You know I don't do small talk. Present company excluded of course, I don't even know anyone here, and worse, there's the Dean and his wife."

The crowd continued to thin out as Chuck and Sharon mingled and shook hands, making the obligatory rounds. It was mostly regulars, people the Dean counted on for financial support more than friendship. None of the conversations went beyond the predictable topics of weather, sports, and health.

Roger considered the likelihood of her answer and continued to stare at June, holding his daughter's hand. Her reply was so mundane it must be true. "And that explains the message on the airplane?" he said.

"I'm not sure about that one. I still can't figure out what they were advertising. That pilot looked a little young, he must have been lost. I mean, everyone loves the month of June, but what? Homemade pies? I don't get it," June said.

Emma couldn't restrain herself. "It said 'I love YOU June.' That must mean a lady."

"I agree with Emma," Roger said. "Who else but the fella at your diner would have known you'd be here?"

"I was kidding," June said. "You guys have no sense of humor. I was being obtuse. There's a good word for you, Emma. Of course, I figured it out. That poor guy's been holding the blowtorch for me since before I left school. He knows I think of him as a friend, almost a brother, but he won't give up. Not that I mind, I mean, it's flattering and all and he's a nice guy, but it's nothing romantic. What about you, Roger?"

"It's just me and Emma, since, you know," Roger said. "I'm okay with it. I keep busy."

"Well, maybe you should start dating me," June said.

"Yea," Emma said. "June's really nice, daddy."

"Slow down, Emma. June was just kidding again, we hardly know each other. Besides, I'm old enough…"

"What? To be my older brother?" June said. "You're only a few years older than me. I was a freshman in your Lit 101 class and that was your first or second year, right?" Roger conceded the point with a nod. "So, that makes you only 7 or 8 years older than me, hardly a generation. Being married to that..." June stopped herself, not knowing how much Emma knew. She also didn't want to curse in front of the 12-year old. "Marriage just made you prematurely grey. Sad people always seem older." June knew her attempts to compliment Roger were falling short and she looked away at the ground.

"Anyway, our age difference is not the point. Brace yourselves. Here comes my boss and his wife, the Queen."

Roger knew he had to stay and make nice with the Dean or he'd hear about it later in ways not so subtle. The afternoon Faculty Tea would be less formal and he could probably avoid Chuck and Sharon in that setting. On the quad, it was tradition to accept the gracious handshake of his Lord and Majesty, Charles the Dean. Why he tried to extend his East Coast sensibility out here, Roger had never divined. It was clear to everyone but Charles, his obscenely rich family, and his pushy wife Sharon, that Southwestern Community College was never going to compete with the Ivy League.

Chuck and Sharon gave a nearby couple their uncomfortable, stiff goodbye handshakes and sidled over to Roger. "Hey, Steadman. Nice of you to show up," Chuck said, dripping sarcasm. The rude display of power was unnecessary but Chuck couldn't resist kicking a downed man. "Where's that mid-term report on the English department? I was supposed to get it Friday."

"Talk to your assistant. I gave it to him after my 1:00 class. He said you were out golfing," Roger said.

"Yea, well, I was," said the Dean.

"Charles, you remember June Turner. She's here for Homecoming. You know my daughter Emma," Roger said. June made a point of not shaking Chuck's hand, as she was still holding Emma's. "And Sharon, you remember June, don't you? She taught in my department for a year and then made a career change, way back when."

They exchanged awkward pleasantries, nodded like boxers before a match and Sharon went to work. "Yes. I thought I recognized you, but you've put on some weight. You'll pay for that airplane stunt, too. Don't think I won't find out who's responsible for ruining the Dean's speech. Maybe the two of you should stop by the buffet table together. Have some punch and pineapple."

"My apologies, of course, but you must know I have no idea what that was all about," June said. She set her face in a pleasant smile and braced herself for the mental beating. "It's my first year back since I retired and noone knew I was coming."

"Isn't it a bit pretentious to say 'retired' after a one year stint? Call it was it is." When June failed to react, Sharon went for the kill. "Admit it, you were rightly fired for incompetence. And what's with the dresses, you two? You look like you're about to stamp out a vat of grapes." June and Emma looked at each other and both failed to suppress a giggle. Emma thought it sounded like fun to make some wine like in the old days. June was entertained. The day was turning out more worthwhile with every minute. She couldn't imagine how someone could be so blatantly rude. It had to be insecurity or some other major character flaw.

Sharon went red with anger at their giggling, but held her composure. Who were they to so openly defy her, the wife of the Dean?

And to thumb their noses at the serious nature of the occasion was more than she could abide. "Aren't you a little old to be holding the hand of an adult?" was the best she could throw at Emma.

Emma was visibly hurt and brought her free hand over to June's for support. "To answer your question, not that it deserves one, the dress is from France," June said, mustering her best calm and rational tone.

"I didn't know they sold crap on the Champs Elysee," Sharon said.

"I said France, not Paris. Truth be told, it's from the coast. I got it for a story at a farmer's market."

"You mean you got it for a song." Sharon's expression added the word "idiot" even though the 3 syllables never passed her lips.

"No, a story. I shopped there most days for groceries, bread, wine, you know, like a local. Anyway, there was a lady there selling handmade dresses and we got to talking. She spoke English better than I spoke French. I told her I thought she was undercharging. It wasn't about the money of course, I was just trying to compliment her. Well, she said she'd take a story instead."

"Was it something you made up or did it have to be true?" Roger said. The idea was fascinating to him as a teacher, a reader, and a writer.

"I can't tell you," June said.

"Why not? That's the most retarded thing I've ever heard," Sharon said. "Did she put some sort of evil gypsy curse on you?"

"No, of course not. We made a deal," June said. "I got the dress, she got the story. You see, it wasn't just that I had to tell her the story, I had to give it to her. I remember it, but to tell anyone else would be to go back on my word. I'd have to give back the dress and I like the dress. Plus, it's fun, like sharing a secret with a friend, even if I never see her again. You know about secrets, right Chuck?"

The Dean was barely paying attention, and she'd caught him daydreaming, just like the teacher she used to be. "Um, yea, whatever you say," he said.

"Well, I think it's fascinating," Roger said. "I want to meet this lady. She must have collected dozens of great stories over the years. That is, if you're not the first person to trade her for a dress."

"Sure you'd like to meet her. Maybe she'd sell you one and you could pass it off as your own," Sharon said.

"Is it tiring to be so persistently cruel, Sharon?" Roger said. "You used to be fun to be around." Since their divorce, she seemed to abuse him at every possible opportunity, just to prove to herself and to anyone within earshot that he wasn't worth marrying in the first place. He was a spectacular failure as a father, a teacher and a writer. "Now that you've succeeded at insulting all 3 of us in the space of 5 minutes, can you move on to your next project? Maybe there's a stray puppy you could give a good kick."

"As usual, you're as spineless as you are worthless. Come on, Chuck. We'll leave the pathetic little peasants to their whining," Sharon said. She steered him away to the next group with a dismissive wave of her hand and a harsh cackle at her pun on the word wine. "And be sure to grab some pineapple."

June and Roger could only stare in disgust as the Dean and his wife walked away. Shaking her head in disbelief, June offered, "Any chance I could talk you into skipping the Faculty Tea? You're right about earlier, by the way, I was joking about dating. But I could always use a friend and I'm afraid Emma may never let go of my hand. Come help me open the diner for lunch. I'll pay you in food." Before even waiting for his answer, June grabbed Roger's free hand and dragged him off the quadrangle. They walked 3 abreast with June in the middle, more comfortable than she could have imagined herself feeling when the day started. Emma skipped and Roger's stomach did back-flips.

8

A Tale of Two Classrooms

June lasted one week before she found herself in Roger's office in tears. It was her first real job out of graduate school and she had high expectations. "The apes didn't even have the books I'd assigned. I'd expected a few of them wouldn't be prepared, but this is ridiculous," she complained to Roger. She envisioned her classes as riveting and memorable, not just educational.

She was seated in Roger's overstuffed armchair, the one usually reserved for students. It was most often occupied by those flunking out of one English course or another. Rarely, it was a junior pre-med student begging to change majors so he could take more of Roger's higher level courses.

"What did you expect? They're only 18 years old, June. You can't expect them to love the Classics as much as we do. Face it, they're fresh out of high school and more interested in where the free beer can be found this weekend." Roger was relaxed behind his modest desk which faced the door. His office was unusually clean for a college professor, not just because it was the start of the semester. One wall was filled floor to ceiling with his favorite books, many first editions, the rare one signed if the author were still alive. A single filing cabinet contained all lesson plans and tests in four drawers. The opposite wall carried only a picture of his bride Sharon, wearing her wedding dress and the last smile he could remember her having. Behind his swivel chair was a view across the quad and up the green hill to the Dean's mansion. From this chair the shortcomings of his life were documented as neatly as his filing cabinet.

"How do you do it? I'm exhausted after one week trying to get them to open their eyes. You've been doing it for years."

"I don't know. Believe me, I've had my rough semesters. There were times when I begged for just one student who'd exhibit some convincing level of feigned interest. Then, there are students like yourself. I remember not too long ago a certain undergrad who loved to read and think. It's the rare student who can take the lessons to be had from a 100-year old novel, combine it with her love of history and economics and then apply it to a career in international law. So tell me what happened this week, I'll tell you what happened in my class and we'll leave the analysis for later."

June started the school year by making sure all the students in her Introduction to Literature 101 class had her summer reading list. When they signed up during orientation week they were given her curriculum, a list of local bookstores, and their first dreaded assignment: Tolstoy. She'd done her Masters on the Russians and figured since it was her personal strength in knowledge, it would likely make for a good introduction for her students. Plus, no one could likely challenge her expertise. She packed her briefcase for class a week early. It included the class roster accompanied by their senior pictures, a lesson plan, and a well-thumbed and highlighted copy of *War and Peace*.

The night before her first class she agonized over the details. She went to bed earlier than usual to ensure a good night's rest. It was only after the first half hour awake that she found herself staring at the ceiling and realizing the sun wouldn't be setting for another hour. To occupy her mind she reviewed the lesson plan for the umpteenth time. Sure, she had an idea of what books she wanted to cover and what she wanted the students to take from each one. Beyond that skeleton curriculum she was lost. How does one actually start? Never in her student teaching was she required to address a class from day one. The teachers had set the curriculum and she needed only to follow the plan. As a substitute, the job was even easier: maintain decent order until the teacher was back. Do I introduce myself? No, they know what class they signed up for. But it seems kind of rude to just enter the room and start barking out lessons. Do I sit at my desk or stand? How much should I write on the chalkboard? Should I ask the students to lead the discussion or just lecture? June made the mistake of looking at her bedside clock. It was worse than passing too many road signs on a long car trip. Every half hour only reminded her how much sleep she was missing. If I don't fall to sleep soon, she thought…

As a result of her worry, June failed to get a good night's rest. She slept through her alarm. Fortunately she didn't have to worry about her choice of outfit. Months prior she'd found a sensible outfit on sale and purchased it for the occasion. It was a navy blue business suit with a knee-length hemline and more importantly, a loose fitting coat to camouflage her bust. A clean and freshly pressed blouse and sensible pumps completed the effect. June was the picture of the academic. She didn't want the women in her class to be intimidated nor the men to be distracted. In the interest of time, she skipped her usual morning shower, just splashed water on her face and tied her hair in a bun.

JUNE'S DINER

When she stepped out of her apartment the air hit her like opening an oven door. At 8:30am it was already approaching 90 degrees. June began to sweat before she even reached her car. The campus was too far to walk but not a long enough drive to cool herself with the air conditioning. Sweat was dripping from her neck and down the front of her white blouse before she was half way to the English building. She rolled down her window thinking it might help but the wind merely undid half of the hair in her otherwise tightly wound bun.

She parked her car and noted the time. It was 8:47. Breathe. She could still make it to the bathroom and freshen up before class. If only she hadn't forgotten her briefcase. With her hand on the door of the building for a full 30 seconds, June contemplated the options. Was it worse to be late or show up unprepared? Either way she realized it was no way to begin one's career in academia. She opted for the drive and the relative safety of her lesson plan.

June removed her blazer for the ride, unrolled all the windows and raced through a few stop lights. Her blouse was drenched through with sweat and stuck miserably to her back. At the apartment she ran up the two flights of stairs and threw open the door. There was her briefcase on the kitchen counter where she'd packed it a week ago, next to her cold cup of coffee. She dumped the coffee in the sink, replaced it with a fresh cup from the pot and bounced back down the stairs.

Back on the road to campus the clock told her she was only 10 minutes late. Things were going well until she had to swerve to avoid a woman in curlers outside the beauty parlor. The woman had crossed the street to get a newspaper and failed to look either way before casually walking right into traffic. June swerved violently with one hand and with the other emptied the contents of her coffee cup onto her right breast.

At the English building she ran in the back door and straight to the bathroom to survey the damage. The pain from the burn was nearly as bad as the pain of embarrassment she suffered upon seeing the dark brown stain spread slowly as she tried lamely to dab it with cold water. Not able to spare any time standing under the air-powered hand dryer she replaced her blazer and saw the stain was mostly covered. Down the hallway she could hear the din of her class chattering, no doubt wondering where their teacher was. A look at her watch showed 9:22. Outside the classroom she took one deep breath and pushed the door open into the noise. And realized she'd left her briefcase in the bathroom.

In horror, she walked directly to the chalkboard and wrote the words, "Miss June" and under it, "Intro to Lit 101." Somewhere in her broken sleep she must have realized it would be silly for these students to call her by her last name. Yet "Miss June" sounded like she'd won a beauty contest or was about to address a group of second graders. She rubbed it out with the palm of her hand but couldn't think of anything better to write. Too late to change it, and too nervous to improvise a better solution, she rewrote the same words. She turned to face the classroom and repeated the words, "I'm Miss June, your teacher for Intro to Lit 101."

The ensuing stillness was as painful for the students as it was for June. Without her briefcase she didn't know what to do with her hands and held them clasped awkwardly over her crotch. Only later did she realize the smeared chalk had made a bulls-eye of her privates. She tried a joke and instantly regretted it, "If you thought this was Underwater Basketweaving, you're in the wrong room."

Silence.

The class was now more on edge than if she'd said nothing at all. It got worse from there. "Alright, take out your *War and Peace* and let's get to work."

More silence.

In a vain attempt to act casually, June sat uncomfortably on the corner of her desk and pleaded, "Did ANYone bring in their copy?" As the words left her mouth she remembered her own edition was still tucked neatly in its briefcase, five doorways down the hall in the bathroom, next to a pile of sodden, coffee-stained paper towels. "Excuse me."

June literally ran out of the classroom and 6 doors down the hall. Realizing she'd overshot her mark, she tried to stop, twisted her ankle and snapped the heel on her right pump clean off. She retrieved the heel, her briefcase, and limped back to the classroom. Without a word of explanation, she walked back to her desk and slammed down the case. She tried stupidly to open it with one hand, one clasp at a time, until she realized she was still holding the broken heel. She threw the pump heel into an empty metal wastepaper basket with a loud clang. The students jumped in unison. When she finally opened her briefcase, the brand new spring loaded lid popped open with a loud snap, sending droplets of coffee onto the first 3 rows of students. They ducked too late and were splattered from the waist up. "Does anyone know who Tolstoy was?"

This time the silence was accompanied by gaping mouths.

June turned to the board but not before the class witnessed her exasperated expression, one part frustration, two parts disappointment. She tried to salvage something of the last ten minutes of class by writing some basic facts about her favorite author on the blackboard. Standing as she was with one broken heel, her right calf muscle twitched in a particularly attractive way. There was no chance any of the men in the class knew what she was writing. Unable to stretch comfortably to the top of the board, June unwittingly removed her blazer and placed it on the back of her chair. The sweat rolling down her back rendered the blouse transparent and revealed the full width of her lacy bra. Turning to face the class and explain her motive she began, "Count Leo Nikolayevich Tolstoy was born in 1828 and died in 1910…"

All eyes were on June's right breast. The coffee stain, mixed with water and perspiration, had now spread from her collarbone to her waistline. Moreover it was clammy and cold in the air conditioned English building. Not only was the front of her blouse as transparent as the back, the lacy bra showed off her erect nipple to stunning effect. Nobody breathed. All eyes were riveted on June's breast. Prayers were answered.

June looked down at her own breast. She looked up at the class but nobody's eyes were there to meet hers. So she decided to look again at the object that held their attention so tightly. She saw the bulls-eye of chalk on her skirt and it barely registered. I've got lovely breasts, she thought. They're right to stare. No one can argue that my first class wasn't memorable, that I didn't have their full, undivided attention.

She chuckled to herself, looked up and smiled in defeat. June tucked one strand of unruly hair behind her ear, and walked behind her desk again. She picked up her navy blazer and made a point of not putting it back on. At the door she turned to address the class one final time. "I trust you'll all be here tomorrow to resume our discussion?"

With that she walked defiantly to her own office and brewed a fresh pot of coffee.

The rest of the first week was a blur of exceeding frustration. Not only had they not read the work as she instructed so clearly in her summer reading list, many of them didn't even own the book. Some of the students had read it in high school and attempted to skate on their memory of it from last year. She quickly ferreted out the poseurs with a few well-placed, incisive questions. As a result even those few students began to revolt and her hopes of worthwhile dialogue quickly faded to impersonal lectures. On Friday she broke down her facade with a stream of rhetorical questions. "What does it take to wake you guys up?" "Are you the least bit interested in my class?" "Is it me, or is it just the material you find boring?"

From the back of the room came a single tentative hand. "Yes?" said June a little too harshly.

"We're not English majors."

"What? Who said that?"

"I said, we're not English majors. Most of us are pre-med, some are in business and pre-law and I'm pretty sure the girl by the door with the paint on her pants is an art major. We're just here for the basic credits. I personally spend 12 hours a week in chemistry lab, I can't read a 1,424 page book in my spare time. Comprendo?"

Now it was June's turn to be silent. It never occurred to her that a book as important as *War and Peace* would fail to force its way into her students. "But don't you…what if…it's not about…" she tried to start and held herself. She knew any arguments to the value of reading such a tome would fail to convince these future doctors, lawyers and artists. She gave in, defeated. "Forget the Tolstoy. It's just my life's work to this point. On Monday, if you care to show up, I'll have a new lesson plan. Nothing over 200 pages, I promise. Maybe a comic book." And she stomped out in tears and into Roger's office to pout.

"That's a great idea." Roger was trying to be helpful.

"What?" June stopped crying long enough to be confused. Reliving the entire week in one sitting had left her drained and unable to breathe, let alone think. She couldn't imagine going back to the classroom ever, let alone with a whole new lesson plan and only two days to prepare.

"The comic book idea. They're not all about men from space with super powers. There are whole series of adaptations of the classics. Not only can you probably find a 50-page distillation of your beloved *War and Peace,* some of the contemporary stuff is worthwhile literature on it's own merits."

"Oh please, Roger, I have a Masters Degree in the Russians. I can almost read it well enough in the native language. You expect me to stoop to giving my students comics?"

The way she scolded him reminded Roger for a brief moment of his increasingly annoyed wife Sharon. "All I'm saying is you asked for my advice. If you want to try something new at least give 'em something they can digest in a single sitting. You've read Solzhenitsyn?" June nodded. "Well if you insist on wowing them with the Russians have them read *One Day In The Life Of Ivan Denisovich.* Compared to a Stalinist work camp, your classroom should seem like a walk in the park."

"Very funny, Roger. So how come the Department Chief has to teach Intro to Lit 101 like he's fresh out of grad school?"

"Oh, I don't mind it so much. You learn to reach the back of the classroom. Don't forget, it's called Introduction to Literature, not The Complete Written Word. If they take a piece of my class with them to medical school or law school, I like to think they'll be better at whatever they choose to do in life. Once in awhile, I make a convert out of the more open-minded and in that one success, I can forget about the rest."

"I'll take that as a compliment."

"You should June, you were always one of my favorite students. Now I hope you'll be one of my favorite colleagues."

"But you lied to me."

"Huh?"

"Yea, you said you'd tell me what happened in your class and leave the analysis for later. Well, I've heard the analysis."

"Oh, yeah. Right."

Roger's week started the same way it had every Monday since he was married to Sharon. He was up an hour earlier than he needed to be in order to drop his wife off for her weekly salon appointment. When asked why she couldn't drive herself or even just walk, Sharon retorted angrily, "You expect me to walk all that way and ruin my toenails, just because you're too lazy to drive me there and pick me up at lunch? Besides, it would ruin my massage to drive in this traffic, not to mention the effect on my color and facial."

Hearing this bit of private news June realized just how close she'd come to ending Roger's weekly obligation by making him a widower. A hit and run would have saved her new blouse and likely her first day as a teacher.

Because of her early appointment, Roger found himself at class a full hour ahead of schedule. He dressed casually not out of a plan, but because it was still ghastly hot and he preferred not to sweat on the way to work, then shiver in the air-conditioned building. With the extra time he reviewed his roster and tried to put names and faces together. With practice he had a way of remembering names that served him well.

Fifteen minutes prior to class Roger positioned himself outside his classroom door with a mug of coffee and greeted the students by name as they entered. The effect was that of meeting the Captain prior to a luxurious cruise to a tropical paradise. "Good morning Mr. Brown. Please, sit anywhere. Hello, Ms. Capshaw, how are you today? Mr. Green is it? Glad you could make it."

When the last of the class had settled, Roger pulled his chair from behind the desk, positioned it so he could see everyone and welcomed them again. "Hi. I'm Roger. You may call me Roger, or whatever you like. Over the years I've been called Prof, teach, and hey you. If I don't answer at first, call me something else. My office is down the hall. It's got my name on it. My home number is in the book but if my wife picks up you'd better try to order a pizza and claim you got the wrong number. If you'd like to be called anything but your first name, now's the time to let me know. I've heard it all. There was once a bright fellow in here who insisted I call him Critter and he never explained why." There were polite chuckles while Roger sipped his coffee and everyone was awake and at ease.

"This is Intro to Lit 101. If you're supposed to be in Economics or Chemistry or Biology, just stay where you are, they won't miss you and you might learn something. Did anyone bring their curriculum with them? What are we reading first?"

This last statement had the desired effect of scaring the pants off the entire class. "I'm just kidding, I didn't publish one. But, since there's no point wasting your parent's tuition money, we're going to jump right in today. Please take out your copies of Charles Dickens *A Tale of Two Cities.*" This time Roger got the chuckles he wanted. "Oh, sorry, forgot to tell you to buy that one and bring it in. Fortunately, I've got all you need right here." From his back pocket Roger produced 25 copies of the first page of the novel and proceeded to distribute them. He then began to read: "*It was the best of times, it was the worst of times*...Isn't that a great beginning? I wish I wrote that." More laughter from the class. "Does anyone want to continue for me?" Hands went up all over. "Mr. Brown, you were first in today, please proceed."

"*...it was the age of wisdom, it was the age of foolishness, it was the epoch of belief, it was the epoch of incredulity, it was the season of Light, it was the season of Darkness, it was the spring of hope, it was the winter of despair, we had everything before us, we had nothing before us...*"

When Bruce was done reading, the class looked anxiously to Roger for guidance. He just looked back at all of them with his eyebrows raised nodding his head, as if they'd all just shared a particularly ribald joke. "I'm out of coffee." Laughter. "Go ahead and read that paragraph again to yourselves. Those who've already skipped ahead to paragraph 3 know that Dickens is writing about the year 1775. Some pretty important stuff happened back then. Think about why and how it could be that it was both the best of times and the worst and I'll be right back." With that, Roger exited the silent classroom to freshen up his favorite mug.

When he returned, Roger entered quietly so as to not disturb the spirited discussion of Dickens first paragraph-long sentence and took his seat. The students argued gently back and forth for the remainder of the hour while Roger sipped is coffee. At the end of the hour, Roger rose, announced, "I'll see you all tomorrow," and the discussion continued out in the hallway.

Later in the week, with no further reading assignments, the class needed only gentle nudging from Roger. They talked about metaphors, similes, foreshadowing, symbolism, and a few of the students even bought the book and read ahead so as to argue back to the first page with more force. When Roger announced after two weeks they'd be moving on to the first 3 words of Melville's *Moby Dick,* there were groans all around the classroom. He reminded the students the class was called "Introduction" and all they had to do to succeed was to develop an appetite for more. Of course, if they wanted to read more on their own time, well that was their prerogative.

9

Bedtime Ritual

It was bed time again. Emma had this notion that she wanted to be a pilot and she was asking for a "flying story." Roger knew it was because of the plane that buzzed the quad on Homecoming weekend. He'd never flown in such a plane and had no intention. The closest he'd come in real life was a ride in a friend's convertible way back in college, for gosh sakes. But that's what writers do, they make stuff up. You don't have to get pregnant and have a baby to write about having a baby. And if Sharon thought he was going to buy a silly convertible just to impress the Dean, well he could think of ten different things on which it would be better to spend that kind of money. Besides, what's wrong with the reliable station wagon he drives? That old car outlasted the marriage by 12 years.

"Daddy, are you going to tell me a story or what? You're staring," said Emma.

"No, I wasn't, I was thinking of a story about a pilot," he lied. "Only this one is a different kind of pilot."

"Ooh, tell me about him."

Nausea

    Ross is a pilot. But he doesn't fly a plane or drive a car or a boat or a train. He flies a pod attached to the end of an enormous arm, like the biggest cotton candy machine you've ever seen. He flies for the government and he holds a position of respect if not admiration. Plus, it's not a bad-paying job. Most people don't want to be pilots because of the risks involved but he considers them minimal.

    Every workday for Ross is the same. He packs his lunch in his government issued lunch box. It's sturdy, made of some kind of metal, with a handle that's indestructible. He never wonders why he was given a lunch box. He just follows the protocol. Take the food from the food slot by the living unit door and put it in the lunch box. All of his food is prepackaged in efficient foil wrapping. The food is dry. So why a lunch box? One of the first rules of piloting is "No liquids allowed in the pod." With nothing to spill it's hardly necessary to have a watertight lunch box. But then, all employees of the government have one, so what's the use in questioning?

    He takes the mobile sidewalk to work. When his building glides near he hops off with his lunch box and the momentum carries him into the revolving front door. Having an important job he enters the first bank of elevators marked "Pilots" which carries him to his floor. He's sure it must be one of the higher ones, though they're all designated with letters. The only number on the panel was #23. No one ever goes to that floor.

    When he steps off there's only one passenger getting on, the pilot from the previous shift. They recognize each other but have never spoken. A mutually respectful head nod is sufficient. With only 5 minutes to pause the pod for shift changes, there's no time for idle chat. The exchange is the same when Ross' shift ends.

The pod waits near the elevator door. It's egg-shaped with a single seat and is attached to a mechanical arm by a ball and socket joint. The arm is 60 feet long and anchored to its axle at the center of the circular room. The pod rocks slightly when Ross gets in with his lunch box. He straps the harness around his chest and attaches it to the lap belt. He slides the door closed and places his lunch box on the floor between his legs. There's a shallow, square depression molded between the footrests for just this purpose.

When he's ready, Ross pushes the button marked "Launch" and the pod begins to move. Takeoff is his favorite part of flying. He never grows tired of the punch of force which hits him as the pod gets up to speed. The acceleration centers just behind his harness in the center of his chest. Unlike some other pilots about which he's heard rumors, Ross has never lost his lunch. For him the intense nausea feels more like falling in love. Not that he's ever been in love, but he's heard about it and gets to simulate it every day for a living.

As the pod accelerates it swings out from the force and circles the room horizontally. If Ross had a window he'd see the axle directly overhead, the floor to one side and the ceiling to the other. Instead he concentrates on the panel in front of him which he knows is the real purpose of being a pilot. At random intervals lights on the left side will blink, requiring him to push buttons on the right side. He imagines this function causes wonderful things to happen in some other room of the great government building or better yet, prevents some serious mishap from occurring.

When the lights pause, he knows it's time for lunch. Without lifting the lunch box or leaning forward, he reaches to the floor, opens the lid and takes out his lunch. A typical meal tastes something like beef with a sugary coating. It's crunchy on the outside with a chewy center. It's not entirely unpleasant and quenches his hunger for the remainder of the flight. In fact, he often jokes to himself that chewing lunch is usually the most difficult part of his day. He seldom has an appetite due to the wonderful nausea of acceleration. And he knows to vomit would break the cardinal rule of pilots, "No liquids allowed in the pod."

The landing comes automatically at end of the shift and is always a surprise to Ross. He can't feel the pod swinging back to vertical but the feeling of deceleration takes much longer than the initial thrill of takeoff. He exits with a smug feeling and lightly grins to himself that he must be one of the best. He's never vomited. With a nod to his replacement he's down the elevator, out the revolving door, onto the conveyor and back to his living unit.

One fine day things began to change for Ross. Upon exiting the elevator he was met not with a courteous nod of mutual respect but a playful, "Hi there. I'm Rebekah, what's your name?" He was too stunned to answer. He'd heard there were some female pilots but he'd never met one. And pilot or not, he'd never met a woman so attractive.

It was all Ross could do to step backwards to the pod while he stared at her with his mouth open. He tripped and fell into the cockpit still staring as she entered the elevator. He'd never seen a jumpsuit so nicely curved at the backside. On entering the elevator she turned and caught his eyes staring at her rear end. Ross was sprawled awkwardly half hanging out of the pod and she giggled at him, blushing with her chin to her chest. Ross was staring so intently at her that a ghost image remained in his vision when the elevator doors closed. Her long red hair, deep green eyes, full red lips and voluptuous figure were burned into his memory. Her sweet scent still lingered in the pod.

Ross' stomach churned in a way it never had. The acceleration of takeoff was more cruel than usual. He skipped lunch knowing the results would be disastrous. His mind raced with questions he'd never contemplated. The panel of lights became a blur and he was certain he'd missed many of the important signals. Upon reaching his living unit after work he was only partly relieved to find no notice from the government that he'd been fired.

The next day was worse and better at the same time. When the elevator doors parted, Rebekah was standing with her lovely head bowed, coyly cradling the handle of her lunch box. Ross managed to both introduce himself this time and stay on his feet. He murmured some lame apology for not talking the previous day. "Oh, that's okay. I still think you're cute. That's why I transferred to this pod." And she kissed him lightly on the cheek, backed into the elevator with a wink and was gone.

The entire flight was a blur. Ross couldn't remember the takeoff, a single signal light, or even whether he ate his lunch or not. When he exited the pod his lunch box was sitting by the elevator door where he'd dropped it in shock after the kiss. He was sure when he got back to his living unit there would be a note requesting his resignation for having failed so miserably in his duties. It would detail in horrible misery his failure as a pilot and the disasters his inattention had caused. He'd likely be given some position in food service, or worse, the finance department. That is, if he weren't sent to exile for his crimes against humanity. He would never see Rebekah again.

Back at his living unit, Ross experienced a shock more significant than the one he was dreading the most. Nothing happened. Nothing at all. His accounts were all intact. The dinner arrived in the usual manner. The lights came on, the water flowed and he sat up all night thinking about the meaning of his life. What did it mean to be an attentive pilot who never vomited? For years he'd never missed a signal light. Then he missed two flights' worth and nothing seemed to have happened. Did he over-estimate his own importance as a pilot? Was Rebekah some sort of test from the government? He vowed to return to his job with renewed vigor, perhaps even volunteer for additional missions if needed.

For the next few weeks he returned to work as usual. When he passed Rebekah at the elevator he gave a respectful nod as if she were any other pilot. She continued her playful "Hey Ross" greetings without any acknowledgment that he was acting differently.

One month after meeting Rebekah, Ross broke his vow to be more attentive. Upon exiting the elevator he was surprised to be greeted with the customary nod, rather than her usual cheerful greeting. He stepped mechanically into the pod, strapped himself in and looked up at the control panel to push the launch button. Taped over the panel was a nearly life-sized portrait of Rebekah, nude from the waist up. Beneath it she'd written a note in perfumed ink: "You need to stop taking yourself so seriously. Go to floor #23."

Emboldened by her provocative portrait and the fact that seemingly nothing could get him fired, he unsnapped the harness. He took down Rebekah's picture, folded it twice and gently slid it into his jumpsuit, next to his heart. He stepped out of the pod for what he guessed might be the last time. Half way to the elevator door, he felt strange. He looked back to the pod where his lunch box sat in it's holder. He walked back and leaned in to pick it up. Feeling mischievous, he pushed the launch button and slid the door closed as the pod took off for an unmanned flight.

At the elevator he paused to watch the pod. He'd never seen one fly before. The speed was tremendous and with every pass a cool, stiff breeze pressed him back to the wall. Around and around it went until he became dizzy trying to follow it's flight. At full speed it was just a white blur and silent but for the wind.

A different kind of nausea hit Ross as he stepped onto the elevator. His life had been so ordered for so long, he'd never before felt the fear of the unknown. He took a deep breath and felt and heard Rebekah's portrait crinkle lightly against his bare chest. He pressed #23.

Rather than up or down, the elevator seemed to travel sideways. Ross had to brace himself to keep from stumbling. The ride was longer than any he'd taken but just as quiet. He could hear only his own heartbeat.

At location #23, the doors parted as they always do. His first impression was of an industrial noise so loud it pressed him back into the elevator and forced him to cover his ears. Rather than seeing the familiar cramped, circular room with pod and mechanical arm, Ross was greeted by the vision of a vast chamber. It was many stories high and humming with activity. At the center of the enormous room was a tremendous revolving shaft which went up through the ceiling. On the shaft was a grinding wheel as large as the entire room where he used to fly his pod. From all directions grain of various kinds was being delivered through large chutes. The grain was ground to a fine powder by the wheel and carried along a conveyor belt to another large machine. He traced the path of the grain from chute to wheel to processing machine and finally to the finished product. His lunch.

At the far end of the warehouse dry food was coming out in neat foil packages, the same ones he'd been eating on the job for years. Then it hit Ross. The meaning of his life. Pack the lunch, fly the pod, eat the lunch, turn the wheel, grind the grain, make the lunch, and so on. A fresh wave of nausea overtook him and he barely had time to open his lunch box and vomit neatly into it. The vomiting continued until his eyes were swollen with tears. On his knees he continued to dry heave until he passed out.

When he awoke Ross sat back and watched the spinning grain mill wondering what to do next. He finally gathered up enough energy to rise to his feet. He picked up his soiled lunch box, closed the lid and clutched it to his chest. Feeling the picture of Rebekah crinkle again only brought on a more deep misery. Somehow he managed to get back to the elevator and shuffle himself back to his living unit.

Ross slept for two days. He ate poorly for two weeks and realized again that nothing seemed to have changed. The food still came, the water ran, the lights worked. His melancholy deepened. He had hung Rebekah's portrait in a prominent position so that it could be seen from anywhere in the living unit. Then, he realized he didn't even need to look at it. He'd long since memorized her smile, the slightly irregular smirk, the firm curve of her shoulder and every other detail of her porcelain flesh.

Finally, out of sheer boredom he decided it was time to go back to work. One day he had read the caption written in her rounded hand and decided it was time he followed the first advice she gave and not take himself so seriously. He always did like that first acceleration after all, and decided he missed it. So what if he only drove a pod which turned a wheel and made the food he ate.

Ross got into his jump suit and proudly picked up a lunch bar from the food slot. He stepped firmly onto the mobile sidewalk and hopped playfully off at his building as lightly as he could manage. He traced the familiar path through the revolving door, directly to the first bank of elevators that read "Pilots." He barely glanced at the button reading #23 and calmly pushed his letter.

When the doors opened it was Rebekah's turn to feel nauseous. She'd been waiting for this day with high anxiety wondering how her portrait would be received. When Ross failed to show up for work after that day she correctly deduced he'd been to #23. But what he did next put all her fears to rest. He said hello and spoke her name. Rebekah dropped her empty lunch box by the elevator.

Not wanting to assume too much Ross then proceeded to the pod and set down his own lunch box in its usual place. He risked a glance back to the elevator and was surprised to find Rebekah was on the wrong side of the closed doors. Moreover, she was walking towards him showing no signs of slowing down. Without a word she climbed right into the pod of top of him and kissed him firmly on the lips. "Welcome back," she whispered.

Instead of getting out she then removed Ross' harness. She sat in his lap facing forward and returned the pieces of the harness to their storage compartments. "Did you ever notice you don't need the belts?" she asked. Ross said nothing in reply as she slid the pod door closed and settled back against his chest. Rebekah took Ross' arms and wrapped them around her in place of the harness. She let her head fall back against his shoulder and reached up with her foot to hit the launch button.

The familiar punch came up in Ross' chest. This time it was augmented by the delicious weight of Rebekah pressed against his front. She held his hands in hers and squeezed them gently against her own chest. He continued to hug her tightly long after the pressure from the acceleration had eased. When the pod was at full speed Rebekah again turned to face Ross and this time kissed him more than once. Before lunch both occupants had violated the rule forbidding fluids in the pod.

Ross was no longer worried that any of his actions would be detrimental to his livelihood. After his shift, rather than part ways again, he suggested she return with him to his living unit. Ross offered to give up his missions in order to spend his life learning more about Rebekah. Since learning his actual place at #23, Ross figured he could do anything for work as long as it involved Rebekah. She declined saying they should continue to contribute as they've always done, but should transfer up to the larger two seat pods and work as a team. Ross wondered if they'd be given a single lunch box to share or whether he could keep his sturdy dependable model and she could keep her own.

10

Humors

June had a particularly rough Saturday night. Try as she might to make the Diner unpopular, new people kept showing up. She hadn't changed the menu in years and made sure she ran out of favorites on a regular basis. People came, and then they became regulars. If she needed the money it might be flattering but instead the crowds just meant more work. The diner was paid off years ago. She had changed her hours, gotten rid of the 4-course dinner specials, and locked down the juke box to play only her 10 favorite sad songs. The slower she served, the longer they stayed. Nobody complained. After the second dinner rush was cleared and cashed out, she looked forward to a quiet night with the Diner's Club.

In the corner booth Will was finishing a pile of french fries and a pile of homework. He'd arrived early for Diner's Club to do both of these things. At the counter by herself was Danny, slowly nursing a black coffee, no sugar or cream, and reading the editorial page. Paul came in fresh from another routine shift for Campus Security, still in uniform, with a large duffel bag over his shoulder. He nodded to Will who returned a genuinely cheerful hello, and to Danny who merely grunted her acknowledgment. He headed to the bathroom to change into something he hoped June would notice.

Josh and Courtney arrived charging through the door using each other for balance, giggling and screaming punch lines from a movie at each other. They'd planned a formal date earlier in the evening, making sure not to miss the Diner's Club. Courtney chose the most inane trifle of a teenage demographic movie she could find at the local multiplex and Josh acquired the fifth of cheap liqueur from a sympathetic party store owner. June cleaned the last of the dirty dishes from the tables and pocketed some small change. Then she turned her attention to cleaning the grill.

When everyone was seated Courtney started to talk. The alcohol made her bold. She had an idea at the theater that teenagers and bad movies are in some kind of symbiosis. By way of introduction she launched into a story she read in the obit page about a man who died of liver failure. "I heard from a friend who works in the hospital that the whole debacle of his death started with the treatment of a toenail fungus, see the man had this funky toenail that was entirely taken over by this fungus ever since he dropped a book on it as a kid and the nail split, the fungus got in and he'd carried it around for the next 60 years, then he heard a treatment for the fungus was available so he went to his doctor and started taking it, then he turned yellow, but not until after the toenail had started to clear and in the end, it was blamed on a rare side effect of the medicine, but I think he and the fungus were living in some kind of harmony, like maybe helping each other out and not even knowing it, like the way bees make honey from flowers and help them pollinate and when the fungus died, he died."

She was met with raised eyebrows and silence. Courtney had never had more than a few words to say and usually in response to someone else's point and then only in agreement. The club was stunned. She completely forgot about her original idea regarding the movie complex as breeding ground for teenagers.

Danny broke the mood with, "Did you just use the word *debacle*?" which almost got as big a laugh as, "and why do you smell like rotten fruit and paint thinner?"

Paul tried to help by saying, "We all appreciate your contribution, even if it is the apricot brandy talking. Any comments, thoughts?" He got only more silence from the group. Courtney just let out a hiccup. "It might just be the way you presented your idea. You sort of summed it all up. Next time just try a question and we'll answer it or expand. Plus, we kind kicked that medical horse last week with the Four Humors discussion."

Josh just stared at Courtney's lips the whole time with his eyes at half mast.

"Hey June, help us out here," Paul said. "Josh and Courtney are full of evil Humors and need a blood-letting. Got any good ones?"

June turned around from where she'd been scrubbing the grill. She'd bailed them out at past meetings. She blew a single dangling strand of hair from her face and crossed her arms. It was an excuse to take a break and stretch her back, but at the same time she had work to do for closing. She resisted the urge to make a sarcastic remark knowing it would only make them more insistent on a contribution from her. "Okay," she said. "Betelgeuse is the single biggest thing you will ever see. If placed at the center of our solar system, earth's orbit would easily be contained inside of it." She paused to wait for a reaction. When noone spoke she took their silence to mean she'd never get back to her work. "It's also a variable star, like most red giants are.

When it pulses up to its maximum diameter it would stretch out to Jupiter. Much like Josh's liver."

"Ooh, zinger," Josh said. "I get it, I drank too much. Excuse me and my Phlegm."

Will liked that idea and said as much. "Orion was the second constellation I learned after the Big Dipper. We can see it great from the farm in the winter. Betelgeuse is the right shoulder."

"Yea, so the idea is we're puny?" Josh said. "How thought-provoking. Wake me if I say something interesting in my sleep." He faked a yawn, leaned back and closed his eyes.

Will said, "Well, the Sumerians thought the stars looked like a big sheep. We could talk about how different cultures view the same things through different eyes. Hardly even similar to The Great Hunter."

"I'm guessing you'd prefer the sheep," Danny said.

"Cute. I get it, since I grew up on a farm I have sex with sheep, right? Well, I also grew up with guns. I hunt. Watch yourself," Will said.

"Okay, okay, settle down or you two can just go get a room," Paul said. To June he asked, "What else have you got? It's a little hard to have a spirited argument over the sun rising in the east. Maybe fewer facts and more controversy."

June filled a bucket for mop water. The teacher in her wanted to help. "In Laos there are so many bombs on the ground farmers use the unexploded ordinance for fence posts. School kids are routinely blown up on the way to class. Is that enough controversy for you to get started?"

This topic was right up Danny's alley. "I was just reading an editorial about the government interfering in every little dictatorship," she said. "The author said we shouldn't be bothering to risk our young men every time there's a hint of some human rights violation. After all, we ended slavery here without any outside intervention. The tree-hugging moron even said we could have dealt with Hitler the same way Ghandi got rid of the British Empire. Can you believe that crap?"

Courtney was back in her old form, ready to agree. "That's ridiculous," she said. "First off, Hitler would have mowed down the poor suckers like so much grass. Maybe the Muslims in India would have stood a chance, but the Hindus would have died in huge numbers. They don't have our tenacious grip on life, let alone all things material."

"Did you just use the word *tenacious*?" Danny said.

"I think we've all got pretty much the same views on that issue," Paul said. "Maybe Josh has something to add that'll get us going."

Josh opened one eye at Paul and answered with a fruity burp. "Look, religion and politics. I can get those on public radio," he said. "Let's go back to talking about my black and yellow Bile."

June wanted to try again but she had work to do. She had reasons for encouraging their group, but she was exasperated on the nights they couldn't self-sustain. She grabbed the coffee pot and another soda for Will. She poured two large mugs for Josh and Courtney, regular for Paul and Danny. She shared the most inane idea that popped into her head. "I'll bet none of you would admit to being superstitious." There were nods around the table. "I'll also bet you'd all like to have a blood transfusion if you needed one. But I'll bet you all a cup of coffee you know your Astrological signs but don't know your own blood type. I'm

Type O Negative, the Universal Donor. I give and I give and I just keep on giving."

There were general murmurs of agreement and a few thank you's for June. Then she went back to her mopping.

11

Chuck's New Job

On the occasion of Chuck's 40th birthday his mother surprised him in two ways. The first was that she instructed him to meet her in the library of her home on 5th Avenue promptly at 6pm. The second surprise was what she told him.

Chuck sat nervously in an overstuffed leather chair looking out over Central Park at the sunset. His mind raced with wonderful possibilities of what his mother might have to tell him. The only other time he'd been invited to the impressive room was when they'd chosen his first wife for him. The announcement of his second marriage didn't warrant the necessary gravity. But Chuck was wrong in assuming his mother had anything resembling good news for him.

The library of Chuck's family was akin to the Oval Office of the White House. Only slightly more important things happened in the latter. His family's legacy was sealed in that impressive room. His grandfather was well known to have purchased the building after the War specifically for its unobstructed view of Central Park on the Upper East Side of Manhattan. Situated just north of the Metropolitan Museum of Art, one could not only view the sunsets over the Park but also see the impressive facade of the Met. Family legend had it that the

Indiana limestone quarried specifically for the Museum facade was provided by one of his grandfather's growing business interests. The profits from that construction deal had allowed him to secure his first piece of Manhattan real estate and begin the rise of Chuck's family in the New York elite.

Countless deals had been sealed in this room. Some with a pen and rumor had it, some with blood. Chuck didn't think a child had ever been allowed in the room. It positively reeked of old money and success with its high ceilings, tall windows and somber lighting. Oversized family portraits adorned the dark walls. As orchestrator of the accumulation of the family fortune, his grandfather's stern gaze occupied the position most commanding of respect. The portrait was larger than life-size and hung overlooking the Park above the massive fireplace. The latter was wide enough to burn a large couch or cremate a body, Chuck morbidly mused.

He realized he was sitting forward in the chair. It was impossible to relax waiting for his mother to arrive. The big room was too quiet. She was never late—a family dictum—and the 8-foot grandfather clock had already marked the quarter hour. He risked her disapproval by getting up and making a quick drink at the modest bar. For his trouble he deserved the best bourbon money could buy and knew there would be an unopened bottle in the bar. Chuck felt he had a slight upper hand since she was choosing to be fashionably late for what could only be a meeting of great importance.

Chuck was certain as any school child he'd get what he wanted for his birthday. It had gone well beyond dropping hints that he desired most of all a certain classic car, a 1962 Corvette Convertible. He could picture its candy apple red paint gleaming in the sunshine on a warm

Spring drive to their place in the Hamptons. But his mother wouldn't call him to the room just to tell him that. The birthday party itself was no surprise and would be held in the ballroom and on the roof, weather permitting. It couldn't be to announce another wedding. Not at his age. Maybe the family had chosen him to run the newly acquired restaurant business.

As always, they were looking to diversify. Construction had its ups and downs. Oil seemed too volatile and too closely tied to politics in this country and unstable governments in the Middle East. While the family was rich, they didn't quite have the foothold in politics to ensure stability on all economic fronts. With his less than impressive social record, Chuck knew there was no way they could be asking him to run for a public office. The weight of his own guilt began to grow under the disapproving stare of his dead grandfather. He'd never make the impact on the world that would demand his portrait be hung in this room.

At nearly half past the hour, and with his first double bourbon on any empty stomach already beginning to make him brave, Chuck got up for another drink. He used the same glass, this time skipping the ice and filling it nearly to the rim. He'd down it quickly and wait for his mother to arrive and clear his head. Speculation on the family legacy and his place in it was starting to ruin his own delight at turning forty and hosting the birthday party of a lifetime. At the precise moment he tipped his head back to throw down the oversized drink, his grandmother entered the room. She glided in on the thick carpet so quietly he hadn't known she was there.

When his mother saw him at the bar, she slammed the huge oak door behind her, to announce her presence. Chuck was so surprised he spilled at least half of the drink down the front of his crisp white shirt, permanently marking his transgression. To make matters worse, his mother made a point of not mentioning his failure to wait before being offered a drink. Any moral advantage he had secured was worse than lost for good. He was doomed.

His mother started with a backhanded compliment, contrasting his weakness for liquor, "Hello, Charles. Thank you for meeting me on time. Please sit down." He slunk to his former seat and failed to make eye contact.

"Well, it would have been nice for you to show up on time. I've been sitting here for 45 minutes." Chuck tried to get the upper hand again, then quickly regretted his rudeness. He had no where else to be and she was hosting his party.

"I distinctly said 6:30, Charles. Please accept my sincere apologies for any errors of communication which may have caused you suffering." Her insistence on such stilted language and manners only made him lose more ground. Chuck had a realization in his slightly fogged brain and knew he'd been manipulated. It could only get worse.

"I'm sure you're wondering why I asked you to this historical room on the night of your 40th birthday. So I'll get right to the point. We've secured you a position at the College."

"WHAT?" Chuck screamed. His voice echoed off the walnut paneling. "You got me a job? What college? We don't own a college." This possibility was the last thing he had considered. Were they making him a janitor? "A job?" he repeated weakly.

"After a fashion. You'll be the Dean at a small college we've acquired in the Southwest. Frankly, your antics have become an embarrassment to the family. We couldn't have you killed conveniently, so we thought this was the next best thing for all of us." Her dry attempt at humor hardly helped to soften the blow. Chuck felt sick to his stomach and the acid bourbon rose to sting the back of his tongue. The mere possibility of his demise at the hands of some thug hadn't until then crossed his mind. He felt sure the family was capable of such a diabolical plan. On the whole, he'd have to reconsider his mother's generosity. But what did he know about running a college? He had an MBA. Maybe he could take over a branch of the restaurant expansions.

"When you were younger, Charles, your presence in the tabloids was amusing. It may even have kept the family name prominent enough to assist in the acquisition of some of our holdings. When your first marriage ended, it was almost predicted. Who doesn't get divorced these days? We were able to spin the separation and hide your infidelities with only modest amounts of cash. Besides, her family was of no more use to us. Then you went and ruined a second marriage. And to think we allowed you to marry for love. All you did was ruin your trust fund in the process. Thank goodness you weren't foolish enough to have any children."

Chuck sunk back in his large chair like a fish being slowly eaten by an anemone. He was helpless to stop the recitation of his life's failures. He stayed quiet and tried think of a way out. His mother went on with her rationalization for ruining his life still further.

"As the playboy of the family you've had a good run. We were able to keep the drugs and the gambling quiet, but we're running out of favors with the national publications. It's one thing to spend the weekend in Vegas and lose a little money. It's another to be blackmailed by a prostitute. Why couldn't you just let her steal your watch like a regular john?" This rhetorical question stung enough that he was almost compelled to defend himself. Chuck's tongue was held still by the large portion of his brain which was amazed she knew of that particular event. Was there anything the lady didn't know? He didn't have the capacity for real shame but was beginning to think he'd be lucky to get the car.

"The family is moving in a new direction. One I'm afraid will not include you. You are aware we are looking to diversify still further. We have two immediate goals, one in government, the other in education. Our financial security is now dependent on our entering into politics. We can no longer run our businesses without local, state and national governments interfering with our profitability. Regulations, taxes, and simple red tape are hindering our expansion. We need lawmakers on our side and we aren't quite wealthy enough to buy them." Another dry joke. Chuck's mind was turning off. He'd heard all this on the golf course.

"A presence in education will afford us no small amount of cachet. Endowments and grants hardly buy one the prestige they once did. We don't just envision a building with father's name on it, we plan to form and run a virtual competition for the Ivy League. And we plan to win." The woman just went on and on, he thought. Chuck was having trouble staying awake. Thankfully, she waltzed over to the window during her monologue allowing him to adjust in his too-comfortable chair.

"Part of making our family respectable again involves getting you off the East Coast," she said. "Besides, the local colleges are frankly, out of our league. We couldn't get you a job as janitor in an Ivy League school. Not with your infamous reputation."

That comment was a gut punch. As sure as his mother had said they were sending him to Siberia, a job in the Southwest was social suicide. He made an attempt to be helpful and beg for his life. "What about the new restaurant chain? I'll be more useful in Boston, don't you think? I can straighten up. I love those little diners. It was my idea to go with the retro rail cars and logos. Remember? Let me run the expansion in the Northeast." His babbling failed to garner any sympathy.

"I'm sorry, Charles. Our decision is made. While it may shock those who know you, it's time you grew up. A life in academia can still be one of leisure for you. You don't even have to teach. Just keep your hands off the undergraduates and don't get into any trouble. We've already hired a Board of Directors we trust, so you don't have to concern yourself with the actual work of running the College. Plus, they'll be keeping a close eye on your progress to adulthood. The occasional homecoming and graduation speeches will be your most pressing obligations. You'll take a comfortable salary and live in a nice house on a hill above the quadrangle."

His mother had stood through this entire exchange. She turned from the view of Central Park and bent over to give him a polite birthday kiss on the cheek. Her precise control of the conversation was only obvious to Chuck in retrospect, from the false meeting time, to the bar stocked with his favorite bourbon. "Happy birthday, son. I expect great things from you. Have a nice party and tomorrow my assistant will give you the details on your move." She turned to leave, then turned back with her hand on the door. "Oh, and the keys to your new car. You'll have to drive something across the country after all."

Getting the beloved convertible of his dreams served more as an insult at this point. Couldn't he fly and have it shipped? Why put that kind of mileage on a car designed for cruising Central Park? It stung as certainly as if she'd slapped him on the cheek, rather than dismissed him with her usual peck. Driving 2,500 miles by himself to the middle of nowhere was not the vision he had in mind when he dreamed of the Corvette.

The rest of the night was a blur. Chuck's party had the feeling more of a wake than the bachelor party mood for which he was hoping. Everyone in the room seemed to already be aware of his fate. In conversation, he tried to make it sound like it was his decision but all his friends and family knew the truth. His insistence that he was "excited by the challenge" and looking forward to "avoiding any more East Coast winters" was only fooling himself. With his life half over, Chuck knew he was not capable of making a change this drastic.

He wore a mannequin smile and nodded politely at the vapid comments he heard. All the while he vowed to himself he'd be back. This college thing was just a temporary sabbatical. He'd prove his worth to the family and soon they'd be begging him to come back East and take his old place. Then Chuck had a sickening revelation. He had no place in the family. His mother was right about one thing and wrong about another. He did need to grow up, but he knew it wouldn't be into her vision of what he should be. What form his life would take he didn't know, but on the night of his 40th birthday, slightly drunk on the best bourbon money could buy, Chuck decided he'd make something of himself.

Chuck was wrong again.

12

Starry Flounder

Emma was lying in her favored position—supine, legs straight, arms at her sides. Roger was in the process of tucking her in, pinning her arms when a single strand of hair fell across her nose. She wriggled and blew from her bottom lip, but it wouldn't move. As he straightened it back along her forehead and rubbed her soft cheek, Roger thought to himself how lovely Emma was already. Compared to his ex-wife, whose beauty was severe and a little intimidating, Emma had the potential to be lovely at every age. She'd even be pretty with wrinkles.

With her eyes closed, Emma began the bedtime ritual, rigid as a mummy with, "How come so many people end up dying in your stories?" She paused, but when Roger answered with only a raised eyebrow, she tried again. He was still thinking how much he'd like to meet her biological mother. She must be stunning to have had Emma, no matter who the father was. "Can't you just write a happy ending? Why does it always have to **mean** something?"

"Well, Emma, sometimes a cigar is just a cigar." She opened her eyes, looked at her college professor dad without turning her head and gave him a look that was both confused and exasperated. He'd made the mistake of forgetting she's only in the 7th grade and immediately regretted his obscure joke. It was a good question from a 12-year old and he wanted to give it an appropriately thoughtful answer. Roger spends too much time with college students who appreciate or at least understand his dead-pan irony.

Plus, it's not true. She's right. All of his stories start out as trifles but end with layers like a complicated burial ritual. The body of the story is preserved, wrapped in fine silk, and placed gently in a velvet-lined, golden sarcophagus. He then places it in a room filled with treasures, fine scents and foods. Before it's finished there might even be false passageways to fool the unworthy looters. Only then will he complete the pyramid shape and finally, the outer facade. Before he puts it to rest, a story evolves. Emma sees the evolution every night and by the time they're finished and written down, invariably they touch on deeper issues. Deep inside the deceptively simple triangular shape of the pyramid, the body of the story is surrounded by valuables like a revered Egyptian ruler.

"Dad? Your stories? The cigar?" Emma caught him daydreaming again. At least this time he wasn't thinking of his ex-wife.

"Well, a long time ago a doctor named Freud…oh never mind. Do you want to hear a story or not?"

"Yea, sure, of course. But don't you have any happy stories? With say, animals? Fluffy little teddy bears? Maybe one where nobody dies?"

"Okay, okay, a happy story. But everybody dies you know, and it's not always sad. And hey, don't be so smart. They're just stories."

Hyperopia

Regis was a fish. Specifically, *Platichthys stellatus*, a Starry Flounder. He was born in California a long time ago. Actually, he wasn't born so much as he was abandoned by his mother along with 11 million siblings. Mom was about 2 feet long and lovely. For a fish, that is. In open water on sunny days, she would even display her handsome orange banded fins. Most of the time however, she was careful to blend with the rocky or sandy bottom over which she was swimming at the time. Her scales were star-shaped and sturdy.

One late winter, large with eggs, Mrs. Flounder ventured a little further up the coast than she usually went for meals. There she spawned near a mud flat at the mouth of a clear, fast-running river. Dad came along later and finished the job.

You could say Regis was lucky in some ways and unlucky in others. Like his other pelagic brethren, he floated vulnerable for a period of time and finally hatched after what seemed like forever. In fact, it was only 5 days. But the water was cold, and some of his siblings who hatched in only 3 days near the warmer shoreline were quickly eaten by other inhabitants of the estuary region. His cold water incubation period, though extended, may have saved his life.

But his misfortune was to be cursed with lousy vision. Regis couldn't see anything within 50 feet of his lips. If the water were more clear, like say, in the Caribbean he might have enjoyed the occasional panoramic view. But there was nothing to see along the muddy coastline anyway.

As a juvenile, he was careful to stay in the intertidal zone. Too near the shoreline and he might be stranded if the tide went out too quickly.

Too deep and who knows what larger fish would consider him a tasty snack. It was a good place to spend his youth, so rich with plankton he could simply open his mouth to eat. Poor vision was hardly a drawback.

Regis did well for himself as a far-sighted fish. Far from floundering, like his name might suggest, he became a strong swimmer. He was only a little disappointed when his useless eyes migrated to the left side of his head, and yet his vision failed to improve. He'd wrongly assumed all flounder were basically blind until this wonderful metamorphosis occurred. But, no matter. He developed other skills. His powerful swimming allowed him to avoid the nets set for other fish. He could smell a fisherman's hook from miles off and so had no reason to fear a meal from the pier. His strong jaws were extremely efficient at snipping the clams and barnacles off the pilings. For variety he'd swim as deep as 900 feet just for fun. There, in the dark, icy depths off the coast of California, he was on a par with the other sightless creatures. To finish the exploration of his world, he even ventured up the river of his birth, albeit avoiding the shallow mud flat.

In time, Regis grew restless. He'd mastered the life of a flounder and wondered if there was more he could do. Fertilizing a few million eggs hadn't quite given him the satisfaction that his spawning female partner had promised with her flashy displays. He'd been to the bottom of the bay, eaten the most succulent morsels of food in both river and ocean, and sired a few million children. Was that all there was? Shouldn't his life have some deeper meaning than to live, eat, spawn, and die? Didn't his poor vision allow him to develop skills his siblings didn't possess? He'd swum deeper and faster. He'd eaten better, traveled further and still avoided the nets and hooks. Yet Regis still felt hollow inside.

One day, and without joy, Regis found himself cruising up and down the coast. He would eat or not, speed up or slow down. Passing a harbor seal he didn't even bother to hide. A nearby halibut became the unlucky dinner choice of the sharp-toothed predator. If only that could have been me, thought Regis.

Somehow he found himself at his old spawning grounds and cruised up and down the river at the entrance to the mudflat. It was the one place he'd never explored. What did he have to lose? Maybe there was something he could learn up there. He crossed the rocky and narrow threshold to the mud flat and immediately sensed a different world. The water was warmer, but also a pleasant mix of fresh river and open ocean. It was just right. He sensed an abundance of crabs and succulent sand dollars. He even tried a brittle star—a shape he'd never eaten—and despite the furry legs, found it delicious.

For the better part of the afternoon, Regis forgot about his quest for meaning. He simply cruised the warm, shallow water and tried not to think.

Waking from a nap, he noticed casually that the sky was a bit more colorful, signaling the end of another day. Regis began paddling to look for a snack. Maybe one of those tasty, fuzzy starfish. Then suddenly, his reverie was broken by a disturbing sensation. Pushing off from the muddy bottom his left pectoral fin broke the surface of the water. The tide was going out. He beat his tail frantically to move and managed only to become tangled in some weeds. He paused to catch his breath and think of where the exit back to the river might be. He slowly cruised the shallowest portion of the marsh in a wide circle but no opening presented itself. Rather than panic, he turned and went round the other direction, thinking he might have simply missed the outflow channel. If he were still he could sense the movement of the water.

Holding his gills, Regis trained all his powers on finding the exit to the safety of the river. No sounds were coming into the marsh. No other fish were entering or exiting. The water continued to recede from the mud flat but not in any tributaries or streams. It was filtering through the muddy bottom and out to the ocean. He was trapped.

Regis wondered how it would end. Would a hungry heron take him to feed to her young? A cormorant perhaps? He'd heard tell of such flying beasts but of course, never seen one. He wondered what it would feel like to be lifted by the tail and swallowed whole, or pierced through with a razor sharp beak.

And then, nothing. The sun continued to set in a blurry ball to the West. Unable to stay completely submerged, Regis pointed himself in that direction and watched the vague changing of the colors. He'd never seen a sunset before, in focus or not. It was lovely. No, stunning. Having lived his whole life in mud and silt, even to see the colors of the fading light was a revelation. Maybe this was the meaning of his life. If only the birds would let him live a little longer. He continued to sip water from his little pond and admire the changing light on the clouds. The water seemed to hold steady at a level where if he were still, only his pectoral fin and eyes were exposed. If he didn't use much energy, maybe he could last the night and find his way back with the rising of the tide in the morning.

It was soon after twilight when Regis finally learned the meaning of his far-sighted existence. A bright, blue-white dot took shape above the setting sun. It didn't register at first, but then became more obvious. The few clouds he'd been admiring, for all their color, weren't something upon which his eyes could naturally focus. The sun itself, of course was too bright. But the stars, slowly appearing, one by one, were a sight to behold. As the sky darkened, Regis became more and more amazed at the vision of the sky above him. When the Milky Way rose, he thought at first it was another cloud obscuring his vision. Little did he know he was looking at the combined light of billions more stars.

Towards dawn, the stars began to fade. Regis was getting low on oxygen in his rapidly vanishing pond. His eyes, so long out of water, were drying and clouding up. The sun was slowly rising and beginning to brighten the sky above the power of even the largest stars. Regis had only a few moments in his fading consciousness to be thankful for his life. Complain though he might about living without sight, in his death, he was given a gift no fish had ever seen. As the mud slowly dried around him, he imagined with one fin free he cold gain flight. In the end, he was lifted by a heron for breakfast, but imagined himself to be lifted by the sun, to become part of it, and the eternal firmament of the stars.

13

Bachelorette Party

June's mind was not on her work. She'd messed up multiple orders, given the wrong change, and it was all made worse by the conspicuous absence of even a single complaint. Towards the end of the dinner rush, one of the new regulars joked, "What's his name, June?" as he was cashing out his tab. To that moment June had failed to realize how much Roger had been on her mind. Like a defensive child she lashed out only to confirm the joke had some truth.

"Shut it, Tony or I'll have you banned for life," she said. "And take your lousy 12% tip with you." She slammed the register shut and threw his change at his head as he ducked out the door. The money clanged on the glass and clattered to the floor. Problem identified, nothing solved.

Josh was early to the diner. He was the first to arrive and early enough to order dinner with the regular crowd and witness her tantrum. He had his food at the counter. June served him like any other customer because she knew he wanted to be treated that way. He lingered when his plate was emptied, reading and not reading what was left of the paper. When the crowd had cleared and there were only a few stragglers, he took his coffee over to the empty Diner's Club booth and took a seat in Paul's spot. It was the one that with the best view of June.

Danny arrived next, this time with her entire head shaved to ½ inch and the stubble dyed a sunshine yellow. The contrast with her dark brows was overwhelmed by her red lipstick. June had her coffee ready and she grabbed it off the counter and slid in next to Josh in what was usually Will's seat.

Will came in accompanied by his pungent odor. Hunting season was opening in a week and he planned to continue the ritual he set with his father since he was old enough to hold a rifle. For him this ritual was as important as any other meaning in his life and he'd gladly miss a week of school to spend the time with Marvin and his father. They'd have to sell to their butcher friend what they couldn't store comfortably. They'd never failed to bag their limit.

Danny couldn't help but stare at a spot on Will's forehead. By not showering to avoid perfumes and scare off deer, he'd managed to grow himself an enormous pimple. Without a word and before Will could sit, Danny took him by the hand, dragged him to the restroom and locked the door. She had a purse made from an old license plate. From it she removed a single pad with an astringent cleanser. When Will flinched back from her hand she reassured him, "Don't worry, it's unscented." She gently wiped the oil and dirt off Will's forehead. She removed the safety pin she was using as an earring and wiped it with the pad. With the dexterity of a trained dermatologist Danny emptied the contents of Will's pimple, wiped the pin and returned it to her ear. Then she took a combination foundation and benzoyl peroxide makeup and covered the light pink wound. "There. Now you're presentable. Nobody would have had a single thought tonight but that pimple exploding and I can hear Josh calling you Cyclops already. By the way, I like the way you smell. *Mui macho.*"

Back at the table Paul was already seated but still in uniform. He apologized for being late and asked for Courtney. Josh explained she'd gone to a bachelorette party. No guys were allowed.

"Oh, who's getting married?" asked Danny.

"Tonight it's Courtney," Josh said.

"What?" they all exclaimed together.

Josh explained how she and a group of friends had been having sham bachelorette parties since high school. It all started when somebody's older sister was getting married for real. The bride backed out or the groom backed out, they couldn't recall and it didn't matter. The point was, they all decided to go out anyway, to drown their sorrows in Shirley Temples and diet soft drinks. Then a curious thing happened. Wherever they went they were treated like a queen and her princesses. At the restaurant they were given the best table right by the musicians. Men sent them drinks. At first they thought it was out of sympathy that they were being treated so kindly. Half way through the night the queen suggested they make a social experiment. She took off her makeshift veil and put it on Courtney's head. She said, "You be the bachelorette at the next bar" and she was. The results were the same. The entire group was wined and dined by everyone they encountered. The single women of the group, assumed to be bridesmaids, were lavished with attention they only imagined was given to superstar A-list actresses. They'd been doing it periodically ever since.

"And the best part is, they've never been found out. They don't even have to lie. People just assume they're getting married because they wear stupid matching hats and one of them wears a veil. No one would be rude enough to actually ask when the wedding is or doubt their integrity as they buy them drinks."

"Maybe it feels chivalrous to be a good loser," Will said.

"What do you mean?" Danny said.

"Well, if you see a beautiful woman who so proudly announces that she's made her choice of males and is out to celebrate that fact in front of you, you're obviously not the lucky guy. So, you make yourself feel better by buying a round and raising your glass to the unseen groom. Plus, the issue of rejection never comes up. She's already made her choice, you're not a threat. There's no reason to be rude. Everybody wins."

"I can see that," Paul said. "But having seen dozens of these parties over the years, it makes me wonder how quickly we all jump to these conclusions. You'd never think to question someone in a situation like that."

"Well, it's like the deer we hunt, in a way," Will said.

"Let me speak for Josh on this one," Danny said. "What the hell are you talking about farm boy?"

"I know it's a stretch, but Paul was talking about making assumptions and in this modern day that translates into judgements about a person or situation. I think in the history of our evolution, it's been a useful adaptation to make quick decisions. You don't want to wait around trying to decide if the saber toothed tiger really is a threat or not. Best to get up the tree at the first flash of light brown in the corner of your eye. You can then live to laugh about it later when you realize it was only your uncle falling down the hill towards you."

Paul motioned to June and she brought him a large mug of black coffee. "What bothers me, besides the underage drinking, is the casual lie."

"There's no lie," Josh said. "I told you, they just accepted what was given. The hats just get the attention and the apes who buy don't want to know otherwise."

"I disagree," Paul said. "It's a lie of omission, which is still a lie. Danny here wants to get noticed, that's why her head's shaved, right? She doesn't say it, she looks it."

"Yea, but it's not working. I still had to buy my own burger tonight." Danny ran her hand through the stiff stubble and went on, "Nah, that's not it. I just like the way it feels." She leaned to the center of the table and they all took turns running their palms over her scalp. "Plus, I can feel the wind, sort of like the way Josh can feel the breeze blowing from ear to ear behind is eyeballs."

"Oh, zinger. If only Courtney were here to defend my honor," Josh said.

Will took a sip of soda and turned to Paul, "So you're saying all lies are created equally? If they went in with a sign that said 'Bachelorette Party-Buy Us Drinks' that's as bad as accepting unsolicited charity? What about restriction on yelling 'FIRE!' in a crowded movie theater?"

"I'm just saying a lie is a lie, and wrong, whether it's verbalized or not," Paul said.

"No, no, no, no, no, no, no, no," said Danny.

"Ooh, here's where it gets juicy," Josh said and rubbed his hands together.

"It's easy to differentiate that some lies are worse than others and I don't mean in a Biblical sense," Danny said. "But you can't say all lies are wrong. What about a lie that saves lives? Say you tell Hitler that a 100 people he has lined up for execution aren't Jewish? Maybe he lets them live. And they don't even have to denounce their faith. You've all heard of the 'little white lie,' right?" They all nodded. What about 'victimless crimes?' You know the whole Seven Deadly Sins thing. As bad as they might be none of them made the list of Ten Commandments. You've got to admit murder is worse than pride."

"Yea, but they're all wrong, is all I was saying," Paul said. "No one's doubting there are grey areas."

"What you mean to say, Paul," Josh said, "is that LYING about murder is worse than pride. Since its covered under the Big Ten, you know. I have to give this round to Danny."

"Not even remotely funny," Paul said. "Move it," and he got up to freshen his coffee himself. Josh stood to let him out and waited to give him his seat when he returned from the pot near the counter.

June was nearly done with the clean up but didn't want the night to end. She was craving company, even another customer would have been welcome. She could fire up the grill and take her time cleaning it a second time. She offered the group a basket of fries and they accepted. She dumped a bag of fries in the basket, lowered it in the oil and got Will another soda. Danny pulled a compact from her license plate purse and checked on the safety pin earring. She pulled the pin again, replaced it with an opened paper clip, and closed the purse. Josh and Paul watched the process with bemused smiles. "What?" she said. "Josh wipe that stupid smirk off your face before I slap it off."

"Nothing," Josh said. "Really, I...nothing."

"That won't do. Not nearly good enough. What is it? You think all liars go to hell?"

"No, it's not that. I can see your eyes." he said. "With the short hair and all. That's it."

A car pulled into the gravel parking lot but didn't stop. Instead the driver turned too fast, threw up dust and headed in the direction he'd just come. "Hey, June, any help here would be appreciated as usual," Paul said.

June took the last mangled wedge of apple pie from the display case and served herself. She took the dirty pan and tossed it into the dishwater to soak. She grabbed a spoon, held it up to the light, then wiped off a water mark with her apron. She pulled a stool up to the business side of the counter and started to twirl the gooey filling around the plate. "June? You still with us?"

"Huh?" She looked up and didn't even register that she should explain how distracted she was. They were staring and she was thinking about Roger. "Oh. I guess I'm more interested in the sins of omission. Like the old saying goes, it's better to regret something you did, than something you didn't do."

"I think that saying is more about adventure," Paul said. "Better to have loved and lost, you know? That sort thing."

"Well, how about the Train Track dilemmas? Anyone heard of those puzzles?" Danny knew the gist of the idea and raised her hand out of reflex, then lowered it feeling foolish. "Take it away Danny, I'll throw things at Josh if he interrupts you."

"There are probably dozens of versions, but the idea is to tease out the subtle variations of what people think are such simple decisions. Life's not always black and white I guess," she said.

"Okay, we're all about that, but what are they?" Will said.

"The simplest version puts you at a switch on a train track. If you don't throw the switch to move the train, 5 people tied to the tracks will die. Everyone would agree, if you're able-bodied, it's your duty to save the people." Everyone nodded, so she went on. "But what do you do if throwing the switch causes the train to roll over, say a single person on the other line? You're still killing one person and it's murder. Well, most people would say it's better to let the one die, and save the 5." She paused to let the group digest and take a sip of her coffee.

"I get it," said Will. "But what if the one person on the other track were a VIP like Einstein, and he had the cure for cancer, that could save millions. Shouldn't you kill the 5 to potentially save the millions? What if the one person were your husband or wife or child? Could you just as easily let the train kill the 5 people you don't know?"

"If it were Josh," Danny said, "I'd probably save the strangers."

"Exactly," Will said.

"Very funny," Josh said, "but completely unrealistic. You just act in the moment. You can't know if the one person is Einstein or a serial killer. He might have HIV and spread it to hundreds of people out of spite or something. You've got to assume an equal risk for the 5 people. Some of them might be future world leaders or completely worthless."

"So what you're saying is, you'd base your actions on whether you think people are basically good or evil?" Paul said. "I think the point of the exercise is to start with the assumption that allowing people to die is a sin of omission. Everyone is basically worth saving, am I right, Danny? Letting more people die is worse than letting one die. Sort of like a little white lie is less offensive than telling someone they'll be rewarded with an eternity of virgins in the afterlife. All they have to do is fly a plane into a building."

June took a little more interest in this line of discussion. She threw the dregs of her pie in the trash and put the plate in the sink. She went over to the table with a fresh soda for Will, topped off the others' coffees and sat back at the counter with a mug of her own.

"I've got one," Josh said. "What if there's no switch available, and the only way to stop the train and save the 5 people is by pushing some innocent bystander onto the tracks? Could you do it then?"

"That would definitely be harder," Will said. "Pulling the switch is action at a distance, like a rifle shot from 150 yards. Try taking down a deer with a knife and your bare hands."

"I think that situation would be best answered by suicide," Paul said.

"Yea," Danny said, "you should throw yourself on the tracks, Josh. Your big head would have no trouble stopping the train and saving the innocent bystander. Six lives saved, plus you rid the world of yourself. Those virgins will be yours in no time."

"Geez, Danny. That was a little harsh, even for Josh," Paul said. "And what if your carcass derails the train? Maybe you kill 400 passengers to save the 5 tied to the tracks."

"Well, it's not like Josh needs defending. You're a big boy. Whatever."

The Club went through a few more iterations and then lost their steam. June got up to get the french fries and brought them back to the table in a paper-lined basket. She pulled a bottle each of ketchup and mustard from her apron and set them on the table. Paul pulled napkins from the dispenser and passed them around. June turned her attention to sweeping the floor behind the counter. She swept up a small pile and went to the back room for some mop water. Josh was first to speak with a mouth full of french fries, red and yellow at the corners of his mouth. "You've got two kidneys, right Danny?"

"This better be going somewhere, Josh."

"What's keeping you from donating one to a needy party?" he said. "Isn't that a sin of omission? Shouldn't we all be donating blood every 56 days?"

Danny had to think of a response and she dunked a fry into her coffee to buy some time. "You got me there. But it makes me think that the train track business is obviously artificial. Some injustice put those people on the tracks in the first place. It's no shame if you're unable to reach a completely satisfying answer. Plus, humans have been around for thousands of years and we're trying to argue ethics with a technology from barely 150 years ago. Blood transfusions and kidney donation are even more recent. Maybe there are similar situations from Egyptian times but it's starting to look like a debate over self-preservation versus survival of the species."

"If I protect myself first, then I can take care of everyone else, do my farming, hunting and gathering, support the tribe," Will said. "Otherwise, I'm a burden to society."

"But we're assuming that stuff is already in place," Josh said. "You've got to have a level of sophistication in your society, otherwise it's survival of the fittest at it's worst. Ethics takes a back seat to survival, right? Only the big dogs eat, might makes right. Otherwise, what are we talking about? The train is a given. Death is a given. End of story, how do you minimize the suffering? Is that our job?"

June was standing behind the counter, leaning on her mop, staring at the intersection of some old and new tiles. There was a worn spot where she'd rounded the counter thousands of times to deliver food or clean a table. "Hey June," Paul said. "You're doing it again. What do you think, you want to get in on this? Have you got a sin of omission? Should we pull the switch on Josh? What's it gonna be, June, self-preservation or self-sacrifice?"

June looked up and met their eyes. "I'd like to meet that guy who tied those people to the tracks. We need to talk." The Club chuckled and went back to the last of the fries. June went back to her mopping and finished up around the tables, then turned her attention to the last of the dishes. She cleaned off the pie pan and the plate, rinsed them and put them in the rack to dry. She dumped the mop water and then scrubbed the sink. Staring at the blank wall above the hot and cold water faucets she dried her hands. Nothing like repetition and menial tasks to stimulate the thought process. June folded the dishrag and set it on the counter. She turned to the group. "I've got it. It hit me like a train, pun intended. I don't know if it qualifies as self-preservation or self-sacrifice but here it is. I'm going to start dating again."

14

Happy Hour

It was 2 months into his appointment as Dean before Chuck started making errors in judgement. His mother had assigned him a completely superfluous "personal assistant." In his denial and ignorance, Chuck thought Carl was provided to make his administrative life easier. To anyone who knew Chuck, the presence of an assistant at his side was more a sign of his need for a babysitter. After all, his role as Dean was more as figurehead than actual director of the college. Chuck saw Carl as breaking him in to the new adult responsibilities his family was giving him. Carl was barely ½ Chuck's age and thought of himself more as successor to the position rather than as a butler or handyman for paper pushing. With his Ivy League background and the fact that he was hand-picked for the position by Chuck's mother, Carl was more than willing to act as spy and give her weekly reports on his activity. The goal of course, was that there would be no activity.

By October, Chuck determined there were far too few social events of any meaning on the calendar. There were fraternity and sorority parties, Homecoming, but only intramural sporting events. Besides the sun-baked golf course there appeared to be not a single location where adults could mingle. Chuck hadn't been with a woman since the half-hearted groping at his 40th birthday party. Two months into his new career, it was time to get laid.

Chuck didn't have any real work to occupy his mind. It was painfully clear to him that he was merely decoration at any meeting of the various counsels on campus. Important financial decisions and their consequences were already in place prior to his arrival. Attempts to make a suggestion or two in his first week were met with condescending rebuttal. When he first spoke up he was met with gentle reprimand, later with outright derision. He was the 8-year old at the cocktail party when someone's sitter cancelled. Further outbursts were simply ignored by the trustees with exasperated sidelong glances.

It was Monday morning and Chuck had just spent another dreary weekend with his television. The joy he initially derived from driving his Corvette to the campus was beginning to wane. Once everyone knew who he was and had finished gawking, he was just another balding old fart in mid-life crisis. He'd begun arriving late for no good reason. Carl was already there with the week's agenda and a pot of coffee. "Good morning sir, how was your weekend?"

"Same as always. It sucked, princess. How was yours?" Then he added without a pause to wait for an answer, "If New York is the City That Never Sleeps, this one is the City That Never Wakes. Please, Carl, I can't stand the suspense any longer, which old folks home do we visit today?"

Carl was all too familiar with Chuck's situation. Getting him used to a more mundane and less tabloid ready lifestyle was part of his mother's plan. He was also secure enough to ignore the insults and outbursts. "It was great, thanks for asking. I took my nephew to the zoo. Today we'll be thanking the alumni for another wonderful Homecoming weekend at the Plaza downtown."

"You've got to be kidding me. Another luncheon? Let me guess: Southwest chicken on the menu? Watered down, lukewarm lemon tea? Some pasty vegetable side dish to keep everyone regular. I give one of your canned speeches and we press flesh 'til the fossils head off to nap time."

As usual in his life, Chuck could readily identify the source of his irritation, he just lacked the skill to find a solution. Things had always just happened around him, and he was more or less satisfied with the results. Now for the first time in his life, his mother had parked him in a location where he could be nothing but inert. He had to think of a way to get back a shred of his former glory, find a piece of the lifestyle he'd made for himself on the East Coast. It was Carl who unwittingly assisted Chuck's continued modus operandi of poor life choices. "Why don't you get to know the faculty? You are the Dean after all. You might find some common ground with one of them, spark your creativity. Who knows? You might even decide to audit a class, expand your horizons."

Carl had in mind one of the male professors. Maybe start with a little golf, from there get him interested in something, anything besides drinking and womanizing. Maybe something that wouldn't involve Carl paying bail or contacting lawyers to discuss worst case scenarios. Still at a loss and in a rare desperate plea, Chuck inquired, "So? What do we do? I can't just parade them all in my office and tell them to entertain me."

"I don't know. It doesn't matter. Host a book club, meet for coffee in the library, start a workout group at the gym, have a faculty Midterm Dance."

"You mean like a party? With actual booze? I was beginning to think this was a dry county."

"No, I was thinking more along the lines of punch and cookies. And something right after school. Remember, these are the working professionals who are running the business of your family's college. Emphasis on 'professionals.' They have families of their own and would likely appreciate not having to spend a week night or weekend in service to your ennui."

"My what? You make it sound like I've got a bladder problem. I'm just trying to have a little fun here and you're sounding a lot like my mother."

They compromised on an end-of-week "Happy Hour" faculty mixer. The rationale would be to welcome the new faculty, albeit somewhat belatedly and Carl would write some sort of speech for Chuck to read outlining the "new direction" the school was heading. It would likely have the words "vision" and "future" sprinkled liberally throughout. Chuck lost his negotiation for alcohol, this being a college-sponsored event, but did manage to convince Carl to include a catered buffet of finger foods. If they had nothing but punch and cookies Chuck knew exactly how many people would show and how long they'd stay. He'd need time to impress the ladies, allow the men to admire him. Any loud or distracting entertainment would only hinder his chances to spread the wealth of his personality. If Chuck was lacking in social graces privately, he knew how to throw a party to his own advantage.

On the night of the mixer, Chuck was careful to arrive fashionably late. The event was held in one of the all-white meeting rooms of the administration building. The white walls, white carpet, and even the white podium were designed to give the room maximum flexibility in its various functions. A long buffet table was set up by the entrance with plasticware on one end, food in the middle, desserts, then a large bowl of fruit punch. There were circular tables, folding chairs, table cloths, and tasteful if forgettable centerpieces. Being on the second floor the room also had a number of large picture windows which could be blinded for video or slide presentations. At this event they were not only open but freshly cleaned and afforded a view of the Dean's mansion.

Chuck made sure Carl was there to get things started on time, so he would have the advantage of making an entrance like royalty. His mother had taught him this East Coast trick. Unfortunately, these were not society people and his tardiness had the effect of irritating one and all. Many of the professors had even arrived early with the misunderstanding that there was some business to be done. An early start would mean an earlier finish. Chuck quickly sensed the negative vibrations and stepped things up on the agenda.

Many of the faculty had brought their wives, husbands and significant others as the memo had stated. Not knowing what type of event it was, they'd generally dressed in clothes appropriate to the weather. In other words, they all came straight from work, Southwest casual. Chuck was somewhat overdressed in a sport coat, but he didn't mind as it helped him stand apart as more of a leader, not just a figurehead. Cliques formed along department lines and conversations were more or less continuations of the same discussions the professors were having just hours before. The spouses looked supremely bored and gazed around to find the exits in the likely occurrence that they'd want to make a quick departure.

His first 10 minutes in the room confirmed what he was dreading the most. Despite the presence of a relatively even split of men and women, those females attending who were in a reasonable age range were clearly linked to the men at their sides. Only one woman stood out and he was careful to save his introduction to her for later. He thought it might build his mystery in her mind and also deflect any criticism that he'd arranged the party solely to meet women. Even if his lechery was the reason for the mixer, one had to maintain appearances, if only for Carl. He also wanted to save his best prospect for last.

Of all the women in attendance this one was most his type. She'd dressed smartly and didn't appear to him to be local in the least, more an unwilling transplant like himself. She was taller, darker, and had more angular features than the other demure professor types. How could he have overlooked such a stunning teacher? He wondered what department she occupied and whether he could start attending her classes. He hoped she didn't teach something difficult like a language. His happiness lasted about one hour until Carl introduced her as Sharon, the wife of Roger, his English department chair.

How did this statuesque lady of class end up with such a frumpy dud? Could he be any more boring? Questions of virtually no consequence flitted through his tiny insect brain. He rationalized if Roger really was Sharon's type, then she and Chuck would be unlikely to have anything in common. They'd never have a relationship, reach an understanding, as it were. Sour grapes and denial were Chuck's best allies in ego preservation. After he had sensed they'd made enough small talk, he decided to bring the disaster to a close and have Carl introduce him formally to make the speech. While chatting with Roger and Sharon he'd already gone over the speech in his mind and decided where he could cut it short.

Soon after he started his canned speech, in the now quiet room, there came a banging at the door. It wasn't a knock of any sort, but rather the obvious distress of someone repeatedly pulling on a door that opens with a push. When the intruder finally figured out the mistake, the door opened with such force a disastrous chain reaction was set into motion as it crashed into the buffet table. The pile of unused plates toppled into the Southwest chicken. The large metal lids slid sideways knocking the Sterno cans over igniting the tablecloth into 3 miniature bonfires. The finale came when the 3-tiered cookie tray fell into the punch bowl. It rocked back and forth several times picking up amplitude with each swing until it dumped its contents into the shifting syrupy liquid. The impact caused the hanging glasses to sound ominously until the end table legs collapsed, rolling the bowl onto its head in a final, catastrophic crash.

June, phenomenally overdressed in high heels, black stockings, pearls and tight black evening dress, made her stumbling entrance landing in the pile of broken plates. Fortunately her dress was so tight it was kept from flying completely over her head and exposing her new underwear. Unfortunately, it made the task of rising from the shards of porcelain as delicate as performing dentistry on a shark while wearing, well, a tight black evening dress. Seeing the spreading blaze she kicked her legs out and managed to rise to a seated position. Feeling the sharp plate fragments cutting into her dress and rump, she rolled over onto her hands and knees. The cuts there were hardly an improvement but allowed her to then rise to her feet and attend to the holocaust. June knocked the chicken out of the way onto the carpet and snuffed the fires out by inverting the chocolate cake over them and spreading it with her bare hands. The cool frosting was quite soothing to her hands so she dabbed a little on each knee. When the blaze was extinguished, she stepped back with her hands on her hips and took a satisfied pause suggesting she'd planned the spectacle and it all went perfectly according to plan. At this point she was unaware the entire crowd now had a view of her new red underpants as clear as any catalog spread. Feeling the wet cake soak through to her hips, she looked down, saw the mess and thoughtfully took a napkin to wipe her hands. She turned around to see a now silent room full of open mouths staring back at her.

Chuck forgot Sharon ever existed, never mind the rest of his speech. He looked to Carl for an explanation of this human calamity, but Carl had already risen from his podium-side seat, removed a tablecloth from an empty side table and proceeded to cover June's ample and exposed bottom. She stood there with her makeshift sarong and managed a sheepish smile while Carl introduced her. "For those of you who don't already know her, let me introduce June Turner, the newest member of our English Department, a graduate of this fine college and our resident expert in Russian literature."

The group rose and formed around her as if Chuck had started performing a mime routine. She was the diminutive waif of the playground who had finally put the bully in his place. She managed a shy wave with her bloody, chocolate-covered hand and briefly accepted a chair. Upon rediscovering the injuries to her bottom she sprung to her feet, reached up under the back of her tablecloth dress and produced a triangular sliver of plate the size of a thumb. Holding it up she began to produce genuine tears, only one tenth from pain, the rest from pure public embarrassment. The men all wanted to be with her, if only to help nurse her wounds. The women all wanted to be her, if only to be the undiluted center of attention for once in their lives.

It was generally decided that Chuck's happy hour get-together was the most memorable faculty function in the history of the college. It was there he begrudgingly admitted he must start getting into Russian Literature.

15

Ypsilon Mountain

"Tell me something real, daddy."

Emma was heading off to bed again and was hoping to learn something more about her dad. She liked his stories and the way they changed over time and got more detailed. But she was lost in the deeper meanings and frankly, fell asleep before they were finished most nights anyway. "What do you mean, Pumpkin?" asked Roger.

"You know, about yourself. Tell me about my mom. Or an adventure you've had," she insisted.

"You know everything there is to know about me. And you also know about Sharon. Plus, I've never had any adventures." Roger had not told Emma she was adopted and now wasn't the time to go into that subject.

"Then tell me about a trip you took sometime. Didn't you and mom go to Mexico once?"

Could she really be like his ex-wife? Were all women destined to be the same? Why the insistence on adventures? Couldn't he just live his life? If she thought they needed to constantly have some major trip planned, just to satisfy some twisted idea of hers about what successful people did, well…it's just Sharon going off on an ego trip.

"Dad? Are you listening? You're doing it again."

"Never mind Mexico. I did hear a story about a hike my friend took once. Can I tell you that one? It's sort of an adventure, but it ends a little strangely."

"Oh, all right. But all your stories end a little strange. And if his name starts with an 'R' I'll know you're just making it up."

"Emma, you're getting too smart for your own good."

Headache

A few years ago a friend of mine named Robert asked to borrow my car. This happened when we were still in college together and it was still a big deal to have a car. Even if it was an old, beat up, rust bucket like my faded, gold Ford Galaxie. Cars back then had seats so big you could stretch right out across them like a couch. Heck, many of today's cars could fit in the trunk of that old beater. Anyway, Robert said he needed it for a road trip. The big seat would come in handy if he had to pull over and rest. When I asked him where he was going he pulled a folded page from a calendar out of his pocket and showed me a picture. It was Ypsilon Mountain, up in Colorado.

You know how hot summers are in the Southwest. Sure, other parts of the country have humidity, but there's nothing like the scorching furnace of 110 degrees in the shade. With the bright blue sky, the cool green trees and deep mountain lake at its base, the mountain sure looked inviting. I even offered to come along but he said it was something he had to do on his own and we left it at that. He used the word "discontent" and said he was going to find answers. With a promise to return it in one piece with a full tank, Robert was off for

Rocky Mountain National Park. He told me the story of his trip as part of the deal.

He started at dusk and planned to drive overnight. That time of day has many advantages for travel, some of them obvious. He avoided the heat of the afternoon and also the worst of the traffic. He packed the bare minimum: a road atlas, his small cooler with soft drinks and water, some sandwiches, a trail map, and GORP for the hike.

Robert's world was defined by the small arc of the headlights. This narrowing of focus allowed him to let his mind wander. The luxury of time was exactly what he wanted. With no worries about registering for classes, coming up with tuition, or his parent's expectations, he was free to dream about the rest of his life. He'd counted on the hike as a way to do his reflections. He hadn't counted on the drive itself as a form of meditation. The miles melted quickly away and he had to remind himself to check the gas gauge every once in a while. Running out of gas wasn't part of his plan for adventure.

Robert stopped to stretch, relieve himself, stock up on caffeine, and buy some sunflower seeds to occupy his mouth. Back on the road he saw a light on the horizon. There weren't any large towns around and it was too dim to be an oncoming headlight. As he got closer, the light began to brighten and spread across the width of the road. It went from deep orange to dark yellow in the space of 16 minutes. Robert had to chuckle to himself that he hadn't figured it out sooner. By the time he'd reached Albuquerque the moon was fully risen. It was only a few days past full and looked enormous. This trip was feeling like a better and better idea all the time and he was only just getting started.

Robert had the pleasing sensation of watching the moon travel across his windshield and over to his passenger side. It became an unexpected but welcome companion for the next leg of his trip. With each degree the moon rose, he pictured the sun floating opposite, under the other side of the earth. The highway turned to the north and he was soon in Colorado.

Things continued according to plan. Robert breezed through the major cities, beating rush hour in Denver by a good two hours. By the light of the moon he could see the outline of the mountains all along the front range. There was no detail revealed by the silvery light, but the view held the promise of revelations to come. These were not the dry hills of New Mexico, that much was clear. North of Denver he turned west and noticed for the first time the unmistakable flat top of Long's Peak jutting up above the rest of the range. He knew it to be the highest and therefore, most popular peak in the region. But the last thing he wanted to see on his journey was 300 other hikers out to enjoy the solitude of nature.

At the still-sleeping town of Estes Park, Robert had the first clue that he might be in over his head. The sign at the bank said, "4:45" and "42 degrees." He convinced himself that his light cotton clothing and windbreaker would be adequate. After all, adventures and surprises went hand in hand, and not always the pleasant kind, like his encounter with the moonrise.

Robert breezed through the gate at the Horseshoe Park station, saving himself the entrance fee. No Rangers were on duty at that early hour. The moon was setting to the west, once again visible above the end of the road, this time on the side of a mountain. The sky was already brightening with twilight, and he envisioned the sun again, this time coming up to his rear.

At the Lawn Lake Trailhead he was surprised to see other cars, then remembered it was a popular activity to get lost in the woods on purpose and camp overnight. He parked, stuffed his pockets with GORP, grabbed his water bottle, and stepped from the car to stretch. The cold air hit his bare legs like falling through thin ice. Equally overwhelming was the stench of pine in the air. The combination of these two strong sensations left him momentarily unable to move his feet. Robert put on a baseball cap for what little body heat it would preserve. He checked his pocket for the keys to the Galaxie, locked the doors, and forced himself to start moving.

On the trail he wasn't 100 steps into the hike when the thoughts began to flood his mind. What a sheltered place a car was. While driving, he was completely unaware of the outside temperature. The only thing he'd smelled for hours was coffee. Now the pine scent was so strong he could taste it, a sticky film in his mouth. He couldn't see any birds but they made a racket that almost hurt his ears after the silence of the car. Then he began to feel the altitude and notice every breath.

The trail was steep and he was immediately thankful for the feeling of cold air on his hard-working legs. Funny how one's perspective can change in the course of an hour. Robert was worried it would be too cold to hike, now he was dreading the heat of the impending sunrise. He felt no wind but heard a sound like breezes high in the towering pines. Then he realized he was approaching a series of cascades. Like his drive, the hike was going more quickly than he expected.

The moon followed him as he traversed the first ridge. His view was obstructed occasionally by bluffs across the valley to the south. Then the moon would reappear and he could see his own shadow on the trail. Despite the cathedral of pines overhead he could sense the sky was brightening.

As he approached the Roaring River and the first of two bridges on the map, the din of the rapids drowned out the cacophony of the birds. This high in the mountains he hadn't expected such a powerful river blocking the trail. The bridge was made of a single enormous log, splint down the middle, flat sides up, and anchored only at the ends. He could see the matching grain as he stepped gingerly onto the right side log. Despite its size, the log flexed under his weight. With the river rushing by and unable to hear his own footsteps Robert became disoriented and a bit dizzy. Half way across he had to stop, look up, and gather his composure. The thought occurred to him that a simple slip at this otherwise benign and picturesque spot could be fatal. The water was no doubt barely above freezing. Though not deeper than two feet, he could easily be dashed unconscious against the rocks.

On the other side, he jumped off the logs and realized he was holding his hands out like a gymnast. He looked back and realized he'd have to cross it again to get back to the car. He was tired from the drive, high on caffeine and altitude, and getting dehydrated. In his excitement he hadn't taken a single drink of water. Robert stared at the boiling rapids, untwisted the cap on his water bottle and took twice the water he needed. Safe on land again he chuckled inwardly at the irony of his need for water and the simultaneous risks it presented. He needed water to survive but too much of it could be deadly. Like waking up from a nightmare, drowning now seemed like such a silly fear when he was standing on the riverbank.

The next few miles of the hike traversed a moraine through a monotonous forest of lodgepole pine. The sun rose and cast his shadow ahead of him along the trail sometimes for a length of 15 yards. He realized he'd missed the setting of the moon. Hiking at this point became like the driving he'd already done. Without focusing he was able to step over rocks and roots without them registering. Robert thought about his life, his future, his plans for college and where that might take him. The sun began to warm his back and he took another swig of water, his eyes never leaving the trail.

Without warning, the trail began to descend. At a small clearing on the side of the ridge, he sensed a brightening of the light, like exiting a long tunnel. He looked up and there it was, Ypsilon Mountain. The view was partly obscured by the pines but it was definitely the mountain from his calendar. Robert quickened his pace and 40 yards down the slope came to the forested shores of Chipmunk Lake.

His plan had worked to perfection. Here was the spot from his beloved calendar photo. The early morning alpenglow lit the mountain in almost identical fashion. Not a single cloud marred the deep blue sky. The Lake, really a pond no bigger than a two car driveway, was smaller than he imagined but so calm it appeared frozen. The reflection of Ypsilon Mountain was picture perfect, an upside down twin of itself. The two deep couloirs full of snow stretched from the summit, joined half way down the impressive east face and ended out of sight behind an imposing ridge of unbroken granite. Combining the snowfields and their reflection in his mind, Robert imagined a stick man with legs spread and arms raised in triumph. It would be his new personal symbol. Like the universal symbols used for restrooms or pedestrians crossing, Robert would be Triumphant Man. It was his third chuckle of the trip and he noted it without embarrassment. In a fit of inspiration he spread his legs, raised his arms to mimic the image before him, and let out a whoop as if he'd just scored a winning touchdown.

But was that it? It seemed too easy. Beside his little self-induced scare at the bridge, in the end, this was no adventure at all. He'd had time to think as planned but hadn't reached any useful conclusions, let alone any grand ones. He could imagine telling the tale to his grandchildren. It would take about a minute: he drove, he hiked, he drove back. Thrilling.

He decided to keep walking. There must be more to see. He had a topographic map after all, plenty of food, it was only 6:30am, and the weather was perfect. Despite the overnight drive, he felt energized by the decision to keep moving. He downed a handful of good old raisins and peanuts.

The trail continued to descend and he soon heard the now-familiar sound of rushing water. This time it wasn't a single river or stream but an entire hillside. The map said he was approaching Ypsilon Lake but the trees were so dense he couldn't see it or the cascades until the trail was upon them both. Another bridge, this time half the length of the first and twice as stable spanned the gap where the cascades gathered, before plunging the final 10 feet to the lake. He felt immediate gratification for going on with his hike. The sun was angled so that its rays reflected off the lake, directly up the small stream and onto the cascades. It was still early enough he could stare at it without blinking. When he looked east he was blinded by the beauty of a lake ten times the size of the one in his calendar picture. Up the ridge to the west, sparks and diamonds of water were jumping everywhere over rocks, downed logs and his own shadow cast up the hillside. He stood on the log bridge wishing he had eyes in the back of his head so he could view both directions at once. Considering such little additional effort had such a great payoff, he continued over the bridge. And he immediately regretted it.

The trail was nonexistent. He could see where people must have milled about and trampled the duff under the trees, but apparently everyone turned back at this point. Robert decided it was all the more reason to continue. He consulted the map and decided the best route up the ridge was to follow the cascades to the next plateau. He stepped over countless downed logs, ducked under low branches, and around massive boulders. With the sun rising higher and the route becoming more steep he began to sweat. Robert's mind was occupied so much with finding a way through the obstacles he neglected to drink any water. At one point, he found the way required him to simultaneously step over a branch onto a wet rock and duck under an overhanging pine bough. Before he knew it the wind had been knocked out of him and he was staring up at the thick crown of branches over his head. His tennis shoe had slipped on the rock and he'd landed square on his back at the foot of a boulder. He'd been lucky enough not to hit his head or fall backwards down the slope. Like his sensation at the first bridge, Robert realized again he was only one misstep from complete disaster. He vowed to be more careful.

That obstacle proved to be the crux before he scrambled up to the plateau and his next reward. The scene at the clearing made him feel as if he'd entered an amusement park or zoo. The tallest pine was no larger than a Christmas tree, a perfectly shaped, bristly cone. The stream was small enough to hop across, and divided by a single boulder in two neat halves which met downstream. The rivulet paused at a small pool before tumbling over the hillside to form the cascades he'd passed earlier. The pool reflected the granite bluff he'd seen at the first lake. Instead of pine needles, the ground was covered in a thick carpet of deep grass. The pine smell was gone and a gentle breeze descended from the cliffs above and cooled him back to a state of complete comfort.

He remembered to drink at this point but then realized only one quarter of his water remained. He'd have to ration it.

Robert attacked the ridge above the garden plateau with gusto. He made what he thought was good progress, until his breath became heavy. He stopped to look around and rest but was disappointed to see he was only about 20 feet higher than his last stopping point. Progress was going to be slow now that he was at tree line. He tried to follow the stream directly as he'd done above Ypsilon Lake but the boulders were too large. So large, that the stream was lost to his sight if not his hearing. He veered to the west and decided to ascend a low angled wall of smooth granite. There were a few boulders strewn about and the occasional grass-choked fissure but otherwise the wall was unbroken for the width and length of a football field. The rock was dry and sharp and his shoes gripped the face in a satisfying way. He balanced himself with his hands but advanced quickly up to the next plateau, 300 feet higher.

This effort necessitated a pause longer than he'd hoped, but the views were enough to keep him occupied for the entire recovery. To the south he could see the flat, 2-acre top of Long's Peak, 15 miles away. The entire valley of Horseshoe Park was spread before him. Robert could trace the route he'd taken over the moraine back to where the car was parked and it gave some significance to how far he'd come. To the west he could trace the entire spine of the Continental Divide as it tracked away to the southwest. His only disappointment was to the north, the direction he still had to go. Ypsilon Mountain was completely blocked by yet another ridge, just as steep and just as high the one he'd struggled so mightily to summit. He took a cautious sip of water and headed up more slowly this time.

At the top of the next ridge, Robert realized he'd miscalculated again, but this time in a more favorable way. Instead of delivering him to the base of the Spectacle Lakes with the view he expected, his route had taken him part way up the southern arm of the cirque. His view was not of the flat lakes with a blank east wall rising behind. Instead, he was treated to a full panorama from his position half way along the lower lake and at least 75 feet above the surface. To take it all in, he was forced to make a full head turn from the lake outlet on his right to see the bluffs over his left shoulder. The snowfields were nothing at all like his calender picture. In 3 dimensions the scale was much more impressive.

Robert couldn't get his mind around the idea that the upper lake was nearly a half mile lower than the summit. He was only used to thinking of distances in the horizontal direction. To see that much rock piled up was more than he could comprehend. What would it look like to roll a 1/4 mile track up the face two times? How much did it weigh? And those hanging snowfields were something else. Why didn't they just slide down? Or melt? The sun was beginning to pound on his bare head even though it was only 7:30am. It was then that Robert realized he'd lost his hat.

It was decision time. He was low on water. His hat had mysteriously disappeared and he had no sunscreen. Every step was starting to take more out of him. He wasn't certain he could reach the summit. But the weather had held, he hadn't gotten lost, and it was still early. Hadn't he already come over 5 miles in just 2 ½ hours? How hard could it be to summit? Plus, he lied to himself, he could always turn around. Life gives you choices and all you have to do is keep making them.

Robert started up the south ridge and immediately began to suffer. The sun was merciless on his neck, back and legs. Finding a route was more difficult than he imagined it would be. The rocks and boulders were of all different random sizes, with no reference for perspective. There were no cairns, trees or even any grass. For all he knew, Robert was the first person in the history of the mountains to venture this way. He needed a hiking technique to be sure he was on the right path, something to gauge his progress. He decided to pause and pick out a rock a few hundred steps away. He chose one that looked like it would make a good seat upon which to rest or an easy step to advance up the route. By the time he reached the rock, it turned out to be larger than the Galaxie. It was no good for a seat and too tall to climb over. He had to walk around it, increasing the overall distance of the hike by a few more precious steps. His thighs began to burn out of proportion to the effort of simply lifting them and putting them down. At times he knew he was extending himself beyond the ability to retreat. Doubt filled his mind and at every corner he expected to reach an impassable crevasse or wall with no exit. Sweat stung his eyes and his mouth took on a dry metallic taste.

At the summit of a house-sized block he paused to rest and check his progress. Looking down to his starting point above the lake was a disappointment. North to the other ridge he leveled his gaze and estimated where he'd be standing on that side. Tracing the ridge over impossibly tall buttes and yawning chasms to the summit was a further disappointment. Not only did he have thousands of vertical feet to go, if he encountered any of those obstacles he saw on the opposite ridge, he wasn't sure he could descend to safety.

Robert took an inventory of his pain. After looking down for over 3 hours at trail and rock his neck muscles were stiffened into two solid cords of steel cable. The pain crept over his head to the front and came to rest behind his eyes. Besides the sweat, the sun was reflecting off the rock and burning his vision. His lungs ached with every breath, now averaging two unsatisfying gasps to every step. The muscles in his arms were fatigued but not painfully so like his thighs and calves. A sunburn was gathering on his legs and neck, echoing the pain in his muscles with every heartbeat. His right shin bled from a wound inflicted by a particularly unforgiving rock when his toe slipped. His hands had shallow scratches which slowly oozed a mixture of blood and serum. The sharp rock was starting to sting the balls of his feet with every step, through the soles of his inadequate footwear. Still he pressed on without a thought of how he was going to get down.

Robert was no longer thinking about the importance of his climb. He didn't think about his life, his future or his worries back at college. He was solely pondering each and every step. A change in the granite from a band of grey to a band of pink or white was hardly enough to rouse him from his mindless scrambling.

Further up the ridge, the angle of the mountain eased off enough that he was able to rest his scratched hands. The plodding course continued with no change in scenery. He'd mark a rock at the top of his field of view with nothing but blue sky above it. On reaching that rock invariably it would be 10 times the size he'd predicted, taking 4 times as long to reach, and revealing only more rock, higher on the ridge. Robert would venture to the east and look down the face to the lakes far below to gauge his progress. They were so far away he felt he must be close until he looked at the north ridge and saw there were hundreds of feet left. He reached a point where his will to go higher was only equal to his will to retreat. The only reason he kept going up was that he was facing that way.

Suddenly he found himself on a rock with nothing to climb. A brief moment of elation was quickly replaced with the realization of yet another sickening miscalculation. The true summit was still a 1/4 mile away. Most of it horizontal, true, but on the other side of the two couloirs. To reach the true summit he'd have to trudge around the two wide snowfields which gave the mountain it's name.

Robert took a small sip of water and saved his two remaining mouthfuls-one for the summit to celebrate and one for the hike down. It occurred to him at that moment, that as far as he'd come he was only ½ way to his true goal of getting back to his bed at the college. Not only would he have to descend the vertical mile and 6 miles back to the Galaxie, he'd then have to drive all the way through 2 states before he could consider his mission accomplished. A deep fatigue set in, bordering on depression.

Heading west around the first snowfield was a particular torture for his feet. The rock was thrust up into vertical spines, like books standing on their bindings. There wasn't a flat spot to be found. He contemplated for a moment venturing out onto the snowfield but had no way of knowing it's integrity. The last thing he wanted was an unplanned, ½ mile slide to the lake.

At the first couloir there was a gap between the rock of the summit ridge and the top of the snowfield large enough to hold a truck and 30 feet deep. The north side of the couloir was vertical rock, the south was a windblown snowdrift. Robert ventured as close as he dared, to try and see through the gap down to the lake. Fear got the better of him and he backed away from the ledge without seeing the bottom. He rationalized that the edge might be unstable and there was little chance he could climb out of the bergschrund even if he survived the fall. The view would no doubt have been stunning, but was it worth it if the outcome could be a painful, frozen, death by starvation? Even if 99 times out of 100 he'd be fine, would you make the same play knowing it would be the last thing you'd see? Who gets into their car thinking they'll never reach their destination? Some payoffs in life may not be worth the risk.

The rest of the hike to the true summit was something of a letdown. The way was flat, the views, no different from the ones he'd had at the south summit, some 40 feet lower. He attempted to jog the last 100 yards to the true summit, but at 13,514 feet he paid the price with a raw throat and stomach cramps. Windblown snowdrifts blocked the view of the lakes to the east. To the north were endless forests interrupted only by rare, rocky outcrops and some distant mountains he estimated must be in Wyoming. To the west were more mountains, but down a gentle slope, and too far to appreciate the distances involved. He might as well have been looking at the moon again.

The implications of his brief time on the summit were not lost on Robert. It's one thing to recite the cliches, another to live them. Summits are nice but it's the sides of the mountain which sustain life. Getting up is optional, getting down is mandatory. It's easy to be a holy man on the top of a mountain. A nice place to visit, but I wouldn't want to live there. He took his celebratory mouthful of water and started down.

The way back became an effort of will. Robert's trip had started out with all the noble intentions of the Crusades and devolved into the act of merely continuing. If he stopped to rest, even on a flat rock, his legs shook uncontrollably. His balance was far from reliable and more than once it failed him. It was all he could do to keep from plunging headfirst down the slope.

Knowing he'd be unable to reverse his exact route, Robert veered more to the south hoping to find a more gentle descent. In the end, he probably doubled the distance of his direct ascent. He couldn't keep his mind from thoughts of finishing the hike. He imagined himself getting first to the flat plateau at the bottom of the ridge. Then he pictured himself splashing cold water on his face at the stream. Over and over he reversed in his mind the ascent route. Instead of having grand thoughts of life, working through great problems, his goal became one of simple, sustained motion.

A single cloud formed and blocked the sun from his baking head. The relief to his eyes and overheated body were as complete as if he'd stepped into a cool shower. The image made him think of the moment when he stepped out of the car to begin the hike. An involuntary chill came over him, not from the memory or the subtle drop in temperature but from the failure of his body's temperature regulation, an effect of the severe dehydration. As quickly as he registered the benefit of some clouds he realized their danger. He was still hundreds of feet above the protection of tree line and miles from help should it be needed. A hail storm, or worse lightning and he'd literally be toast. Despite the danger, the image and pun made him chuckle out loud. The sound of his voice was startling. For the first time he felt more lonely than alone. He mused again how not only plans change, but perspective. He was just as pleased when the cloud blew past and he was in full sun again.

Things were going well on the southern flank of the mountain but the view was far from inspiring. Instead of the yawning chasm and sheer east face of Ypsilon Mountain, he was treated to an endless moonscape of rocks, uniform in color and shape. The only break in the monotony was also the most dangerous spot of the descent. He found himself on a ledge, two feet across above a wider, sloping ramp the size of a couch and just as inviting. Under other circumstances it would have been no trouble to simply jump down the 6 feet to the ramp and continue. However, he knew his shaky legs wouldn't hold and if he missed or lost his balance, well, they'd never find the body. To his left was a featureless wall he could traverse with hands and feet to gain the top of the ramp 20 feet away. The further he made it in that direction, the shorter the potential fall should he slip to the ledge. To his right was a tumble of rocks stacked up such that they resembled a ladder. He could hear trickling water underneath them and it would get him closer to the bottom of the ramp which was his immediate goal. Should he venture onto the rocks to save some time, risking a disastrous fall? Or should he stick with the relative safety of the traverse, adding vital steps but risking nothing? With a pounding head, shaking legs, and parched throat, Robert stood on the ledge paralyzed, unable to decide.

In the end it was simple inertia which led him across the traverse and down the ramp. When he reached the point on the ramp below the rock ladder, he turned to look up and said aloud to himself, "I could have done that." He knew he was deluding himself and had no idea what it would have taken at this point in his journey to put out that level of physical effort. Turning back down the ramp he found himself at the top of a narrow gully filled with snow and completely impassable.

Robert grinned at the irony of his agonized decision, knowing either route would have delivered him eventually to this exact spot. The trickle of water he heard showed briefly where the rocks ended and dove under the top of the snowfield. The rocks on the right looked somewhat more stable and without thinking this time, he began to pick his way through them. He reached a cliff and knew he'd have to cross the snow to the other side. When choices are removed, it's easier to just keep going.

He kicked two small steps and stood in them, facing the snow. It was so steep he could dig his fingers in for balance without leaning forward. The surface was slushy with a harder layer underneath. Robert briefly contemplated a controlled slide to the base but knew he had no way to stop before hitting the rocks at the bottom. The snow numbed his swollen hands and felt briefly inviting. Then it began to sting and he was happy when he reached the other side of the snow and was back on rock again. Yet again he noted the change in perspective. Compared to the danger and discomfort of traversing the snow, he really was glad to be back on the hated rocks.

The rest of the way down was a blur of discomfort. He was out of water and food. The pain in his feet was throbbing up his shins and landing on his knees with every step. He might as well have been crawling. Suddenly, out of the corner of his right eye, he saw another hiker passing him. When he turned to look and say hi, there was only a windswept tree, 4-feet tall with no branches on the windward side. Far from occupying his mind with deep thoughts, Robert was starting to hallucinate. The rocks appeared to have shifting insects on them. The moment before his step fell on each one, it became solid and accepted his foot. Dying in the mountains would be easy.

Robert reached his goal of the shelf above the lakes without further injury. He turned to look back at his mountain and couldn't imagine having been up that high. Considering how far he had yet to go, it was ludicrous to think of the summit as his goal just a short 4 hours ago. More clouds were forming and he welcomed the shade. It did little to comfort his pounding headache, rather he began a recitation of his regrets. Losing his hat was the first one. He should have packed 3 times the food and water. He should have brought better footwear. Sunscreen is a must in this thin air. Camping overnight would have allowed him time to acclimatize and not suffer as much. A camera would have been nice. What about a lady for company?

The rest of the way to the Galaxie was uneventful. He couldn't imagine how the trip up the moraine seemed so short in the morning and now was interminable. When he finally reached the Roaring River, he waltzed across the rickety bridge without even a thought of his earlier trials.

At the car he treated himself to his remaining bottle of water, draining it in one breath. Considering the magnitude of his accomplishment his arrival was oddly anticlimactic. He'd been in motion for 9 hours and for all his trouble was back where he started. And with nothing to show for it.

On the drive back to college, Robert experienced acutely all of the disadvantages of traveling by day. He hit rush hour in Denver at it's peak. His brake foot shook violently from the sustained effort of driving in the stop and go traffic.

When night came he could no longer drive. The fatigue was overwhelming. He found a rest area, pulled over and stretched out in the back seat. After the constant motion of driving, hiking, then driving again, Robert's sleep was less than fitful. He dreamed he was still driving. The road was smooth, it was daytime again but the air was cool, and he was hanging his arm out the window feeling very satisfied with his progress. He didn't know where he was driving but in that way we think in dreams, he just knew it was good. Looking over in his passenger seat he was pleased to see a beautiful young woman appear. He recognized her as his wife, and everything was as it should be. A moment later a child was in the back seat, and Robert was grinning in his sleep, driving along on the smooth road.

A fancy sports car came up behind them and flashed it's bright lights. Robert slowed to let it pass, but the driver held his position. He turned to his wife to make a comment about bad drivers but she was no longer there. Nor was his son still in the back seat. After a mile, the sports car passed him on the left and there was his dream wife in the other car, laughing with her head tilted back as they shot past.

Better rested despite the strange dream and with his headache subsided, Robert woke with renewed optimism. His mind returned to deep thoughts of his life and goals. Mountains and roads were wonderful metaphors for his journey through life. He'd had countless ups and downs. Some plans worked out and others didn't. Surprises were sometimes pleasant and other times downright dangerous. The gray fog of his random thoughts began to coalesce into a more solid theme. He wasn't sure what it all meant but it felt right. He became content, not because it was the best possible life but because it was the one he was having.

16

Newcomer

The Diner's Club was in full session when a strange car pulled into the parking lot. The driver got out, slammed the door in a hurry and rushed up to the entrance. She paused at the top of the steps as if waiting for something to happen. She could see June and the other patrons bathed in bright light but couldn't figure out a way to get in. The neon sign blinking "Open" mocked her. She leaned back a step, looked up, and waved at some invisible thing noone else could see. After a minute of this strange quest, she had the attention of the rest of the diner's occupants. She was petite, with brunette hair and with a Hollywood-thin figure which suggested she'd never laid eyes on Diner food. Her makeup implied she was on a date but the jeans and t-shirt revealed her to be another tourist to the Club. June saw her frustration and watched her stomp back to the car. At the driver's side door she held out her arm, holding the keyring and gestured like a King bestowing the rank of knighthood. When nothing happened, she did it again, then a third time. The driver stood there looking defeated, let out a visible sigh with her hands on her hips and tapped her foot. There appeared to be some great internal battle taking place.

She walked back to the door of the diner and knocked a little too loudly on the glass considering she was in plain sight of each and every occupant. June gestured to her to come in and mouthed the words in encouragement. The girl looked back at June with her palms to the sky, key ring in one hand and shouted, "Your door's broken!"

June left her perch at the counter, walked around to the far end of the diner and gently pushed the door open. "Hi. I'm June. This is my diner and you're welcome to come in. Sorry, the butler's on vacation."

Without a word of thanks, the girl stepped in and surveyed the room looking not for the friendliest face, but the one she thought might be most helpful. Paul was still in uniform and she addressed him directly. "Officer? Is there any chance you might be able to let me back in my car?" To the rest of the room she spelled out her problem. "The battery on my door opener has been dying for a month and now it's completely dead."

Josh was the only one who laughed out loud. Paul waved him quiet and said, "Sorry. I'm just a campus cop. No tools for breaking and entering. Have you considered calling a locksmith?" When she said no, she didn't have a cell phone, his decency got the better of him and he had to end the farce. "Have you tried your key? It's that shiny thing, next to the dead remote on your ring."

She looked at the key ring in her hand, outside to her secured car and back at her hand. It took a moment for the dome light to come on in her head. "Coffee?" said June.

The girl accepted a cup, confessed her real reason for coming and pulled up a chair. Introductions were made and the astonishing entrance was forgotten. They made space between Danny and Josh. Will resumed their discussion of the latest trends in advertising. After

20 minutes and without contributing a single comment, the newcomer could no longer restrain herself. "So," she said. "Don't you guys ever talk about big stuff? You know, the existence of god, the meaning of life, stuff like that."

Every few weeks this happened. This month's version was named Alyssa. She'd no doubt heard about the weird group of mental freaks who get together on like, Saturday to just sit around talking about things. She was there to check it out for her clique. She'd report back on this strange land like an explorer, and for once be the center of attention. She considered herself open-minded, like they all do. Also, of above average intelligence, and wasn't intimidated that they would touch on any topics she couldn't easily handle. She was captain of her debate team in high school after all.

"Well, it's like we told you when you first asked to sit in," Paul said. "We never set up any rules. We don't even consider it a club, that was a label someone else gave us. My feelings aren't hurt if you or anyone else shows up or not. I eat here after my Saturday shifts. The talk is just a bonus."

Alyssa fit in very nicely with her own group and would never understand the main cement in the foundation of this group was the fact that its members don't fit anywhere else. They're joined ironically, by their individuality. Will's stems mainly from his unique farming background. Josh fits because he's trying to separate from his past. Danny is trying to find something with which to identify and is still on her quest. This week she has a streak of green along the left temple where she'd shaved the hair to within ½ inch of her scalp. Paul's just too plain old to fit in with the college crowd. The uniform doesn't help. Courtney is an underachiever, her intellect far outstrips her ambition.

June owns the place and by default plays whatever role they assign her whether she knows it or not.

Will added, "Frankly, it's never come up Alyssa. We've only been meeting for a few months and some weeks it's only me and Danny. Paul covers a lot of extra shifts and these two have a life." He gestured to Josh and Courtney. "Besides, I personally finished all the metaphysics in high school."

"What do you mean by that?" Alyssa said.

"Just what I said. I was raised on a farm and Sundays are just another work day. We didn't go to church but my parents were spiritual without being religious, if that makes any sense. The nearest church was an hour away by car. Ever see a dairy cow that hasn't been milked for a day?"

"Thanks for that image, Will," Josh said. "What farm boy here is trying to say is we've all been through the pony stage." He got blank looks from everyone. "Oh come on, don't tell me you haven't heard of the pony stage. It's that age when every girl wishes she had a pony. Then she discovers boys or cars and gets over it. Isn't that right, Danny, didn't you have a pony stage? Or was it reptiles for you?"

"Fuck off."

"Try to be nice, Josh," Courtney said.

Paul played den mother again. "I think what he means is that we all go through that stage of wondering about where we come from and the meaning of life. We all reach our conclusions based more on gut feelings than on anything solid. Not to get too deep here but my own path pretty well paralleled the modern Europeans. It's hard to call Descartes modern since he died in 1650 but he set a challenge that was hard to dismiss for those who followed him."

"You mean the 'I think, therefore I am' guy?" Alyssa was proud of herself and figured this trivia would score her points.

"Right, him. He tried to come up with something that couldn't possibly be doubted. If the foundation were solid he reasoned, any conclusions he reached from that place would be equally solid. Unfortunately, he settled on a tautology. *Cogito ergo sum,* I think, therefore I am. It's like saying, 'I'm a circle, therefore, I'm round.' It doesn't tell you anything. From there he took great pains to restate everything the seventeenth century man and woman took for granted anyway."

"I'm starting to get bored," Josh said. "Can we get back to the dish soap marketing?"

Paul ignored the interruption. "We've come to realize there are certain topics that just don't lead to good discussions. We've all heard the old saw about mixing religion and politics with polite company. The problem comes down to a couple of basic tenets that most people seem to have. They just aren't aware of their own prejudice. Politics boil down to whether you believe men are basically good or bad." Danny shot him a look. "Relax, I did just use the word tenet and I mean people in general, women included. If you think people, when left alone to make their own choice will make a good one, for themselves and society in general, then you're a Jeffersonian. If you think people need lots of direction, that they can't be trusted to act responsibly, then you're a Hamiltonian. You know, strong central government and lots of protective tariffs."

"Ooh, tariffs. I just got chills," Josh said. "Can you tell us more about immigration law next Uncle Paul?"

"And don't forget Hamilton got himself shot by Aaron Burr for his troubles," Will said. "Just think if some of our current politicians had the balls to back their statements up with a bullet. You'd probably hear less of this crap about lowering taxes and maybe some real ideas for once."

Josh hated retreading old ground. "Look Paul, I'll explain the problem with religion in simple terms so Alyssa won't get lost. Then she can get back to her sleepover buddies, making friendship bracelets, braiding each other's hair and explain to them why none of them need to bother us any more. Arguing about religion is like arguing why you like the color blue. Since it's not based on any fact, but faith, no one can present any arguments or data that would convince you that no, you don't in fact like the color blue. End of discussion."

"Actually, Josh, we don't braid each other's hair anymore." Alyssa was too smart to be baited by a petty insult. "We tend to get down to our thongs and have hot lesbian sex. Most of the parties are videotaped but we always felt something was missing and thought you might come help us out sometime."

Josh and the others couldn't help but laugh. June came with a round of drinks and coffee. She'd been listening as usual and added, "Congratulations, you've discovered the keys to a good conversation. Don't forget, facts are no fun to argue about either. Two plus two will always equal four and trying to convince a complete idiot of that fact won't be any fun."

"But that's the whole point," said Danny. "Most people don't know where they stand in the big picture. They have little ideas about certain topics but they let the Pope or the President or their parents tell them what to think on the really important stuff. It's the fun of arguing out the points of why you favor say, a certain tax cut or not, that leads people to discover what they really believe."

Josh couldn't resist, "And you believed you'd dye your head green this week?"

"Cute. What I mean is, if we all knew our basic tenets at the beginning, we'd just have to agree to disagree on whatever topic is on the table. I don't want to sound too melodramatic here but the point of Diner's Club is a journey of self-discovery."

Given the unwavering certainty she'd had all her life, Alyssa couldn't wait to get back to the comforts of her own people.

17

Mexican Pineapple

"Look, Roger. Here comes Rufus."

On the horizon was a dark-skinned man with tightly curled hair, sailing a tiny skiff, bobbing on the light surf. He was backlit by the setting sun and leaned to port in order to balance the wind and the weight of his catch. Sharon and Roger were in Mexico with their towheaded son, Roger Jr, age 5. This vacation was designed by Sharon to be the highlight to date, of their perfect marriage. It also marked the beginning of the end.

Roger had just come up the steep beach and collapsed into a recliner next to Sharon. He and Roger Jr had finally given in to a losing battle with the advancing tide. They had built a sizable castle together with the mandatory towers and moat, only to see it gradually slide into the Pacific. Even sacrificing their bodies to make a human shield was hopeless in the face of the advancing waves. Roger Jr had been tossed and rolled more than once but managed to stand up easily before being dragged under the next wave. When his father abandoned him for the safety of his beach chair, Roger Jr simply moved up the beach and started on castle number two.

When Roger and Sharon first met, he was very protective of his writing. Like many aspiring authors he was shy about sharing his ideas. He disliked his own work for many reasons, some of them valid. Either the characters were weak, the story was underdeveloped, or he just wasn't happy with a particular turn of phrase. As their relationship grew, so did his confidence in sharing his stories. Sharon was helpful. She wasn't overly complimentary and offered suggestions in a loving way. On the rare occasions when she did say she liked something of his, the praise meant that much more. It wasn't unusual for her to refer to characters like Rufus. She knew his work as well as he did. At this point in their marriage she still held high hopes for his future as a famous writer. Then she would be a famous writer's wife.

Wiping the sand and salt water out of his eyes Roger squinted into the sun and glare. "Oh yea, yea, I see him. He must still be miles out yet. Thank goodness we're not spending Fall Break in some dreary country like France. Otherwise I'd have missed the inspiration for a story I've already written."

"Cute, Roger. No I brought you here because if you're going to be a great writer, you need some more experiences in your life. Besides, only the little people stay home during the holidays. We're special and you're on the way up. We've had the beach to ourselves all week. Who else can say that? If you fail to return to your class with a deep tan I shall be greatly disappointed." For Sharon, speaking like a dry character from a British television sitcom was the height of humor. Her light tone was a conscious attempt to keep the conversation from taking its usual course straight to a petty argument. "Hey, why don't you give Rufus one blue eye and one brown eye, just like Roger Jr? Then he'd really stand out, be more unique."

"Yeah. Hey, why don't I give him 3 arms? Then he'd be like no character in the history of the written word," Roger said with false enthusiasm. Sharon had a brief moment of glee, thinking Roger was taking her seriously. She mistook his tone for consent to change or add to his story. She not only misunderstood the qualities of good writing, she misunderstood the qualities of a good writer. The greatest stories and novels were not written by committee. Roger knew a superfluous detail would only distract from the main point of the story. It was an inside joke that no reader would understand. Besides, RJ didn't need to be referenced in some second-rate, unpublished short fiction to feel validated. That dubious honor was something Sharon cherished. Roger never wrote about anyone he knew, including his wife and child with the unique eye colors.

Roger waited for Sharon's face to change, signaling that she recognized his sarcasm. "Look Sharon, Rufus already has red hair. I think he's different enough for folks to get the point. But the main reason I'm not going back to change him is that the story is done. If I kept tweaking it, I'd still be writing the first paragraph. Sometimes you just have to be through and done with it." Sharon dropped her chin and gave him a false pout. She knew he was right. Argument avoided, Roger threw her a bone of encouragement by adding, "Maybe I'll use that idea in my next story. If it doesn't work for the flood, maybe a prince and pauper theme. I'll think about it."

"You always do, Roger. You always do." Sharon was pathologically required to get in the last word. On the surface it sounded like a compliment to tell him he always gives his ideas and stories a good amount of careful thought. In reality, she was unable to resist telling him he was already overworking every detail. If he just went with the flow he'd have his novel done and could put his silly science fiction shorts behind him.

Roger was happy to be in Mexico with Sharon but she could easily ruin his good moods without even trying. Roger felt the need to defend himself. "Look, I like seeing my family this time of year. I wrote 'Nausea' long before I'd been to the ocean and besides, RJ is too young to appreciate an expensive vacation like this, let alone remember it."

"Don't call our son 'RJ.' It makes him sound like some uncultured hick, with the maximum potential of a career in the carnival."

Roger was bruised by this attack. Roger couldn't imagine what his son might wish to become when he grew up, but a career in the circus had a certain romance to it. However, Sharon saw herself as the future matriarch of a great family tree. Roger Jr can't be RJ, because he himself will have a son named Roger III. And so on. To achieve this lofty goal, Sharon had unconsciously established a number of rules for nearly all aspects of their lives.

At first, Roger welcomed the control and order Sharon brought. He liked the attention. He liked the way he looked in the clothes she favored. He liked having nice things. But lately, and especially with regard to Roger Jr, her controlling ways were becoming more of a nuisance. Roger wasn't sure whether all the rules made sense. They certainly didn't seem to come from a place of genuine concern and love.

Take his haircuts. When Sharon and Roger met he was perfectly happy getting his hair cut at whatever barbershop or chain store happened to be having a promotion. Any rare, bad cuts would grow out. He'd always said, "The difference between a $40 haircut and a $10 haircut is one month." Sharon said a haircut was an investment. The head is the most important part of the body. If it doesn't look good, how will his students respect him? How will he ever sell his books to a publisher? How will he look as the Dean of the College one day with a bowl-cut mop like that on his head?

Roger and Sharon both knew where this conversation was heading. Only Roger saw their petty fights as something to avoid. They're like bugs under the bark of a tree. Sooner or later, the mightiest oak is overwhelmed by the mass of termites. Sharon saw their discussions as a way to prove Roger wrong for his own good. She saw it as her duty and privilege to improve her man in spite of himself. Sometimes he may not like the process but then, pruning a tree involves cutting some branches so others can grow. That way, the whole tree benefits.

Roger ignored the "uncultured hick" comment, rose from his chair and went back to play with Roger Jr. He knew Sharon couldn't refuse him that simple pleasure. The waves were already approaching the new castle and Roger Jr was once again trying to block them in vain with his skinny body. To keep Sharon occupied Roger asked her to get the 3 of them drinks and they'd take a break and watch the sunset together.

Sharon returned from the poolside bar with 3 drinks on a tray. For Roger she'd purchased a tall souvenir glass imprinted with the hotel logo so he would always remember this time. The glass was overflowing with a syrupy mixture of fruits and rum. The stick of pineapple in it was so large it threatened to topple the entire creation. Knowing she'd been a bit harsh with the carnival comment, Sharon felt the small gesture of this drink would set things right and let them continue the vacation according to her grand plan.

Seeing his wife return with drinks Roger rose to meet her at the beach chairs. He decided to let his irritation go. Walking in the sand while balancing the heavy tray of drinks caused Sharon's hips to swivel in a particularly attractive way. Roger forgot about castle number two and was beginning to look forward to making up after their narrowly avoided argument.

"That drink could feed a small family, Sharon."

"Well, what you don't drink before the sun sets we can take back to the hotel room. Use your imagination."

She set down the tray, pulled the long stick of pineapple out of Roger's drink and seductively cleaned it with her lips and tongue. She gave Roger a sticky kiss with her mouth open and pushed in a large piece of the pineapple. Surprised at both her sudden playfulness and the mouth full of pineapple, Roger giggled as he tried to chew. The first swallow went down easily. But the piece was so large he still had a fibrous chunk in both cheeks. Then Roger felt a strange tingling in his lips. He started to wheeze and put his hands to his throat.

Sharon tried to help by offering to perform the Heimlich maneuver, but Roger waved her off by spitting out the remaining pineapple. He wasn't choking but having an allergic reaction. Susan began to panic and for the first time in her life didn't know what to do. She started to run back to the hotel for help but Roger caught her by the wrist. With one hand on his throat, he pointed down to the water where Roger Jr had just been rolled by a large wave. Sharon ran down to where the castle had been but before she could reach the water she heard a loud crash behind her. Roger had passed out and collapsed into the tray, shattering the glasses and cutting himself.

Midway between her drowning son and her comatose husband Sharon stood paralyzed. Roger was too heavy to carry. If she entered the water and was lucky enough to find Roger Jr, she wasn't sure she could escape the waves herself, let alone with her boy in tow. ~~Susan~~ [Sharon] screamed more out of horror than any intention to call for help. Overwhelmed, she fainted, leaving both men to fate.

In the hospital the next day, Sharon and Roger had little difficulty in piecing together the events that followed, including the fate of Roger Jr. Between the crashing glass and ~~Susan~~ [Sharon's] screams the hotel staff was alerted to call for help. They didn't know to search for Roger Jr and so concentrated their efforts on reviving the two adults. Sharon was easily aroused only to pass out again at the fresh horror of the emergency team performing a tracheotomy to save her already bloodied husband. Unable to put in a breathing tube through his mouth, they cut open his neck and jammed it in that way. The subsequent infection and scarring left Roger with a souvenir of his trip more memorable than any hotel logo glassware. Roger Jr was presumed lost at sea. The stateside memorial service was modest yet thorough. They even buried a short, white coffin filled with RJ's favorite toys and Roger and Sharon's dreams of the ideal family.

18

Evolution Moon

At bedtime, Roger noticed an abundance of room on Emma's bed. He could even sit comfortably while tucking her in, mummy style. It then dawned on him where the extra square footage came from. "What did you do with all the stuffed animals?"

"They're under the bed. I didn't know where else to put 'em." When Roger failed to comment or ask any further questions, she added, "I think I'm getting too old for stuffed animals."

"Ah, now I see. What's his name? Are you ever going to bring him by the house so I can meet him?"

"Dad, geez, it's not about a guy."

"Uh, huh. Sure. Forget any homework assignments lately?" How else to explain her new maturity? Emma paused, bit her lower lip and sighed. "Okay, there is this one guy, but he's a jerk anyway," she said.

"Really. Tell me what he's done to deserve to be called names. And you didn't tell me his name yet."

"Well, his name's Marvin, he lives on a farm and he says we come from monkeys." Roger considered this new information for a moment.

"Biology isn't my department, Sweetie, but wouldn't that comment be insulting himself as well? Plus, we didn't exactly evolve from monkeys. They're still around. Is that what you want to talk about, or are we going to get to a story? Sounds to me like he likes you. "

"I think he just meant to be mean to me, dad. I climb better than him. Way better. Anyway, he said no matter how high I could climb—even like a monkey—he could always fly higher in his crop duster."

Roger was again surprised by the variety of torture and teasing kids could inflict upon one another, especially when it was just to cover up an obvious attraction. Some were so good at it they made a career of tormenting their partners for life. His ex-wife kept trying to change him too. Make him "evolve into a new man" she even said. When are you going to publish your book, Roger? Once you're published they'll have to realize you're more valuable to the school than just any old teacher. You'll be promoted, make more money, we can get a better house, have more kids and they can carry on your legacy of excellence in literature. We'll evolve in one generation to a family of powerful authors. Maybe even a world-renowned publishing company. What a ridiculous idea, as if creativity, success, and ambition could be passed on to children with any more certainty than hair or eye color.

"Dad? Your face looks funny. Are you mad? Can we still talk about evolution or do I get a story?" Then, with false enthusiasm and a hint of sarcasm Emma added, "How 'bout a story with evolution in it? Do you have one of those?"

"Not really. What do you know about evolution? Are you studying it in class or something?" Emma nodded. "Well, the first thing you have to realize is that with evolution, extinction is just as common and important to the theory as the emergence of new species. As for your friend Marvin's attempt to insult you, what he needs to know is that both modern primates and humans probably came from the same common ancestor, now extinct. If we came from monkeys, they wouldn't be around any more." Roger wasn't sure she was following but he went on anyway.

"And new species aren't just bigger, faster, or prettier in coloring than the previous generations. New behaviors can make a group more successful just as much as thicker fur, sharper claws or longer wings. Did you get to that in class yet?" Emma shook her head. "Well, think of an animal like the sloth. They hang upside down in trees and move so slowly that potential predators don't even see them. A faster moving sloth on the ground wouldn't last long looking for fallen fruit. He'd be lion food. The tree-dwellers move slowly and live to make more sloth babies. Like you and Marvin."

"Dad, geez. I don't like him. Can we just get to the story?"

"Sure hon'. This one takes place on the moon."

"Any monkeys?"

"Nope. No monkeys."

Anxiety

Joan lived in a small apartment on the moon. It was modest by Earth standards but she needed little else. There was a place to make and eat meals, a place to sleep and a place to take care of necessary personal hygiene. The kitchen was really only a storage cabinet with dried foods and a sink for preparation and disposal. The dinette barely fit two small stools. The bed was a single mattress in the corner of the room that doubled as a love seat. Just inside the door was a long bank of computers where she did her research. The bathroom was identical in design to those found in jail cells on Earth, but hydraulic and chemical rather than water-based and gravity-driven. Having 1/6th gravity can hinder the most simple bodily functions.

There were two luxuries. Joan would never have left the Earth without a promise of at least the occasional hot shower, even with recycled water. The second was the result of lessons she learned growing up in the suburbs. Joan rightly assumed that on the moon, as on any other planet, the key to real estate value was location, location, location. She occupied one of the few outer apartments with a view through the protective dome in the outer ring of the compound. When the timing was right, no other apartment could beat the view of the Earth through her kitchen window. True the Earth was always in view, but given the slight wobble in the moon's orbit and the compound's location she was occasionally treated to the illusion that the earth was rising over the rounded horizon.

It was a colony of a few thousand, all immigrants from Earth, all chosen for some particular skill they brought to add to the success of the colony. They were scientists and volunteers. Nothing was wrong with the home planet and they didn't choose to live there to escape some political, religious or social persecution. Life was comfortable if a tad boring, but these scientists chose a life of the mind and needed little else. Friendships were mostly casual and aligned along professional interests. Joan's best and only friend was Martha a woman she met on the transport. Joan was the pilot, Martha an engineer. There was enough of an overlap in their training and expertise that they could converse on the same subjects and both respond to jokes about female rocket scientists.

"Good morning human," said Joan's front door.

"Oh shut up and let me in," grumbled Martha. It was the

convention to have any and all robotic appliances address the colonists as human. For a door it seemed rather absurd, but other robots were lifelike enough that confusion had resulted in lawsuits in the past. Martha was there for her morning visit, to update Joan on any new gossip and to hear herself talk. "Did you know you can unhook that ridiculous voice door?"

"Hi Martha. Yes, but I kind of like it. When I come back from my workouts in the gravity room I like to imagine it's my husband or better yet, my lover. When I'm feeling saucy I program it for Spanish." She handed Martha a small cup of coffee.

"Cute. What's new in propulsion? Any advancements in thrust? How's the chassis? Inquiring minds want to know."

"No. I haven't solved that pesky problem about the speed of light." Martha gave her a look of mock disappointment, thrusting out her bottom lip. "Oh, you're not talking about work, are you? To answer your question, no I haven't talked to Ronald yet. Face it, he's not interested in me. Besides he's a ditch digger." That was what Joan called members of the primary settlement team. Putting up a bio-dome invariably involved a lot of excavation and soil stabilization.

"Ditch digger? He's the leading roboticist on the moon. Speaking of which, what time is it?"

Joan's single piece of decoration was a vintage analog kitchen clock she smuggled aboard her transport shuttle. Clocks were hardly needed since every machine had its own internal digital connection to the standard in Greenwich. She had to starve herself for a week to lose the two pounds needed to avoid suspicion at the launch pad. She'd been able to slip it easily in her jumpsuit.

"It's almost 9:00am. He'll be along any minute, Martha. Calm yourself."

It was Ronald's habit to get his exercise in a manner that might prove useful in future settlements. The gravity gym was fine for most folks to maintain their muscle mass and bone density. But in his opinion, it prepared them not at all for the different environments and topography of the planets and moons to be settled in the future.

"Why can't he just exercise in the gym like everyone else? And that suit looks ridiculous."

Joan had to agree. On cue, Ronald rounded the corner on his usual clockwise route as if in slow motion. Between the #300 weight suit and the 1/6 gravity, his stride made him look like a bobbing jellyfish. Despite their derisive comments, both women were riveted to the window. Here was a man who clearly stood out from the crowd. His intellectual prowess was well known and he was a certain pick for the Jupiter mission. But add to that quality the fact that he was an obviously fit specimen in his prime, and his good points more than made up for the minor eccentricity of his choice of exercise.

What happened next was so obvious it could only have been planned months in advance. The Earth stood on the horizon like a giant beach ball. Ronald began to lengthen his loping underwater stride. Thirty feet before eclipsing the magnificent view of the Earth, he spread his arms, took a mighty leap and launched himself clear over. He landed with perfect symmetry on the other side making a small cloud of dust rise. Joan and Martha traced the entire arc of his display with open mouths. They followed his progress around the compound until he was out of view and they were both left with their heads leaning against the tiny kitchen window.

Martha broke the silence with some defensive sarcasm. "Well, Joan. If you like a show-off, there's your man." She knew the display could only have been for her friend. There was little chance Ronald knew Martha was there for coffee. Martha drained her lukewarm cup and excused herself with a promise to engineer a blind date with Ronald if Joan wouldn't take the initiative. *"Buenas tardes, senorita,"* said the front door.

"Oh, shut up," barked Martha.

Joan decided she must meet Ronald as soon as possible. Despite her best judgement she knew it would have to be out in the relative exposure of the compound's outer rim. The robotics laboratory was out of the question. She had no reason to show up there unannounced or without an escort. He didn't use that natural meat market, the gravity gym. Steeling her nerve she resolved to jog the compound the following morning. She cleverly deduced a counterclockwise route would increase her chances to 100% of meeting Ronald with minimal effort.

With her anxiety over what to say and worse, his possible reaction, Joan accomplished exactly nothing that day. She even failed to eat. She barely slept overnight playing the encounter with Ronald over and over in her mind. Despite being out of bed in plenty of time she still risked missing her "date" by agonizing over what to wear. Suddenly nothing in her wardrobe was adequate for the simple task of a slow jog once around the compound. In the end, she decided on the outfit she'd normally wear to the gravity gym—running shoes, loose long pants, matching long-sleeved, zippered coat, and ponytail. She thought the color was most flattering to her eyes, skin and hair but agonized further over the location of the zipper. Too low and she risked showing too much of the minimizing sports bra. Too high and she may get no reaction from Ronald at all. In the end she decided on a mid-chest level so as not to appear too desperate, but allowing some ventilation in case she overheated. The last thing she wanted was to appear distressed about a simple jog in front of a man carrying 300 pounds.

Her knees were shaking when she bounded out the apartment door, but the motion helped calm her nerves. The same anxieties plagued her mind that had kept her up all night. Suddenly she realized she'd made an entire loop and was back at her apartment. She immediately felt foolish when she realized in thinking so intensely about meeting Ronald, she'd copied his clockwise route. Turning around to retrace her steps actually helped her settle down. Joan was one who could laugh at her own folly.

The correction soon paid off and she saw Ronald in the distance, instantly recognizing his confident, loping stride. As they approached each other Joan made the wise decision to let him speak first. Clearly the fact of her mere presence would signal to him that she'd seen his display the day before. Also, by mimicking his eccentricity she was signaling not only interest but approval of his behavior. Plus, as Martha always said, better to remain silent and have people think you're a moron than open your mouth and remove all doubt. She couldn't trust her voice she was so nervous. When was the last time she'd had a date? Even spoken to a man? She was embarrassed to admit to herself it was back on Earth, not in her graduate school or college days but early in high school. Now here she was, approaching the most intelligent and handsome man of the species, 235,000 miles from home.

As the gap between them narrowed she slowed her own stride to prolong the encounter. What would he say? Would he stop or just fly right past? Should she speak first? Doubts began to re-enter her fragile mind. When he did speak, Joan couldn't have been more surprised. "Good morning, human," said Ronald the Robot.

When she awoke from her fainting spell a few moments later, Ronald the Robot was looking down on her with a concerned expression. Her mind filled all at once with a dozen emotions. First was embarrassment at getting so worked up over a robot. Imagine finding out your future love, the father of your children, is a toaster. The second was astonishment. She'd never seen a robot so advanced and easily forgave herself for making the mistake of lusting for this perfect specimen. Then came doubt. Was there really a Ronald the Man? And if there was, what was he doing leading on poor defenseless rocket pilots? Her final emotion was anger and she got up off the dusty floor of the compound, brushed herself off and demanded, "Take me to your creator."

Ronald the Robot turned in silence and led her to the opposite side of the compound. At Ronald's apartment the door opened with its usual greeting, refreshing Joan's anger at having been manipulated. She burst into the room prepared to deliver a good lashing and was stunned to silence by what she saw. The size and general layout were the same as her own apartment. There was the kitchen, the row of computers and the personal area. But every square inch of the floor, walls and ceiling was covered in some sort of mechanical device. Seated in the center of the floor was Ronald, wearing a magnifying, lighted headset and fiddling with what looked like a mechanical arm. He looked as artificial as the creations around him. To complete the contrast to her own austere dwelling was the view out the window. Instead of looking back to earth, Ronald's vista was of the cosmos, the parade of planets, the constellations in all their brilliant luminescence.

When the door closed behind her and Ronald failed to look up from his work, she found herself feeling more awkward than ever. Her embarrassment soon turned to fascination as the scientist part of her became interested in his contraption. It was some sort of arm and hand assembly but the digits were paired and of various sizes. As he put it through its functions, Joan began to regret her thinking of him as a ditch digger. This arm was clearly designed for more versatile capacities than your average shovel. It's balletic movements were likely for some kind of repair manipulation but so smooth as to suggest they were part of an expressive human dance. Joan found herself hypnotized by the sheer grace of it. Ronald the Man broke the spell by speaking to Ronald the Robot, "We'll download your gross motor program data in a minute. Let me see how this arm fits you first."

Ronald stood up still wearing his headset and goggles and therefore failed to notice the intruder at his door. Joan's anxiety returned when she realized she was standing in a complete stranger's apartment unannounced. She hoped he didn't do anything private while she was there. When he stood to his full height she noticed Ronald the Robot was not only a magnificent creation, but modeled after his designer. They looked like twins. It was Ronald's turn to be surprised when he removed his goggles to fit the mechanical arm to his creation. "Joan, how did you get here? Er, when…I mean, uh. Hello, I didn't hear you come in." She had a hard time retaining her earlier anger and blurted the story in one long breath.

"And how do you know my name?" she said in an accusing manner.

Ronald apologized, "You were the pilot on my shuttle. I'm sorry if I frightened or misled you. That was not my intention. Call it terminal shyness, but I wanted to meet you, too. You don't just walk up to a beautiful pilot and tell her you want to take her to Jupiter." He was hoping she'd notice the double compliment even though he recited the information in a neutral manner. There was a good chance she knew the details of the rumored Jupiter project.

With introductions out of the way, they took a seat at the dinette window. Ronald outlined his plans. It had all started innocently enough. He was working on the new robot technology for an upcoming colony project. When people mistook his robot for him he let the rumors build thinking it might get Joan's attention. When he learned she lived on the earth side of the colony he began to send Ronald the Robot on full circuit training missions only hoping she'd be impressed with the magnitude of his creation. He never dreamed she'd mistake his robot for him.

They shared a good laugh at the situation but then Ronald became more serious. "We need a pilot for the Jupiter mission, Joan, and you're the best." She raised her eyebrows at this roundabout proposition. She was as surprised at the compliment as she was the boldness of his implied intent. There were rumors that this was to be a self-sustaining colony. Her skills as a pilot were clear. He was very careful not to emphasize her obvious assets as a mate. Here was Ronald, a man she'd met literally moments before, asking her to not only risk her life, but in effect, marry him and have children. Her answer came without hesitation.

"Yes."

19

First Memory

After Fall Break the members of the Diner's Club settled into a comfortable friendship. Comments and topics were somewhat more predictable but far from boring or rote. Hence, everyone kept showing up, despite the lack of any formalization of the group. Danny and Josh were still at each other with every comment. It was a friendly antagonism that neither would admit they enjoyed. Paul continued his unrequited love of June. Will kept his interest in Danny a secret as best he could, which meant he had not yet gotten up the nerve to ask her out on a date. Hardly one for tradition, Danny had almost forced the issuing by asking out Will herself. Then it occurred to her that they'd been enjoying the equivalent of dating by meeting once a week at the diner. Courtney got over her initial shyness and started to contribute more both in topics and stimulating comments.

Danny finished her chipped beef on toast, put twice what it cost on the counter and sauntered over to take her seat. The group was literally talking about the weather, like musicians warming up their instruments. She sat down next to Will and said to noone in particular, "What's your first memory? Did it ever occur to you why that particular memory was laid down first? Is it just biology? Does your brain suddenly decide these experiences are worth remembering?"

Will, always the farm boy, came back with the evolution angle. "I think we have to start remembering things that are going to be important to our survival. If your first memory is of your mother it's because you learn she's your ally, not an animal that's going to kill and eat you. We have to reach reproductive age after all."

Josh just needed an opening to start in with the barbs. "Tell me Will, just when will you be reaching reproductive age?" he asked with false concern.

"About the time you start using silverware," Danny said, defending Will. She continued, "That was the first thing I thought though, that the early memories would be useful somehow later on in life. But mine is of no use at all." This confession stilled even Josh's tongue. It was Courtney who broke the silence.

"I have what I'd call early memories but I can't really say which one was first," she said. "What was yours Danny?"

"Well, I'm lying on my back looking up at a picture of some saints from a Biblical scene. I'm about 3 or 3 ½ and I'm in the Crying Room at my parent's church. You know, the place where all the moms and dads with young kids are sequestered so the crying doesn't disturb the worship of the other parishoners. I have my head in my mother's lap and that's the reason I was looking up at this picture. We ended up in the Crying Room because my mom was breast-feeding my younger brother."

"Did you just use the word 'sequestered'?" Josh said. Danny was talking like she was reciting a speech. In point of fact, she'd thought about it for some time and had told the story in the past. This time it was Paul who made the defense against Josh to keep them on track and avoid another round of smart-ass comments leading nowhere.

"Hold on, Josh," Paul said. "I like this. Why do you think you remember it? Why not say, a memory from ½ hour before? Or after? How come you don't remember walking or riding to the church first? What other details do you remember?"

Danny went on with her description. "Well, there was a single tinny speaker at the front of the room so we could hear the service. Plus, a giant window overlooking the church, like the panels you see in hospital nurseries so people can see their baby. You could hear the priest but he was so far away you couldn't put the words onto his mouth. You couldn't see his lips move if you know what I mean. The room itself was about the size of an average bedroom. There were maybe 3 or 4 pews of some hardwood about 12-feet long, with clear coat polyurethane and aged to a light yellow. The walls were white, painted cinder block, that sort of post-War cheap construction, I guess. The floor was linoleum. I don't remember a smell. I think it was summer or fall, definitely not winter. I can't remember what I was wearing. Oh, and the ladies bathroom entrance was at the back of the room. Better for diaper changing, I guess."

"So why do you think that's your first memory?" Will said.

"I don't know," she answered honestly. "Maybe it was just unique enough, different enough from say, having a bath or dinner, that it sticks out."

Courtney had an idea. "How many times were you in that room? 100? 200? Maybe it's the kind of thing that happened more than once, but wasn't so mundane as say, chewing, that your brain decided to remember it. But you have to admit, it's a little sketchy."

"What do you mean? I thought it was pretty detailed for a memory of when I wasn't even 4-years old yet," Danny said.

"What I mean is, you admitted yourself that you can't remember some of the details," Courtney said. "How many pews were there? 3 or 4? You don't remember the season, or a smell. Maybe that memory is a composite of dozens of trips to that same room. Are you sure it was your mother's lap you were lying on?"

"Well, yea. Even if I didn't know it at the time, think of her has 'Mother' then, her presence in my life has persisted in some predictable fashion. So the two impressions are compatible. I mean, the woman I see now is older but it's definitely her. Right?"

"What if you were adopted?" asked Josh in a rare moment of earnestness. They all stared. "No, really. What if your memory of it was not only flawed, but your interpretation of it? Would it change how you felt about it? If on your 21st birthday, a lawyer contacts you, says you're the heir to some huge trust fund you never knew about, would it change things? Would you turn down the money, say it was incompatible with your memory of your true mother?"

"I think I'd be a little more than pissed off," Will said. "Having to work so hard growing up and then finding out I was really born to royalty."

Paul added, "Yea, but can you ever know? You always hear stories about this or that bank robber from the 1800's that no one could track down. You think it could never happen in this day and age what with us all being branded with a Social Security number and tracked in our daily habits by the banks and credit card companies. But think about your most basic assumption: My parents kept track of me from the moment I came out, to the day we left the hospital together, and have made sure I was safe until I could form my first memories of them."

"That's a little creepy," Courtney said.

"Yea," Paul said. "Do the math. Let's say you were born in one of the larger city hospitals. They might have 50 deliveries a day on average. Babies are similar enough that maybe you got switched by accident. Let's say the odds of such a ridiculous mistake are a million to one. That means there are 200 or 300 kids in the U.S. alone who grew up in the wrong family. In China, it would be thousands. Think of the countries where they don't strap a wristband to you the minute they cut the umbilical cord. I love to think of the aunts and uncles all cooing over me a week later, telling me how much I look like my father."

"Actually, you'd have to double it," pointed out Courtney. "With each goof up, there would be two babies switched. Even if the odds are a billion to one, that's 10 or 12 kids right now worldwide who are in the wrong household."

June was at the counter trying not to show much interest. Having had a child and given it up for adoption, she often wondered about the same scenarios, how her daughter's life might be playing out right now. She lazily turned the pages of a day-old newspaper not reading a word.

"But would it make much difference?" Will said. "We're not talking about a Chinese baby being switched for Danny. It's virtually impossible to mess up by switching a boy for a girl. That decreases the odds by half right off the bat. Then, we're talking about babies whose parents used the same hospital. They probably live in the same neighborhoods, have relatively similar incomes, lifestyles and the like. Those kids could grow up as next-door neighbors, attend the same schools, be on the same soccer team. Have you ever spent so much time at a friend's house you wondered why you didn't just move in or were born into that family from the beginning?"

Paul said, "What about the opposite? Let's say a baby is born, kidnapped or lost in some way and ends up in an orphanage. The parents later decide they need to adopt and they go and pick out their own baby."

"That's just ridiculous," Josh said. "They'd just have another one."

"What if the mother had to have an operation, or just couldn't get pregnant again? It's not so unthinkable as babies being switched in a nursery," countered Danny.

As he'd done countless times before, especially when the diner was slow, Paul invited June to join in. "Hey, June, what do you think? Are you feeling confident in those memories of your parents?"

She looked up slowly from the paper she wasn't reading. Always one to go from the concrete to the general, June offered, "What you're all talking about, I think, is what it means to grow up in a family. To think of yourself as belonging somewhere. It doesn't really matter if you're genetically related, right? What intrigues me are the possibilities and variations. I can't imagine a mother not knowing she's ever been pregnant and had a child. Outside of some cheesy made-for-TV movie where she falls into a coma or suffers amnesia from a head injury. On the other hand, it's easy to think of a man who doesn't know he's fathered one, especially if the mother never told him, or thought some other guy was the father."

The group was silent for a minute to digest the details. Paul twirled a spoon in his coffee. Will took a sip of watered-down soda. Danny ran a hand through her stubble and twirled an earring. Courtney and Josh avoided eye contact. In a few short years they'd likely be wondering if a child of theirs was misplaced by some careless obstetrical nurse.

"Okay, I've got one," Will said. "Imagine a man living in say, New York. He's single, and wants to get married and have kids but can't find a spouse. He travels to Paris on business where he meets a model and gets her pregnant. See, she travels a lot for her modeling gigs. She never tells him. She has the baby in New York but gives it up for adoption so nobody in France knows about it. He gives up on the marriage thing, and just adopts the baby, later they meet up again in New York when she's decided to settle down and give up modeling. She adopts her own baby back and marries the father. Only she doesn't recall that he's the one who got her pregnant in the first place, and he doesn't remember her from the first time they met."

Josh can't let this little story go by without a comment. "Oh, please, like you can just push out a baby anywhere you want to. And Mr. Devoted Father-To-Be has one night stands while on business trips? I don't think so."

Will answered, "I don't quite have all the details worked out yet, Josh. Maybe she has dual citizenship. Maybe the guy's frustrated that he can't meet a wife. Or they marry first, then adopt their own baby back. Maybe he's mistaken for a spy and drugged by the Russian mafia. Whatever. You come up with something better. June, tell Josh he's a small-minded fool with no imagination."

"Josh, you're a small-minded fool with no imagination," June said. "Believe me, there are stranger things happening around us all the time. We just don't know about them. Who wants to share their uncertainty about something so basic as where they came from? We define ourselves by where we believe we came from. We judge ourselves and each other by whether we came from poverty or riches and what we did with those tools. These are some of the oldest cliches out there, the rags to riches stories, the falls from grace. And trust me. I know there's nothing impossible about a businessman and a model having a baby."

20

June Gets Some Good Work Done

A week after June's scenery chewing entrance to the faculty mixer, it was business as usual. She found herself seated uncomfortably at her desk after another week of just getting by. The pain in her rear only distracted her from grading papers whenever she moved slightly. In other words, all the time. She paused to scratch a bright, blue stitch on her left palm with the back of her red pen. An hour later she'd only gotten through the first paragraph of the first midterm paper. Between the discomfort of her wounds and her typically restless mind, she found herself accomplishing precious little.

Which isn't to say she was still struggling like she did in the first week. Her job had settled into a predictable rhythm. She had started eating breakfast again and was even keeping it down. She wondered if this comfort level was what people meant by a career. Would she wake up after 20 years and find she was doing the same thing? It wasn't that the material was boring her, after all, she controlled the curriculum. It was just that she had yet to find a student or colleague who would challenge her.

No, that wasn't it. Maybe it was the complete lack of a social life outside of the academics. She'd been so worried about living up to her own high expectations as a teacher she forgot about the rest of her life. Even in graduate school she was able to meet with friends after class. True, they often ended up continuing the same classroom discussions over pots of coffee or pitchers of beer, but at least it was a different setting, some new faces.

It wasn't for lack of choices, despite the provincial size and culture of her little college town. She wasn't a snob about her social life and could enjoy a bowling alley as much as the next person. I'm just too busy, she thought. If the opportunity arose to have an actual date, she'd have a hard time deciding where to squeeze it in. Work took more time than she thought it would to just teach, test, and grade the material she knew so well. June found herself just wanting dinner and a good night's rest at the end of the day. She had to admit, the last thing she needed was a man in her life. Considering how impressive she was at the first faculty meeting she attended, it was probably best she stick to the classroom, Roger's office, and the small upstairs room she was renting in the house off campus.

The midterm papers stacked on her desk were a major disappointment. Still, she intended to make a dent in grading them before the weekend. The more she marked with her red pen, the more obvious it became that most of her students hadn't read the assigned work. None had demonstrated any capacity for critical thought let alone conveyed that understanding in plain writing. She began to get angry. First, at individual students, the ones whose work she thought would be better simply because they were intelligent and excelled in other areas. Then, she started to hate the academic system that allowed them to get all the way to college and consider this work to be adequate.

Chuck appeared in her doorway and casually knocked on the jamb like a neighbor in a sitcom. June thought, the pompous ass must think he's welcome anywhere at any time. Then for no reason, June immediately thought the worst. I'm fired. Well, it was worth a try, this academic life. Some student or parent must have complained already. I wonder if he'll make me pay for the ruined carpet in the meeting room. She heard somewhere that employees should be fired first thing in the morning. Did Chuck know that? Would he care? No, it must be the carpet. He couldn't fire me after just two months. The axe would have to come from the Board, Chuck didn't even have the authority. Roger would have said something. He'd have allowed me a probationary period or some sort of second chance. What else could it be? She concluded her internal argument by deciding she'd better say hello. "Chuck, uh, hi. What can I do for you?"

"Sorry to barge in unannounced. Is this a bad time? I'd be happy to come back if you're busy, but I was in the building and saw your door open," he lied. Chuck had been trying to come up with excuses since the party to risk a meeting. That weenie assistant of his was always on him and today was the first day in a week he hadn't been booked with useless meetings. He figured her injuries were a good place to start and act casual. Ever calculating, he decided he'd sound concerned and she'd appreciate that. "How's your back side healing up?"

"I'm sitting on it, so it can't be that bad," June lied right back to him. What a moron she thought. Didn't he see that huge chunk of plate I pulled out of my ass? What's his game? Thanks for reminding me when I was finally able to forget the pain for 4 seconds. Okay you diabolical waste, go ahead and fire me, I can take it. And stuff your new white carpet, asshole. Despite her thoughts, she smiled at him blankly, wondering if she should plead for her job or thank him for letting her out of this nightmare.

Chuck made an attempt to smile warmly, then proceeded with his script of seduction. "That didn't come out so well, did it? Here I am trying to be charming and I'm coming off like a complete cretin."

Charming? Did he just say "charming?" No, tell me he's not here to date me. Cretin? Can he possibly know that cretinism has to do with the thyroid gland?

In her usual tactless way, June couldn't stop herself from putting it all on the table. "I thought you were here to fire me. I know I'm doing a crappy job, but Roger's helping me and I'll get better." He chuckled and shook his head. That wasn't it. "Then what do I owe for the carpet in the admin building? I have some savings if it needs to be replaced right away, otherwise I'd prefer you took it out of my next few paychecks."

"Not even close," he reassured her. "In fact, Carl tells me for some reason your classes are some of the most talked about on campus. The carpet is as good as new after a steam cleaning. No, I'm not here on formal business at all. In case you didn't know it, we're the only new faculty this year. I figured since we had that in common we should get to know each other better." Chuck hoped she'd pick up on the subtle compliment he gave himself.

"So you want to fuck me, then?" she blurted.

"No, no, nothing like that," he instinctively denied.

"You mean you don't want to have sex with me?" June said.

"I didn't say that," he back-pedaled. "Listen, I just thought we could get a cup of coffee. Or something. Talk." Chuck was way out of his element but by no means giving up.

"Look. Let me make it simple for you. You'd like to think you're here to get to know me. You envision an extended chit-chat, then maybe we decide it's dinner time and go to a restaurant together. Maybe we exchange numbers. We talk later on the phone, have more non-dates. But eventually, sooner or later you hope to bed me. Right? A simple 'yes' will do."

"Yes."

"See how easy that was? Isn't honesty fun? Now, if you'd phrase that in the form of a complete sentence, I can answer your proposal."

"June, will you have sex with me?" Chuck couldn't believe what he was saying. Never in his life had it been like this. She must be toying with him, but what did he have to lose? He'd previously spent thousands of dollars in courtship only to be snubbed at the threshold. The only thing more surprising up to this moment was what she said next.

"Sure Chuck. Let's have sex," June said. When she saw his expression change from surprise to suspicion, she continued, "What? You don't believe me? Well, I can be slutty when it suits me. You've admitted what you want, now what's in it for me?"

"Whatever you want."

"Oh, come on, Chuck. What can you give me? Let me summarize for you. Everyone knows you've been parked here by your mother. You must have done something pretty despicable. You got your fancy sports car, your salary and trust fund, but you're bored. You figured you'd hit on the new teacher for a little entertainment value. But you're just a figurehead. The two things I could use you can't give me. I won't take money. I may enjoy the occasional fling, but I'm not a prostitute. What I could really use is a lighter course load, but that's determined by the board, not you. As for opening my eyes to an enlightened sexual experience, well, let's just say I'm skeptical. So, I'll ask you again, what can you bring?"

Her little speech hit home on some sore spots. Pressed with answering the question of why a woman should want to sleep with him, Chuck came up blank. Back home his money and family name gave him rock star power. He had to come up with something. This opportunity was too good to give up. Thinking wasn't one of his strong points, let alone thinking on his feet. How do you impress a master of Russian literature? In the end, he went for a combination of his old script and calling her bluff. "Well, figurehead or not, I am the Dean. Call it money in the bank. Maybe something will come up in the future that I can help you with. It can't hurt to have the Dean on your side. And don't forget the benefits of my considerable charm."

June couldn't help but chuckle at the last line. "Okay, your amazing powers of persuasion have me convinced I'd be a fool not to sleep with you. When should this momentous occasion take place?"

"Well, how about right now?" Chuck suggested. He knew he was pressing but frankly, he didn't have anything else to do.

"Get real, Chuck. I've got to get through at least a third of this stack tonight."

"Okay. I can wait," he said.

"You're a piece of work," June said. He'd been standing at the doorway for their entire exchange. Now he had his hands in his pockets like he was waiting for the bus. "Go on, sit down. If I so much as hear you breathing, I'm calling it off." She nodded her head towards a chair by the overstuffed bookcase. When he casually kicked the door behind him, leaving it gaping by 4 inches, she rolled her eyes at his smugness.

Then to her surprise, June began to make progress on the papers. The stack on her right gradually turned into a stack on her left.

As the afternoon faded into evening, Chuck was content to sit still and stare out the window. When it was dark, he turned his attention to the outline of June's body. In the four hours she made him wait, not once did it occur to him to peruse her bookcase to entertain himself or pass the time. He had the patience of a hungry dog waiting for scraps to fall from the dinner table. He felt like his silent obedience would demonstrate his devotion and therefore his worthiness of the event to follow.

At about 10pm June put the last of the papers in the stack on her left. One class done. She sat back in her chair and let out a long sigh. Making two fists, she put both hands into the small of her back and stretched. With her eyes closed and head back, the position caused her breasts to jut forward in a provocative way that was not lost on Chuck. She turned to him and said, "Well, as they say, your place or mine?"

Chuck rose from his chair and said, "Right here works for me." He stood her up at the desk, kicked over her chair, and attempted a kiss.

June didn't resist but she couldn't will her body to respond either. A late dinner and a good night's rest were foremost on her mind. By her estimation, Chuck followed a script from a romance novel. Taking her on the desk somehow failed to instill in her the level of passion that was probably intended. He was a bit rough, but not too much so, in tearing her blouse open. He was acting out a part after all. She was pleased she'd chosen one of her prettier, lacy bras that day, as Chuck pushed the cups aside.

As opening night performances went, his was average. He kissed her some more, gently at first, then with more force when she didn't respond immediately. He played with her hair, rubbed her neck, kissed her shoulder, then her breast. She dully noted that he was careful not to overlook any part of the anatomy. June had to suppress a giggle at his clumsiness when that song about the bones went through her mind. *"The shinbone's connected to the..."* The disconnected teacher part of her couldn't help but grade his performance: C-minus. He was thorough, but completely lacking in imagination.

Chuck pressed her onto the desk after a woefully inadequate amount of foreplay. He dramatically swept the term papers and other desktop contents to the floor. He figured the gesture would further demonstrate his true passion. Her calendar blotter dropped with a mild thud. Chuck mistook her groan as one of pleasure. In his immense self-admiration he assumed she must be enjoying him and not in fact, aching from the cuts on her bum.

June grabbed the edge of the desk and tried to brace herself against his thrusts. If he would have made eye contact June could have suggested they move to a new location for their mutual benefit. Thankfully his pace increased and she rightly assumed he wouldn't be taking much longer. She looked around the room bored and was annoyed to see the door ajar. Looking back at her was a wide-eyed security guard. His surprised expression suggested to June he'd only recently arrived. She became self-conscious of her exposed breast and reached over to cover it with her right hand. She squinted her eyes at him like she would a younger brother trying to sneak a peak at her in the shower. Nodding her head once to acknowledge their secret, she motioned for him to go, and he did.

Thankfully for June, Chuck in his oblivion and self-absorption, missed the entire exchange. He exited, zipped up unceremoniously, and let June put herself back together. He tried to make light of it, as if he'd planned on being brief. "Well, now that that's out of the way, maybe we could start dating, ha, ha."

"I don't think so," June said.

"What do you mean? Can't I see you again? It's going to be hard for us NOT to continually run into each other," he said.

"I said we could have sex, but I don't want a boyfriend. Plus, you've got to give the cuts on my ass some time to heal up. Maybe I could be on top. That was a little uncomfortable to say the least."

"Oh, shit. I'm sorry, I forgot about the…uh, your injury."

"It's okay. Or rather, it's too late now. I appreciate your enthusiasm, but let's plan things out a little better next time. Maybe when I'm not so busy, huh?" She was also thinking they were going to have to be much more discreet. In the meantime, she might have to approach the security guard and be sure to arrange some way to keep the rumors quiet. If nothing came of their discovery, she might give the egotistical bastard another shot at pleasing her.

Chuck, let himself out the door. "Well, you know how to reach me," he said.

"Yea, you can let yourself out, you smug bastard," she teased him with a laugh. "I'll call you when I think of what you can do for me. Or when I'm exceedingly hard up."

June replaced the strewn contents of her desk. Collecting the midterm papers into a pile, she saw a grammatical error she'd missed. She righted the chair, sat down gingerly, retrieved her red pen from its cup and corrected the mistake. She put the term paper on top of the newly formed stack, stowed the pen and said out loud, "There. Time for some dinner and a good night's rest." In all, it had turned out to be a very productive day.

21

Counter Entropy

The evening started with June attempting to stump the club. She was in a good mood for the first time since the school year started. A ridiculous grin was smeared across her face during the dinner rush. It can't be confirmed, but she may have had sex on her mind. When pressed for a topic, she asked them, "What's the evolutionary advantage of homosexuality?" Her query was met with silence at first while each member puzzled the assumptions in their own head. The members were seated in their usual stations and she wanted to keep things interesting until her date arrived.

Danny was in the middles stages of crocheting something intricate, with a tiny Number 1 hook. "Yea," she said. "If evolution proceeds by natural selection, which requires mating, reproduction, and mutations, then how do two same sex partners contribute to the gene pool, let alone the origin of species?"

"Maybe it's a dead end, like sponges," said Paul. He snapped a crispy, over-cooked fry and swirled it in ketchup with no intention of eating it.

"But it's not a physical characteristic, like colorful feathers or horns," Will said. "It's a behavior. Like the slow movement of a sloth, there's got to be some reason for it."

"No. Evolution doesn't follow some rational direction," Danny said. "It's not designed to end up with *Homo sapiens*. Some branches have been so successful they haven't changed for millions of years. Sharks and alligators are done, they're not changing. But if some better predator came along they'd starve out or worse be eaten. Kill or be killed, evolve or become extinct."

"How do you know if a shark is gay?" Josh said. "Hey, that sounds like the beginning of a knock-knock joke. Better yet, 'A gay shark walks into a bar...' I'll have to work on that one."

"At least you'll be working on something," Danny said. "By the way, genius. Sharks don't walk, they swim."

"Ooh, zinger, you got me there."

The deep fryer made a beep and June raised a fresh basket of fries out of the oil. She poured them into a paper-lined basket, sprinkled them with salt, and set them on the counter. She made eye contact with Courtney, who got up from her aisle seat to retrieve the snack for the Club. She set it on the table within easy reach of all the members, then made a second lap to the counter for mustard. "But you see it across species," Courtney said. "Wolves have been known to exhibit homosexual behavior. Usually it's the subordinate males in a pack lacking females. It's not like they're sparring rams vying for the attention of a fertile female. That behavior isn't showing anything to a potential mate."

"Maybe it's just about being accepted. Feeling like you're part of a group," Paul said. "There's safety in numbers even if you're not contributing to your own gene pool. The actual sex could be the learned part. Heck, heterosexuals don't know what they're doing when they lose their virginity either."

"You'd have to be a masochist," Courtney said. "Who'd want to be part of a group that's ridiculed, abused, and teased? After racism it's like, the last group you can be prejudiced against and nobody jumps up to defend them. Noone calls you a bigot if you make a gay joke."

"Yea," Will said. "I think it's genetic. Society tells you from the moment you're born whether you're pink or blue. That's why a homosexual has to 'come out of the closet' when they finally realize where they fit in. I think we can argue it's not a choice. But then again, plenty of things we do to fit in are painful. We get tattoos, pierce our ears to be like other people and that doesn't make us a masochist."

June was entertained by the exchange. It made her clean-up after the Saturday dinner rush more tolerable. She wore a smirk while scraping the grille with her back to the Club. "It sounds like you're all lecturing. You're just restating the problem. I ask you again, what good is homosexuality? It must be part of a successful strategy for our species or it would have disappeared."

"No, that's not necessarily true," Will said. "We still have an appendix and that's not helping anyone. You could even argue that it's harmful to the species to have an appendix."

"Sort of like Josh," Danny said, without looking up from her crocheting.

"Cute, I get it. I'm useless," Josh said. "Then tell me why I'm the only one who ever shows up here with a potential mate." He nodded to Courtney while looking around the table and she gave him a playful peck on the cheek. The obvious answer didn't need to be stated. It was only a matter of time before Will and Danny were an item. Paul would continue to pursue June until she was officially off the market.

The question hung in the air until the only noise was the buzzing of the fluorescent lights. June had finished scraping the grill and turned her attention to the floor. She swept up a few stray crumbs and broke the stalemate by offering, "What about ants or bees? Don't they have a caste system? What good is a worker bee, when they don't reproduce? Why would the queen go to the trouble of laying all those extra eggs?"

"So you're saying gays are the slaves of our society?" Will said. " That doesn't seem right. I don't get it."

"No, I'm just saying they may already serve some important purpose. Homosexuality probably isn't some mutation that's leading to a new species," June said.

"What about in the arts?" Danny said.

"Oh, here we go," Josh said. "Grandma Danny here, whittles out a doily and comes up with the most silly cliche out there: All gays are artistic. Next you're going to say they make our lives more meaningful by producing Broadway musicals."

"So I've got a skill, sue me."

"Hey, wait a minute," Will said. "It's like what Courtney said a few months ago about the movies being a breeding ground for teens. Maybe the idea is that if we have more art in society, then we're all happier and more likely to have sex and more babies. It gives us an excuse for going on a date, right? No art show, no movies, no poetry readings, then no dates."

"That's pretty weak, Will." Josh said. "You've got to admit it's pretty prejudiced too. You might as well say all wedding directors are gay, therefore they facilitate the dream of every little girl to have a storybook wedding. We're just aware of who's gay or lesbian in the arts because these are professions for public consumption. It might even be beneficial to your career to come out, simply for the publicity. Hardly something to do with evolution and the creation of new species. What's the purpose of being a gay plumber? You know they're out there." Josh paused to demonstrate his impeccable comedic timing. "Laying pipe. Ha." He ruined the effect by laughing at his own joke.

"And I'm sure there are plenty of people who've had a child without seeing a movie first," Paul said. "So what's your point, June? You've got us stumped."

June bent over and flicked a pile of crumbs into her dustpan. She slid to the back room and dumped them in the garbage, then returned with the mop and bucket. She ran the hot water and turned to the group while it filled. "No point. The best questions are the ones with no answer. Sometimes you need to look behind at the premise. Does my question imply that homosexuality is genetic? The source of a mutation, and therefore desirable as part of evolution? You know, even if it doesn't lead to a stronger species, we need mutations in order to adapt. The same flexibility that leads to cancer cells, leads to other more useful types of diversity, like your immune system. What about the old debate that it's just a lifestyle choice like a preference for heavy metal music?"

"Kind of like your choice to own a diner?" Josh said.

"Exactly. It's not like this place has afforded me the opportunity to get laid with any regularity. But it's become who I am," she said. "Then again, if your only purpose in life is to make more babies, well, how depressing is that?"

"But there you go again, the idea that evolution has some goal in mind," Danny said. "It's a strictly human thing to feel like your life has to mean something, that we have to define ourselves by what we do, whether we're gay or straight, have offspring or not."

"Or shave our heads?" Josh said. "Tell me, Danny. Is your goal to be sure you never reproduce? That'd probably be good for the species." Danny casually reached into the dwindling basket of fries and took out the largest remaining one. Instead of dipping it in her mustard she flicked it at Josh and hit him in the forehead.

"Your goal is transparent," Danny said. "You're clearly defining yourself as an asshole."

"And what of it?" he said. "You've got to be good at something. Now if I could only figure out a way to get paid for it."

June added some soap to the mop bucket and swirled it around. She wheeled the bucket from behind the counter and started mopping by the door. Through the glass, she could see a boxy car coming up the road 5 miles per hour under the speed limit. She saw the right turn indicator come on a full half mile before the Diner parking lot. The driver angled gingerly off the blacktop and into a space, barely raising any dust. June held the door open for Roger and realized her cheeks were hurting from smiling all day. "Good evening professor Steadman," June said. "You're right on time. Watch your step, the floor's wet."

Roger entered as if walking on ice, to avoid slipping on the wet floor, and took a seat at the counter. He nodded to the Diner's Club and gave a sheepish hello. June gave introductions although she was aware Roger knew all the members, if not from his classes directly, then from rumors of the Club and general campus gossip. "Would you like something to snack on?" June said. "I could spark up the grill and the oil's still hot."

"You did it on purpose, didn't you?" Roger said.

"What?" said June with the most innocent grin she could muster.

"You ended that question with a preposition, just to give me a rash."

"Guilty." Roger answered her offer by helping himself to a diet soda from the fountain and June returned to her mopping. Nobody noticed Paul roll his eyes. He was the only one who made anything of the exchange. His reaction was an odd combination of jealousy and condescension, as if he thought the playful verbal sparring was beneath them. They should stop acting like they're on a TV sitcom and just get on with it. Put the dagger directly in his heart. Paul had the odd thought at that moment that it would be less painful being rejected by June if he suddenly realized he were homosexual.

"Hey, professor Steadman, you want to get in on this?" Will asked.

"Please Will, I've told you, you can call me Roger."

"Yes sir. I mean, okay Roger. And that's kind of what we were talking about when you came in. June started us off on gays and evolution, but now we're sort of on the identity topic." They rehashed the earlier discussion while Roger sipped his soda and made a few mental notes. June made her way in and around all the tables with the mop. When she got behind Roger's station she playfully jabbed the mop between the legs of his stool and over his brown loafers. Their giggling exchange was not lost on the Diner's Club this time.

"I think what you're getting at is what defines a person," Roger said. "But nobody labels themselves homosexual or otherwise. Other people give us an identity, whether it's accurate or not. And not everything we do means something to the overall picture. I've been a son, a husband, a student. Now I'm a divorcee, a father, and..." He paused not sure where he was going. "Do they have a word for when a parent loses a child? A kid without parents is an orphan, but what about the other way around? How come they don't have a name for that?"

"Um. Buzz kill," Josh said.

"Is it a disease with you, or what?" Danny said. "Geez, have a little sympathy. You're not just an asshole, you're pathological."

"I didn't mean to be rude, it's a joke to lighten the mood. It's just my way of saying how tough that must be. He brought it up."

"No offense taken, Josh," Roger said. "It was years ago, and I was trying to make a point, not beg for sympathy. Back to lighter fare, I've been a teacher for so long, that's all anybody ever thinks I am. Maybe it's because it's my public identity like your actors, artists and wedding planners. I'd rather be known for my writing, but nobody's read any of it. Then again, there's probably a downside to making one's hobby into a profession. It'd take all the fun out of it. There are lots of days I don't teach or write, but not a day goes by I don't think about RJ. In my own mind, I'm a 'whatever it means to lose your offspring.' Publicly, I'm a teacher." He paused, not sure where this train of thought was taking him. It was starting to get confessional, not at all in the spirit of the Club. "Besides, the end of a line means, no evolution. Why have a name for it?" No one said a word. "You're right, Josh, I'm a one-man buzz kill. Sorry."

Paul tried to play referee and redirect the group. Instead of enlisting June as usual, he tried to help Roger redeem himself. "So what defines a person, Roger? Where he came from? His upbringing, his actions? Or some combination?"

Roger took a thoughtful sip of his soda. "Well, our public persona probably never matches what we think of ourselves. It'll differ between critics, too." The club had puzzled looks on their faces and were looking around the room. The word critic seemed out of place and Josh said as much. "Well, that's what we are for each other, right? Constant critics? And I don't mean to say it's always a bad review. We're human, we can't help but make value judgements. In two seconds a woman will size up a man and determine if he'd probably make a good mate or not. In the same amount of time one man will judge, correctly or not, whether the guy standing across the room is more of less of a success than he feels himself to be. Sometimes the reviews are good and sometimes not so favorable. If you ask my ex-wife who I am you'll probably get a different answer than my little Emma would give. The reality is somewhere in the middle, I'd guess."

"Is there a reality that's not defined by public opinion?" Will said.

"No fair bringing in Plato, *a priori* truths and anything in Latin," June said fully realizing she'd just spoken Latin herself. "Does the falling tree make a noise if no one's there to hear it? Blah, blah, blah…"

"What, like a reality apart from public perception?" Danny said.

"Yea, sort of." Will said. "Let's say you devote your life to charity. For decades you're the most giving person in the community. The go-to guy for local benefits. If someone needs to borrow a gardening tool, you're well-known as the guy who'll bring it over on a moment's notice. You'd give the proverbial shirt off your back. But the community falls on hard times, your family's hungry, but all your friends won't help you. You steal a loaf of bread to feed your starving toddler. Does that suddenly make you a thief with no redeeming qualities?"

"Besides being the most ridiculous example you could come up with, you make the guy a saint, even in thievery," Josh said. "Nobody would say he's suddenly changed. Circumstances forced his hand and he'd likely be forgiven, not re-labeled. By everyone but the guy who's bread he stole, that is."

"But we're talking about how society defines a person," Paul said. "When does what you do, become who you are?"

"Well, suck one dick and you're a cocksucker," Josh said. Danny picked up the dregs of the french fry basket and threw them across the table.

"There," she said. "I'm a French Fry Flinger. Hey, say that three times fast."

"I think Josh is trying to make a point," Courtney said. "Despite his horrible choice of words, the example is valid. There are some actions that trump all the others."

Will interrupted and added, "Yea, I can see it. You can be a saint all your life, steal a loaf of bread under extreme circumstances, and people won't stop thinking of you as a saint. But kill someone in cold blood for no reason and you're forever known as a murderer."

June finished up behind the counter, mopping twice by the grill. She dumped the grey water out and poured herself a cup of coffee. She set the cup down by Roger and pulled up a stool opposite him to join the discussion. With one last look over the Diner before settling, she noticed a mark on the counter, leftover from the dinner rush. Always the perfectionist, she returned to the sink, grabbed a scouring pad and started to work on the offending coffee stain. The mark wouldn't lift and she scrubbed harder and harder until her arm began to cramp. "Ow, ow, ow, ow, ow, ow, ooooooow," she whined.

Roger put down his coffee and asked with genuine concern, "What's wrong, June?"

"Nothing."

"Oh c'mon, don't be so stubborn. Bring it here." Roger reached out and took June tenderly by the wrist. He began to rub out the cramp starting at the base of her thumb and moving slowly towards her inner elbow. June relaxed and took her seat all the while letting Roger caress her arm. He worked his way back towards to her wrist, never taking his eyes from the work at hand. "Geez, the cables in your forearms could hold up a bridge." June stared into the downcast, businesslike eyes of her rescuer as he worked the last of the knots out of her forearm. By the time he worked his way back up to her wrist, June was beyond relaxation. Her shoulders fell as he worked on the base of her thumb. She felt it in her toes when he massaged each finger out to the tip. "There. How's that, now?"

The Diner's Club was silenced. Roger answered his own rhetorical question by ignoring the Club's open-mouthed stares and June's sleepy-eyed swooning. "What about entropy?" he mused. "If the universe is trending towards the same temperature, a kind of boring evenness, maybe evolution, including homosexuality, is an attempt to counter that tendency. What if people choose to get together to make things more interesting as an end in itself? Gay. Straight. Who cares? The quest is the reason. How you oppose the trend towards uniformity becomes who you are, literally, your individuality."

22

Montezuma's Revenge

Roger drove home from work one day after the Mexico trip and found a van-sized Dumpster parked where his car should be. On mental autopilot since the tragedy he pulled into the drive and had to stomp hard on the brakes to avoid a humiliating accident. He put the sedan in park, hefted his suitcase and steeled his nerve. It was time to have a talk with Sharon about her recent behavior. He was stopped short at the sidewalk by the brand new landscaping. The neat row of mature yews was gone and in its place was a pathetic display of tiny boxwoods. The way the foundation showed beneath the white porch made the house look naked, exposed. The weathered mulch was scraped away and replaced with sharp, red, lava rock. Roger had the impression the house was bleeding into the lawn.

The final straw was the last thing he noticed. In the center of the yard was a gaping hole like a land mine had been detonated. It took a moment for Roger to realize his young, red maple tree was gone. He'd planted it in commemoration the week Roger Junior was born.

Roger trudged up the steps and paused with his hand on the doorknob. He stopped, rubbed his eyes and wondered how to broach the subject with Sharon. He looked back to survey the damage that was his yard, his home and was met with the image of the maple in the Dumpster, lying on its side as if in a casket. That image was all the encouragement he needed. He opened the door, stepped inside and slammed it as hard as he could to get Sharon's attention. The response he got was the arc of a sledgehammer crashing from the kitchen through the living room wall. Before he could yell out his surprise, Sharon let loose with another wicked swing and carved out a gaping wound, 1 foot wide and 4 feet tall. Roger saw her through the dusty opening wearing overalls and goggles. "What the hell are you doing" Roger said. "Why is the maple tree in that garbage pile?"

"We can't get him back, Roger," Sharon said and heaved the sledge again. This time it landed with a dull clunk when she found a hidden stud.

"I know that," Roger said. "I don't want him back. I mean, of course I want him back, but I know that won't happen. I just want my life back. Our life." *Crash.*

"You deal with it in your way, I'll deal with it in mine," she said.

"My way is to continue our life together. You're pulling it up by the roots. Literally," Roger said.

"That's right," Sharon said. "I can't spend 20 minutes crying every time I see something that reminds me of Roger Junior. That's why I cleaned out his room, that's why I put down carpet in the hall, and that's why that scraggly tree had to go. Now I'm taking out this useless wall. I have some money left over and I've always wanted a bigger, brighter kitchen."

"That scraggly tree was a red maple and it was supposed to grow with RJ," Roger said. "Wait a minute. What leftover money?"

"Well, I figured he wouldn't be needing his college fund, so I cashed it out," Sharon said. "Besides, there's no way that tree would have lived in this climate. The least you could have done was chosen a native tree."

"And your bushes come from what part of New Mexico? Geez, Sharon, the lawn's not native. What are you thinking?" Roger said. He watched her take a mighty backswing and knock an exposed stud clean off its footer. He could only stand there with his mouth open. Speechless, he slumped up the stairs, closed the bedroom door against the noise and sat on the bed to think.

Even with his fingers in his ears, he couldn't gather his thoughts on how to get through to Sharon. The incessant pounding shook the entire second floor. Roger began to wonder if she weren't removing a load-bearing wall. He hurried down the stairs to intervene before the roof collapsed. "Sharon!" he yelled over the pounding. "Can't we talk about this?"

"What? I know you've always wanted a bigger kitchen, too," Sharon said.

"Not just that. I mean Roger Junior, too. Please take a break and sit down with me," Roger said and sat on the couch. He knew they couldn't converse through the remains of the living room wall. He watched her relax and pull the goggles down like a necklace, never making eye contact. Then she took them off fully and walked out of view leaving the sledgehammer there on the kitchen floor. When she didn't appear around the doorway it took him a beat to realize she must have sat down at the kitchen table. He got up too quickly, hurried through the swinging doors, and fell right over the toolbox. Roger landed on his knees in a full bow before Sharon. More humiliated than hurt, Roger looked up and found no sympathy or concern, only Sharon's scornful look of complete exasperation with him.

Roger stood up, brushed off his knees and took his usual dinnertime seat across the table. "Sharon, I've been thinking for a month about how to get over this and nothing's working. I just want our lives to be the way they were," he said.

"That's your problem, you're always thinking. You never do anything," Sharon said.

"What do you mean?" Roger said. "I'm coping. I'm getting on with my life. You're in some sort of denial. Just because you're active doesn't mean you're accomplishing anything. When's it going to end? After the kitchen, then what? The roof?"

"I'm doing what I can in my own way. How come you're not writing? I think you should write about Mexico. It could be your best story yet. Call it Montezuma's Revenge or something," she said.

"You're crazy. This isn't about bad water and diarrhea. Plus, you know I don't write about myself. Or us. Geez. You know what I think? I think we should have another baby," Roger said.

"What? Now you're the one who's crazy," Sharon said.

"Why not? We always planned to have more while RJ was alive. Why can't we have them now?"

"I don't know. I just don't want another baby," she said. "I'm going to start dinner."

Roger felt the conversation slipping away. He watched her get up and walk to the refrigerator. Even in the overalls and covered in dust, she still had an attractive figure. He enjoyed the way she bent over to look deep into the fridge. To continue the line of conversation he got up and went to her. He hugged her playfully from behind and said, "C'mon, let's get started on that baby right now."

"Stop it, Roger, I can't," she said.

"Oh, I know I can change your mind," Roger said. He tried to undo the strap on her overalls.

"Give it up. It's not going to happen," Sharon said.

"What are you talking about?" Roger spun her around to look at her.

"I can't have another baby."

"Yea, you said that. But with time you might think it'll be okay. I'm not talking about replacing RJ or any of that. We'll never forget him, of course, but there's no reason we can't be parents again. C'mon, what do you say? Work with me," Roger said.

"No. You're not hearing me. I can't get pregnant. I never went back on birth control after Roger Junior was born. It's been five years and I haven't gotten pregnant again. Didn't you ever wonder? I've been to doctors, they don't know anything," she said.

For the second time that day Roger was rendered speechless. He held his wife as tightly as he could and was relieved when she hugged him back. They both had a good cry in each other's arms. Roger broke the silence, "We'll just have to adopt." When she didn't object, he felt a small joy, something like his wedding day.

The next two weeks Roger worked at fostering the marriage back to health. They made redecorating decisions together and he even helped pick out paint. He tried to complement Sharon on her home improvement skills and thanked her for saving so much money on the labor. He noticed her softening a bit but was still too cautious to bring up the issue of adoption again. One Saturday he was surprised when she brought it up herself. They were painting opposite sides of the kitchen trim from the same paint bucket. "Roger Junior was a great kid, wasn't he?" Sharon said.

"The best," Roger said.

"I didn't spend all of his college savings, you know. I'd been saving for another trip when he died. You didn't know about that money. Somehow, I couldn't see us going on another vacation without him," she said. Sharon dipped her brush in the bucket and carefully applied it around the new entrance to the living room. "Maybe we can redo his room for a little girl?"

"They say girls are easier to adopt. Since most folks want a boy, that is," Roger said. He tried to contain his excitement and let the idea simmer in Sharon's mind. He dipped his own brush and painted around the window trim. "Maybe after the school year, you know, when I've got more time, we could look into all that adoption stuff."

"Then again, why wait?" she said. " I hear it takes months or years to apply and get matched and all that. I'll research it. Since the house is done I'll have more time on my hands." He met her at the bucket and gave her a sloppy hug. The hug turned into a kiss and before he knew it they were well on their way to christening the new kitchen. This time she didn't resist when he unfastened her overall straps. *Ding-dong.*

"Of all the lousy times for the doorbell to ring," Roger said. "Hold that thought. I'll be right back."

Roger buttoned his pants and walked to the door. *Ding-dong, ding-dong.* "Alright, alright, I'm coming," he said.

When he opened the door he was met by a man in a work shirt. On the right breast patch, was his name, Tim. On the left was the logo of the airline they'd flown to Mexico. Roger's head began to swim. In Tim's right hand was a clipboard with a pen attached. In his left was a small, brightly-colored suitcase, the kind a child would take on vacation.

"Hi. I'm Tim. You must be Roger Senior. Sorry about the mix-up and all that. I hope you haven't missed whatever's in here." He handed Roger the suitcase.

23

The Cave

Seventh grade was almost over for Emma. Roger was dreading the impending loss of innocence for his little girl. She must have noticed the way June was spending more time around the house. The excuses for getting together, the three of them, were starting to become contrived. They'd gotten through the holiday season without any awkwardness. If Emma knew there was a history between these adults, she didn't let on much. Roger knew she was becoming more precocious and was on the lookout for subtle hints, sarcasm, and outright accusations. It wouldn't be long before their little bedtime sessions would take a serious turn. Sooner or later he'd have to admit that June and he were more or less dating.

Roger tucked Emma in and snuggled her like he was leaving on a long trip. He was delighted when she didn't protest but stayed in her cocoon and smiled up at him. "Dad? Do you ever write any poetry? I noticed you don't teach any classes in it."

"Poetry is for teenagers in love. So, is that Marvin making any progress? You will tell me before you run off to the farm and get married, won't you?"

"Dad, geez!" Emma said. "It's just that they're making us do poetry now for a final writing project in English class. We have to write a poem and read it in front of everybody."

"Hmm. That seems rather cruel. Has the class been misbehaving?" She shook her head. "That teacher must really hate you guys. Well, good night." Roger made like he was getting up to leave until Emma begged him to come back.

"Okay," he said. "I see you're not going to let me off easy on this one. I think poetry and its meaning to readers has changed. Poetry's changed. People don't take it as seriously as they used to."

"Yea? How so? Our teacher told us about all these famous people who did poetry and nothing else." Emma freed her hands from her sides. She clasped them over her chest in the best listening posture she could muster and waited for her father, the man who knows everything.

"Well, it's demanding of the reader. To really get the most out of a poem, you have to study it, word by word, line by line. At least the good ones. It's probably best to know the historical context as well, study the time, study the previous work of the artist. Most readers aren't that devoted, I guess. And I'm sure those famous men and women didn't write poetry to get famous or make a lot of money. That's a sure way to starve, write poetry." Roger let her digest the thought while he composed the rest of his answer. "You can't make a multi-million dollar movie about a poem, can you? I guess like so many things it may all come down to money."

"But how come you never write any poetry?"

"Oh, I've written volumes of poems." Emma gave him a look. "Okay, one epic poem and a few short ones." Her look didn't change. "Okay, I did write a poem once. Well, sort of. A short one. Well, no I never wrote a poem."

"C'mon, dad. Did you or didn't you?"

"Okay, okay. I never wrote a poem. You want to know the real reason? It's too hard. Not as a reader, but a writer. *Roses are red/Violets are blue* is about as far as I've gotten. Then there's a few limericks I heard in a pub in Ireland once, but you're too young. My dad wrote a poem for my mom, once. Do you want to hear it?"

"Of course, yea," Emma said. "Wait a minute." She sat forward and gave him an accusing glance. "This wouldn't happen to have anything to do with a bedtime story, would it? And your dad's name starts with an 'R'?"

"No, no, honest. He wrote it for my mother when they first met. Kind of. You want to hear it or not?"

"Sure," said Emma and she leaned back against her pillow.

Roger started to explain that some background information would help make the poem more accessible. "Ray was the kind of man who…" he started.

"Wait a minute, wait a minute," Emma said. "This isn't really about your mom and dad, is it?" Roger rolled his eyes and shook his head. "And he didn't really write a poem to your mother, did he?"

"No, but we're at that point where I ask you one last time, if you want to hear the story or just go to bed. Got it?" She gave him a fake pout but didn't say anything. "I'll take your silence as agreement and we'll go on."

The Cave

Jenny first saw Ray from behind. He was the kind of man that women fell in love with so easily, they didn't even realize they were ignoring all other men. He exuded confidence the way the sky is blue. He didn't have to work at it and yet he was completely unselfconcious about his power. Ray was so friendly to all those he met, with such a genuinely kind heart that even lesser men felt no jealousy. He was the ultimate big brother and role model. People wanted to be like him but never faulted him for his perfection.

On the late, October day in question, Ray was parked in his 1962, fire engine red, Corvette Convertible at one of those drive-up burger places. A real old-fashioned joint. The waitresses used to wear roller skates, more as a gimmick than for speed of serving. It was a time when you could call a server a waitress. Jenny saw him from behind. It was his left arm she saw first, and that was enough. Ray was seated with his arm propped on the driver's side door. Though it was early evening, the temperature was plenty warm enough to have the convertible top down. It was the kind of fall weather that evokes all the nostalgia of Homecoming Dances and football games. Jenny didn't have a chance.

His arm had muscles. The kind that grow from honest work, not the sissy kind that come from a workout at the gym with a personal trainer, after spending the day pushing pencils at the office. He was tan underneath a light covering of blonde, curly hair. The low angled sunlight grazed his arm, illuminated his angelic face through the side view mirror and sent the virtual image back to Jenny. He glanced down as she approached from behind the car and their eyes met in reverse through the reflection. She tried to act cool and walk right past into the shop but stumbled up the small curb. Like any man, he noticed her trim figure as she pulled open the door to walk in and place her order. Ray didn't flinch or avert his gaze when she turned to catch him staring at her form-fitting skirt. He just gave a sly smile, a slight nod, and resumed his silent admiration.

"You know, you got a lotta nerve staring like that mister," Jenny said when she came back out with her order.

"Hi. I'm Ray. You want to go for a ride to watch the sunset?"

"I should have you arrested. But since I'm a nice girl, I'll give you a second chance."

By the time they reached the hilltop park overlooking the city and the sunset, the two were holding hands. When the first stars came out, Ray and Jenny were already well acquainted. When the moon rose and set, they were making plans to have a life together. They dated nonstop. Except for the times when he was driving, Jenny always grabbed his left arm, a nod to their first encounter. They shared the expected dating experiences, movies, bowling and putt-putt. When those trips became tired, art shows and even a poetry reading. The latter was so tedious Ray made Jenny promise she'd never again inflict upon him that particular torture. But Ray remained a willing and adventurous companion. He was game to try anything once and always let Jenny sit on his left side.

If Ray had one fault, it was his inability to get along with animals of any kind. It wasn't that he didn't like them but just the opposite. He respected all living things, they just didn't return the favor. He never had any bad experiences, he just thought they ought to have their place in the world and stay there. Where humans intersected with animals it was for their utility. Why was it that he was the only person who saw a horse as a terrific tool? At the far end of his tolerance were those people who kept exotic animals with no capacity for interaction. Snakes and reptiles? Fish and coral? He could see someone fawning over a dog and showing off the latest trick. But an animal that spends its day trying to regulate its temperature? What was the point? In the end he realized he'd never sympathize with someone who owned 3 cats and he managed to avoid the inevitable arguments by keeping his opinions to himself. Clearly, the human culture of keeping pets did not involve rational thought.

Jenny was a dog lover. Specifically, she co-habitated with a toy poodle and woe to the mortal who failed to accurately identify the breed. She tended to correct rather sternly anyone who guessed the canine looked rather like a fuzzy Chihuahua. Jenny's pride and joy went by the name Cuddles, but her full name was Stardust & Cuddling Moondancers Dream. There were 3 champions in the line and Jenny would be happy to direct you to the framed four-generation Certificate of Pedigree, should you have missed it in the den.

After a month of more than serious dating, Ray ran out of excuses to avoid meeting the third member of their little family. He'd heard all the stories and laughed the proper amount at all the right times during the endless Cuddles anecdotes. Now he had to meet the little beast. Before dinner on their one month anniversary, Jenny suggested they meet at her place for an apertif. She'd bought a "silly little Cabernet for the occasion with a dry sense of humor" much like her Cuddles. Ray rolled his eyes but agreed over the phone to celebrate the momentous 1-month anniversary any way she wished.

He glided the red convertible into her driveway exactly on time, one half hour late. He opened the storm door to knock but found it completely unnecessary. The faint squeaking of the hinges was enough to set off an eruption of high pitched yelping from the other side. Ray thought it would be amazing if there were any glass in the room which hadn't been shattered. The din brought to mind certain tortures inflicted upon the unfortunates from Dante's "Inferno." Jenny was nearly ready to receive him and answered the door with her hair in a towel. Upon spying the intruder, Cuddles began to leap chest high against the door, causing Ray to nearly stumble back off the porch in surprise. "Down, Cuddles, it's just Ray. You two are going to get along just fine," said Jenny. She then instructed Ray to get down to Cuddles' level and offer a hand to sniff. Ray did as he was told and Jenny cracked the door just wide enough to let a wet nose poke through to do its business. The barking stopped so suddenly that Ray realized his ears were ringing. Maybe this "family" thing would work out after all. "See? I knew you guys would hit it off."

The bite came so fast Ray didn't realize what was happing until it was over. When Cuddles clamped down on the pinky side of Ray's left hand with those razor sharp teeth he froze in shock. A moment later the pain reached his brain and a new signal came telling him to pull his hand away from the stabbing pain. The motion splattered Jenny with blood from the gaping wound and Ray began jumping in circles on the porch. Ray held the remains of his hand to his shirt and a wide, wet bloodstain spread slowly down his front. Cuddles joined the dance on the porch and resumed jumping chest high until a defect in timing caused Ray to step on the creature's front left paw. Cuddles bolted off the porch and down the street in a slowly fading Doppler decrescendo of yelps.

Jenny was far from speechless. She yelled for Cuddles to no avail.

She yelled at Ray for being so careless. She yelled at herself for not inviting Ray into the house before the introduction. Ray could only look at his dripping palm and wonder how many stitches his hand was going to take. He was already dreading the needles the doctor would no doubt have to use in order to numb the hand and put the meat back together. Jenny started to run down the street in her robe and towel, then thought better of it. "Ray, you've got to find Cuddles," she said.

"What I need to do is get to the hospital. I think there's some skin missing. Won't it get hungry and come home?"

"What? You're crazy. Cuddles has never been out of the house. She's scared and it's getting dark. Your hand can wait."

They agreed on a compromise of sorts. Jenny bandaged Ray's hand with a dressing so large it could absorb whatever blood Ray still had in him. He'd gather Cuddles to the car with a seat full of doggie treats, come back to pick up Jenny after she'd dressed, and they'd all go to the Emergency Room together. Ray started off down the road in the direction they'd last seen Cuddles bolt. He slowed at the corner and gave Cuddles' favorite squeaky toy a squeeze. When the dog failed to appear he took a guess and turned right. His left hand, the bandaged stump, could steer somewhat which allowed his right hand the freedom to alternately shift and squeak the toy. Two trips around the block failed to produce the dog, so Ray expanded his circling by large figure eights up and down the hills of the neighborhood.

His mind began to wander thinking crazy thoughts about love and relationships and concluding somehow it was all worth it. That's how much he loved Jenny and she loved him. It was just a dog after all. Then again if the dog failed to appear, he'd undoubtedly pay for it the rest of his life with Jenny. She'd had Cuddles for years, they slept together, something Ray hadn't even been invited to do. He was a speck in her life, a near non-entity. If Cuddles was gone, so was Ray. Sure, she'd get a new dog, maybe even from the same breeder and bloodline but it'd never be the same. Twilight gave way to black night and the streetlights only served to blind him to searching the blackened yards and bushes. He determined to circle the neighborhood one last time, return to get Jenny and enlist her help. Maybe Cuddles would respond to her voice better than the squeaky toy and a pile of dry biscuits.

He rounded the corner at the top of the hill on the far side of Jenny's block. Ray began to speed back to pick up Jenny when Cuddles darted from behind a tree directly into the road. Ray tried to steer but the bandages on his hand slipped impotently off the wheel. He grabbed the wheel with his right hand but locked the clutch in gear. The engine stalled and the wheels locked as he threw the wheel around trying to avoid a collision. The convertible spun perpendicular to the road and began to flip. The last thing Ray saw before he was knocked unconscious was Cuddles cowering on the pavement as the car flipped clear over the canine.

Ray's head hit the ground first and he was forced into a deep crouch. His left arm, bandage intact, was pinned above the elbow between the door and the blacktop. Ray felt nothing as the arm was amputated by the weight of the car sliding down the hill. The skin was lost in the first dozen feet. It took another ten yards for the door to shred through the muscle and down to the bone. When the fragments of bone began to chip away from the elbow joint, the car began to slow and settle. One final shard of humerus caught on a defect in the pavement and the arm was torn free of it's final sinews. The weight of the car acted as a tourniquet for Ray's new stump.

Cuddles ate two of the dog treats and then dragged the remainder of Ray's arm down the hill to Jenny.

Ray spent the next month in a coma. It was for the best that this time seemed to pass in an instant. He couldn't even recall having a dream during his multiple surgeries. He was blissfully unaware of the conversations at his bedside during which family, friends and doctors discussed his fate. Luckiest of all he couldn't hear Jenny sobbing throughout every visit of every day.

Upon waking from the coma, Ray's first two weeks felt like a lifetime in hell. The headache was excruciating and constant. It was much later that Ray learned of the emergency surgery to evacuate the blood that was compressing his brain. He suffered with multiple, daily blood drawings. After a prolonged period on the ventilator they decided to cut a hole in his neck to attach the more or less permanent tubing for the ventilator. Ray was alert enough to sense every insult but unable to communicate. His eyes were taped shut to keep them from drying out. His remaining hand was tied down to prevent him from pulling out any of the life-giving tubes. Ray had the odd realization that he lacked hunger but worse, he had forgotten the pleasure of eating. The level of light through his bandages was constant and robbed him of any sense of day or night. He may have slept or not. Any touch he received brought only more pain. While they meant the best, his care givers couldn't imagine how he craved a touch without needles. The timing of his pain medicines was ludicrously inaccurate. When he had pain or an itch, the next dose was hours away. When he was comfortable, alert and therefore more active, they wrongly assumed he was in pain and snowed him with a double dose of morphine.

One day, he was awakened by the soft sound of a familiar voice.

"Ray? Can you hear me?" Jenny said. "We're going to see if you can breathe on your own." The doctors let his pain medicines wear off and he began instinctively to pull at the ventilator with lame respiratory efforts. The sensation was worse than drowning but he proved he might survive off the machine. Jenny volunteered to take the bandages off his eyes. Once adjusted to the light, he could see Jenny, a man in a white coat and "Maureen, Respiratory Therapist." They unhooked the tube from his neck and he immediately coughed out a large glob of foul slime which flew clear to the opposite wall under the force of his efforts. The next gasp produced a sensation of wondrous release for Ray and the equally odd feeling that no air was passing over his tongue.

Jenny was on his left side and leaned over to kiss him and hold her tear-smeared face against his. He tried to hug her with his left arm but found he couldn't move it. He lamely tried to reach her with his right hand and stroke her hair but the restraints made a clanking sound on the bed railing. More pain shot up his arm from the strain on the IV and arterial lines. Ray dropped the hand to his side, looked at Jenny and gave a shrug. She reached across his body to unstrap the wrist. Ray let the weight of her warm heavy body fill him with the comfort he'd been missing for so long. Her delicious scent removed all traces of alcohol swabs and iodine from his nostrils. He felt as nostalgic as walking into his grandmother's kitchen at the holidays, with a roaring stove and a dozen foods cooking. When Jenny was through freeing his arm and stood back, he tried to tell her what he was feeling but no sound came out. His neck just made a rude gurgling noise and Ray began to cry.

Once again he tried to reach up with his left hand to touch her but nothing happened. He wondered if he was still tied down on that side or worse, if he'd lost feeling and movement in that arm. Ray wiggled his left foot and felt it move against the sheets. No, it wasn't likely he'd had a stroke. He looked down the side of his chest and nothing appeared to be wrong. It took a moment to realize what was missing. He looked at Jenny but she only stared back shaking her head and offering no explanation. When the realization hit him that he'd lost his left arm, Ray let out a scream, but again made no noise. Jenny asked the doctor and respiratory therapist to leave. Since he appeared to be breathing fine, they were happy to go, and closed the door to the nurse's station.

Over the next hour Jenny brought him up to date as gently as she could, with Ray insisting that she spare no details. Ray kept pointing to his neck with his remaining arm, so she started with the tracheostomy. She explained how to plug the hole briefly in order to direct the air over his vocal cords. Ray could then ask questions with the pitifully hoarse growling that substituted for his voice and help direct her explanation. She explained she'd heard the crash but couldn't bring herself to investigate until Cuddles dragged his arm down the hill. She immediately recognized it by the bandage on the hand. She told him how long he'd been in a coma and how they thought he might never wake up. She listed the surgeries, the machines, and the therapies, none of which made sense to Ray but the summary allowed him time to adjust to his new situation.

When she'd finished her forensic documentation of his ordeal, Jenny asked if Ray had any questions. "Yea," he croaked. "When can I get out of here?" Jenny responded by crying.

"I've asked them one hundred times, Ray. They said if you could get off the vent, eat on your own and go to the bathroom, you could leave and do the rest as an out-patient."

"The rest of what?" said Ray.

"Well, you know. Get that hole in your neck closed up and learn how to walk again. You haven't used your muscles in over a month. Plus, they told me we can get you an arm and I can still sit on your left side in the movies."

Jenny said it all so nonchalantly, Ray couldn't help but think for the first time what she'd been through while he was blissfully unaware in his comfortable coma. She must have already come to terms with his loss and moved on to the recovery phase. "It must have been terrible for you. I can't imagine." Ray processed that last bit of news and it made him love her all the more. She hadn't thought of herself once during his ordeal.

"I'll have the nurse remove the other tubes and we'll get you some solid food, huh?"

"No, wait. I wrote you a poem."

"What? Oh, great, brain damage. You didn't really write a poem." Her lame attempt at humor let him know he'd be all right. No way could she joke about his mental state if he'd been losing brain cells for months.

"Well," said Ray, "What did you expect me to do for a month on my back? My thoughts weren't too clear, what with all the morphine, but I sure had some emotions. The worst part was I had no sense of time. I think I slept, but I had no dreams. It was hard to tell if I was imagining say another blood draw, or if it was really happening. When I was awake I tried to sing songs or remember stories from my childhood. Then a fresh pain would bring me back to the present and I'd lose my place, have to start all over again. Did you know the last thing I saw was Cuddles? Upside down when the 'Vette flipped?"

Jenny's eyes grew wide but she couldn't think of anything to say. If it hadn't been for Cuddles… "I kept reliving the crash," said Ray. "I finally resorted to poetry. Don't ask me how that idea came to me. I hate poetry." Jenny failed to suppress a giggle recalling their poetry date. "Yea, tell me about it. I started with limericks and haikus about Cuddles. Then I went into free form verse. I've been under so long I have it memorized. You want to hear it?"

"You're serious," said Jenny. "Yea, sure, let's hear it tough guy."

The Cave

I spend my days in the oblong cave
Life at arms' reach
One day like the next
Easy
In the cave

A point of light shows much too brightly
Hints at another reality
I must turn to look
Marvel
In the cave

The illusion I see, wishing it to be
A close imitation
I strain to comprehend
Doubting
In the cave

JUNE'S DINER

A vision incomplete, from the universal teat
The cave it serves now as prison
Aware of potential
Longing
In the cave

Only the grave gives escape from the cave
One oblong box for another
No light to frustrate
Dark
In the grave

I waste away in the oblong cave
Life a struggle for meaning
Yearn for all I've seen in part
Hoping
In the cave

24

A Tale of Two Saturdays

The Diner's Club was suffering an unspoken fit of nostalgia. Graduation was coming and nobody was stating the obvious. The school year would soon be over. Will would return to the backbreaking physical work of the farm. Danny would resume hating her job at the mall or wherever. Courtney and Josh would switch on the charm for friends and family at the country club. Paul would go back to full-time shifts and enjoy the break from juggling academics and his livelihood. June and Roger were too close to their situation, with too much shared history to realize they were already in love. Making mutual summer plans would be just a formality once Roger and Emma were done for the school year.

When stalled, the Club always fell back on the classics. Paul and June were going over the tired symbol of light as a metaphor for knowledge. For once, Courtney was the leader in driving the discussion forward. "I'm just saying, sometimes the light is so bright you're blinded. The two times you don't know what's going on are when there's no information at all and when you've got too much information," she said. "One situation you're in the dark, the other you're blinded."

June had started them off on Plato's Alleghory of the Cave. "Quickly then, we're all chained together in a cave by our ignorance," June said. "Action happens behind us, lit by a fire, but we can't see it. The only information we get is the flickering shadows on the cave wall in front of us. We don't even see what's going on between us and the fire. Someone breaks the chains, sees the parade and the fire, but doesn't stop gathering information there, no, he leaves the cave and gets up into the sunshine. That's where the real world is. We're twice removed from reality, we only see the shadows of a sham, played out on a wall."

Paul picked up the thread. "In today's world you could be talking about anything from economics to politics. Doesn't matter. It's likely you don't know what's going on, even if you study it yourself, you're only seeing the fire. Someone's got to show you the sunshine."

"So who's the someone?" Will said. "And how do they break the chains?"

"Depends what culture you're in," Courtney said. "If you're a Native American, it might be the Medicine Man who's giving out mushrooms, eh?" Danny got up to get the fries and condiments. June came with a round of drinks.

"So let me see if I've got this straight," Josh said. "If I see a movie, I need to hear whether I liked it or not from a critic? That's good, I was worried I'd have to make up my own mind."

"Very funny," Danny said. "But I think it applies to things a bit more complicated than your personal preferences. That's your own reality. No one can tell you what to feel. This concept applies to the external stuff, like that crap about ranking movies by how much money they make. Are people really fooled by reports of weekend grosses?

Tickets cost 4 times as much as they did just 20 years ago, so I think we should divide by at least 4, then we'll see how movies compare. Don't even get me started on *Gone With The Wind*."

Paul shook his head. "No, you can't compare that far back. That's like comparing a current quarterback to one before the modern football rules favoring the forward pass. *Gone With The Wind* was a great movie in it's time but it was also the only show in town. What else were people going to do for entertainment? What was a ticket then, about 5 cents? Heck, you'd get a newsreel updating you on World War II, a cartoon, and an episode of your favorite cliffhanger series. Licorice set you back a whole penny. Now you have the choice to see twenty different movies at the same theater."

"My point exactly," Danny said. "Did they even have a way to track ticket sales? Of course not. So nowadays they report what they like as a way to further their own advertising. Newspapers pick it up as if its really worth reporting, and the cycle continues. Then again, newspapers aren't giving out any useful information either. It's all just entertainment. Just strip away the pretense of journalism already."

"Okay," Courtney said, "that's one level removed from reality. What's the other? Is it all a government conspiracy to keep us from knowing the real truth about the political world around us?"

"Sounds a little far-fetched," Will said. "But I get your point about the alternate realities. And speaking of newspapers, I've got another example. The Tour de France was started as advertising for a newspaper." All Will got in return was blank faces and confused looks. "Oh, you've never wondered why the leader of the race wears a yellow jersey? The newspaper was printed on yellow paper." There were nods and smirks around the table, then all heads turned to the parking lot.

A car pulled up by the door and a distinguished gentleman got out. He was wearing khakis and a loose-fitting polo shirt. Clearly the man hadn't been out for awhile and had never heard the phrase "dress casual." He took a single jaunty hop up all the steps at once and pulled open the Diner door. He glanced about the room before taking a seat at the counter. June came over with a menu, a glass of ice water and told him to just sing out when he was ready to order. "We don't get too many handsome strangers in these parts," she said.

"Just give me the usual, June. Thanks," Roger said.

"Could you at least play along for once?"

"Oh, sorry. What's tonight's topic? Did I miss anything?"

"Only the entire history of Western Philosophy," Josh said. "But no biggee, Rog. We'll get you caught up." The familiarity of Josh's comment was not lost on a single occupant of the diner. Roger was now an honorary member of the Club. He came with regularity, if not weekly, his comments were learned, non-judgmental, and invariably led down new, unexplored paths. This man was no sorority tourist. They apprised him of the earlier topics and he listened intently. By now he had the menu memorized and June just served him whatever she wanted anyway. He liked her for it the way lifelong companions finished each other's sentences and knew each other's favorite pizza toppings. His "usual" was whatever she wanted to bring him and everyone was in on the joke. Leftovers or not, his ex-wife Sharon never cooked with an ounce of love or a pinch of affection.

"Nice. I like the Medicine Man idea," said Roger, sipping his diet soda. "What do you think about artists? We don't have Sophists and Rationalists nowadays though. I think it's our artists who do the sunshine-seeking. If they're really good we argue for decades over the ideas they present. Even in this accelerated culture, some modern ideas last." Nobody spoke, so the professor continued. "I brought something to share with you all tonight. If it's not too much of a stretch, I'll read you a little quotation." Roger pulled a small card from his pants pocket and apologized, "I'm not much for memorizing. I've never understood people who could put those tedious passages of Shakespeare to memory. Anyway, here it is…"

> *…but I shrink from the harsh cares and turmoils of public and political life at Washington, and feel I am too sensitive to endure the bitter and personal hostility, and the slanders and misrepresentations of the press, which beset high station in this country.*[1]

Roger was met only with silent looks of anticipation, so he read it again. "I know the language is a bit stilted," he said. "But you get the sentiment, right? It could have been some candidate from the last election, bowing out with false humility when his party failed to give him the nomination. It was actually Washington Irving in 1838." The members of the Club just looked around the table. "What? Too obscure? C'mon folks, you all know 'Rip Van Winkle?' How 'bout 'The Legend of Sleepy Hollow?' Right, that guy. He was gracefully declining an invitation from Martin Van Buren, our 8th President, to be the Secretary of the Navy. So what is it that makes a guy decide to write stories for a living? He was one of 11 children, born to a successful hardware merchant in New York. He had it made. Instead he decided to write political satire. Why leave the cave? So that we'd be talking about him 180 years later? I don't think so."

"Now we've got something to chew on," June said. She delivered another round of drinks to the table and a fresh basket of fries. Roger gave her a scowl from his seat at the counter. It had become her habit to tease Roger with intentional grammatical errors. She knew her misplaced prepositions were like nails on a chalkboard for Roger. She dropped the tiny bombs the way more conventional couples would flirt or share bites of food at a fancy restaurant.

Paul chimed in with the first retort to Roger's query. His attempts to woo and impress June would never end. "Art is always derivative in some way. There's no such thing as a truly new idea." He meant it as a not-so-subtle dig at Roger, but noone saw it that way.

"Sure," Courtney said, "Doric, Ionic, Corinthian. The Renaissance, Boroque, Impressionism. Dada, Action Painting, Pop Art and Op Art, we can all see the progression over time and in retrospect. But what I think Mr. Steadman is trying to say is, Why bother producing art in the first place? What makes one think he or she has the vision or idea that noone else has? Am I right?" She looked to Roger who shrugged and nodded as if to say that's sort of what he meant. "You've got to be a bit stuck up and pretentious to think your ideas are worth distributing," she went on. "Otherwise, keep the canvas or movies or whatever in your basement."

"Good one, hon," Josh said and he gave her a peck on the lips.

"Okay, okay," said Paul by way of contrition. "So where does art come from? The term Impressionism was originally an insult. It wasn't Monet's idea, it was some critic trying to belittle his painting. The labels came later, in history books."

Will took a french fry, dipped it in ketchup, and started to doodle on a napkin. He drew a stick man with a spear and a fat mammal with horns that looked like a buffalo. He held it up to the Club and waved it at June and Roger at the counter. "Is this art?" he said.

"Ooh, clever boy," Danny said. "What ancient culture didn't have some visual representation of daily life? But I think cave art is more like a daily newspaper. It says to the rest of the tribe, here's what we did, we caught this many fish, we had a party and all pigged out. No new ideas there, no deep insight. Just documentation."

"The new idea is the representation itself," Will said. "Imagine being the first person to see a pictorial representation of *anything*. I'd argue that's more mind-blowing than a silkscreen print of Marilyn Monroe in cartoon colors repeated 4 times."

"So, art is ultimately just about communication," Josh said.

"No, I was thinking art only comes from the leisure class," Will said. "By definition, the drawings came after the hunt. No one does art when they're running from a predator. No one does art when they're starving to death. People do art when they have the time to sit around and tinker with ideas and materials. We look at an old piece of pottery and think it must have been considered beautiful, but the so-called artist probably just had so much leftover corn, he needed something to put it in that the rodents couldn't chew right through."

Paul signaled June for a refill on his coffee and she brought over the pot. "What do you think, June?" he said. "Does art come from communication? Leisure time?"

"I like the old idea that the best art comes from pain and suffering. You know I love my Russian authors. Did you ever think they didn't know about the topless beaches in France?" she said. "Just think. If Tolstoy ever went to the Mediterranean for vacation…"

Roger laughed out loud and added, "That's why they say the

young can never produce anything of value. They haven't suffered enough."

Courtney shook her head while swallowing a french fry. "But that doesn't explain all the uplifting art that's out there," she said. "It's not all *War and Peace*. There's *Tom Sawyer* and *Robinson Crusoe*."

"Hey, I've got a wacko artist for you," Josh said. "What about Van Gogh? He's not helping any of your arguments. Here's a guy who was born into a pretty good family, pretty normal to start. Decides to become a priest but paint like a Dutch Master in his spare time. He chooses to be poor, suffers, produces crap and sponges off his brother. Next thing you know he's going crazy, cutting off his ear, and decides to kill himself. But he can't even do that well. In the end, he's known by college sorority girls everywhere for his uplifting sunflowers and irises."

"So what's your point?" Paul said.

"Well, he's not communicating anything with his flower pictures. He only drew a bunch of self-portraits because he didn't have money to pay models to sit. He suffered horribly, not because he was poor but because he chose to suffer, thinking it was his calling. He wasn't old when he died but he only sold one painting his entire life. Monet made a fortune in his day, lived to be 80 or 90 or something. Sure, Vince drew some coal workers and inmates, but he's best known for his flowers. Hardly the stuff you'd guess would come from a guy who shot himself in the chest. Probably would have died from lead poisoning anyway."

"Good one, hon'," Courtney said and gave him a peck on the lips. "You started to ramble there at the end, but I got the point."

"You didn't have to go back that far, Josh," Danny said. "Warhol didn't even produce his own work at the end. He just designed it and had some apprentice whip up a silkscreen."

"Let's not even go there," Paul said. "What about you, Professor Steadman? Rumor has it you've been known to put pen to paper. Or fingers to keyboard. Why do you write?"

"Yeah," Josh said. "How come you're always late to Diner's Club? I'll bet you're writing. You're a closet artist. C'mon, fess up." The rest of the Club joined in the jeering with overlapping questions.

"When do you write?"

"How do you pick a topic?"

"Where do you get your inspiration?"

"How much wood could a woodchuck chuck, if a woodchuck could chuck wood?" This last question came from Josh when he saw Roger was covering his face in genuine embarrassment.

Roger turned four shades of red. "Really, I thought we were talking about art. My short stories are just doodlings. I'm not communicating anything or revealing some great truths. I just write to get the ideas out of my head."

"Oh come on, Roger," June said. "Everyone of your stories has some guy searching for the meaning of life. They're full of symbolism. Heck, they don't even happen on earth."

"How would you know?"

"I'll bet you were writing today while you were mowing the lawn," June said. "Tell us what you did today and I'll tell you what I did."

Roger took a deliberate pull off his diet soda, ate a french fry, then drank again too soon. The mixture of the fry and the carbonated drink caused a gagging sensation in his throat and he choked. "Maybe. That's not the point here," he managed after a final, throat-clearing cough.

"What do you know about my stories? Noone's ever seen them. The versions I've told Emma aren't completed and she falls asleep before I'm even through."

"Not true," June said. "I bribed her. While you were at work she gave me the hard copies from your home office. It wasn't that tough, she's still young and trusting. Hey, I hate to resort to cheating but you wouldn't give 'em up and I'm between novels."

"The little…"

Will, Danny, Josh, Courtney and Paul were frozen in mid-thought. Roger's unheard stories were legend around campus, almost as famous as his messy, public divorce. Everyone new he was a frustrated author, noone had heard a single line. The stories may never live up to the hype but they were about to hear the plots-with criticism-from a woman with a Masters in the Russians!

"Oh, come on Roger, it's not such a big deal. I hate to sound like Sharon but what's the point if you never get them published? An artist needs an audience. Who cares if the greatest work ever produced is sitting in the artist's basement? It's the same as the tree in the forest. It might fall over and sing 'Happy Birthday' but if noone's there to hear it, you got yourself a non-event."

"But those are my stories to publish, burn or do whatever I want with them. She is so grounded," said Roger to himself. Then he had a thought. "And what could you possibly bribe her with that she doesn't already have?"

"Nothing much. I just promised her a summer full of adventure if she let me borrow them. Maybe I'll take her to France. So that's what I did today. Read all your stories. Now what did you do?"

"No, no, no, that's hardly good enough," Roger said. "If I'm going to spill my guts here, you've got to do better than that. I want a full 24 hours."

June pulled a stool up to the counter opposite Roger. The Diner's Club hadn't yet exhaled. June started by telling them all how she met Emma after school while Roger was still in his final class of the day. They walked from the middle school to what passed for a downtown on the way to Roger's house. To soften her up, June suggested they stop for fries and a soft drink at a fast food joint. June had the bizarre feeling of dining in a restaurant that wasn't hers. They talked about girl stuff and boys until June got around to the subject of Emma's schoolwork. From there it was a short hop to getting Emma to talk about her Language Arts class, which led to a discussion of Roger's work. June was able to play dumb and casually mention that she hadn't read anything good lately and before Roger's class was even over, Emma was walking June to the Steadman house. June promised to just "borrow" the copies from Roger's desk and return them to Emma before he even knew they were missing.

Her tale of Saturday started with Friday night's closing of the Diner. It was mercifully slow and she decided to close early. There wasn't enough business for the clean-up to take very long. Out of habit she wiped, scraped, and mopped every surface as usual. Her loyal customers would understand if they happened to drive by and she wasn't open at her usual time. She turned off the lights at midnight and flipped the "Open" sign on the door. She'd never posted hours on the Diner, a symbol of the fact that this was no chain restaurant, she was the owner and boss and could come and go as she pleased. She walked home in prickly anticipation of reading Roger's stories. It had been like foreplay to have them at arms' reach all afternoon at the Diner, but to resist looking at even the title of the first short story.

Once home, she bounced up the front steps with a huge grin on her face and skipped in the unlocked front door. It was her policy that she would never own anything worth stealing. The house was decorated in bachelorette chic, which is to say not at all. Rather, the place looked like 5 wrongfully terminated librarians had decided to move in together. June closed the door behind her and took a survey of the parlor. Every horizontal surface was covered in books. The only bare spots were a single file path to the kitchen and a spur to the only chair in the room, an overstuffed and ancient recliner. It sat under a tilting floor lamp with a low-watt bulb, facing away from the front door and windows, the better to read by daylight during those hours and to avoid being distracted by anything outside. The walls were similarly covered with books of all sizes. Dorm room style shelves were sagging under their loads and made of bare pine wood, supported by still more piles of books at either end. June placed the stack of Roger's short stories on the reading chair and smiled at it. She tiptoed through the kitchen and upstairs to the master bedroom in order to clean off the day's work and grease.

June's shower was twice as long and hot as she would normally take. As was her custom, she threw away a partly used bar of soap since the logo was worn off. "I hate small soap," she said aloud to herself. This shower was no mere exercise in personal hygiene. She was preparing for a date with a new author. She had to leave her hair wet since she doesn't own a blow dryer. June put on her most uncomfortable special underwear, a loose-fitting knee-length skirt, and a silk blouse with no bra. She padded down the stairs barefoot and into the kitchen where she took her largest tumbler from the cupboard. She put some ice in her canvas bartender bag and beat it to smithereens with a rolling pin that was never used for anything else. She filled the tumbler with shrapnel of various sizes to one inch from the top. From the pantry she took the half-empty (or half-full she mused) bottle of tequila. June removed the cap, inverted the bottle and counted to four. She filled the remainder of the glass with generic margarita mix, swirled it with a straw and walked into the front room. June sat, read and drank until the sun rose. The room brightened slowly around her until a single shaft of amber light broke the horizon, penetrated the parlor window and warmed her shoulders. She then re-read the stories she liked best.

June didn't tell the Club or Roger what she did in the recliner immediately after she was done reading the stories. She fell asleep in the recliner and woke up later with the wonderful sensation of not having a clue what time it was. She took a luxurious stretch like a cat on a sunny window seat, the smile still plastered on her face. With nowhere to go and zero obligations she deliberately sat in her chair enjoying the fact that she had nowhere to go and zero obligations.

Out of curiosity she took her cup to the kitchen to see what time it was and pour out the melted ice. The analog clock on the wall reinforced for her what a perfect day it was. She'd had a full 8 hours of sleep, finished her reading and still had time to change, get to the diner and prepare for the dinner rush before the Diner's Club members arrived. She walked up the stairs, reversed the procedure of preparing for her "date," put on a fresh uniform and headed to the Diner, stories tucked under her arm. In all, it was just about a perfect day.

"You see," she said in summary to her listeners, "being a student of art, literature, and ideas is a very different thing from wanting to teach them. It's still another layer of insanity to want to produce those ideas and put them out there for public consumption. What do you say, Roger?"

"Well, I'm jealous to a certain degree," he said. "And I wonder how often you do that."

"Pretty much every day. Sure, there's a laundry day here and there, I shop for groceries, pay bills, plan a summer trip, but you can't imagine how nice it is to be able to read for its own sake. No lesson planning, no dissertation to write, nothing to tell me what or when I can read. I work just hard enough here at the Diner to be able to enjoy the time alone."

"So you're saying even your consumption of ideas needs a sounding board, an audience, if you will?" Danny said.

"Yea, you could say that," June said. "But don't be so observant. It's annoying when you read my mind, Danny. Now it's your turn, Roger."

The professor was used to public speaking and even reciting his stories to Emma, but here was a new setting and he was somewhat nervous. He drained the last of his watered-down soda and motioned to June for another one. She got up to freshen the drink and offered to do the same for the Club. The motion and distraction was enough to put Roger at ease, remove the direct eye contact to the matter of the drinks, and allow him to start.

Since there's nothing more boring than saying he woke up, Roger started by saying just that and apologizing for how boring it sounded. No alarm clock was needed, he hadn't used one in years. He checked to see if Emma was awake and ended up staring at her sleeping form for a full 3 minutes. When she rolled over and mumbled something in her sleep, he backed out of the room slowly so as not to wake her and let her know he was staring. He didn't want to scare her after all. He took his usual, brief morning shower. The previous day he'd welded together 3 tiny shards of old soap and was pleased they produced enough suds to complete his lukewarm, 4 minute shower. Roger then proceeded to the kitchen to make coffee and think. He wasn't much of a breakfast person and would have a light snack whenever Emma awoke. He sat in his favorite chair and stared out the window. Emma's soccer game was still hours away, he had no papers to grade and wasn't currently working on any writing.

Back to the question of where his art and writing came from he realized he couldn't give the Club a satisfactory answer. Sure, leisure time was important to think of themes and to accomplish the craft of writing them down, but that begged the question, how did he think of it? Life experience was important—the suffering angle—but hardly explained the process of inspiration, never mind the drudgery of revision and self-editing.

Emma stirred, dressed for her soccer game, came down the stairs and after exchanging hellos and kisses, they had breakfast together. Some days, if they had time, he'd cook a warm meal like bacon and pancakes. Most days, like today, it was cold cereal. Roger had a dry, breakfast bar and a diet soda to take the edge off his hunger, once his coffee grew cold. A single prompt about her upcoming day was enough to start his daughter off on a monologue that continued with no further input from Roger. Emma had plans for a birthday party and sleepover after the soccer game, at the home of one of her teammates. Rides were already arranged, so he'd have the afternoon to himself.

They left the house with time to spare to get Emma to the field for pre-game warm-ups. Leaving the neighborhood, Emma continued her monologue of preteen complaints and stories. All Roger had to do to keep her talking was give the occasional grunt or nod that he was still listening. While he drove, Emma knitted with her fingers, a trick she'd learned at the last birthday party sleepover. The scarf-like chain was already starting to accumulate in her lap as they exited the neighborhood and turned onto the main road. Roger was glad Emma's eyes were averted when he saw a squirrel up the road, dragging its back legs across the pavement. It had been struck at the waist by a car, but not mercifully enough that it wasn't suffering. Then again, how much does a squirrel suffer? Even if it's not the kind of suffering a human say, on chemotherapy has to go through, it's got to be bad on the Squirrel Suffering Scale. For reasons unknown to Roger, it changed directions at the yellow line and he was unable to avoid hitting it when it crossed in front of the car. A sick feeling grabbed his stomach at the tiny thump that came from the back tire. He tried to look in the mirror to see if it had escaped but knew the little guy would be hawk food in a matter of minutes. Did he just commit suicide, to end his own suffering? Squirrels are all around us and yet we don't know a thing about them. Would they miss him back in the tree? Why do I think it's a male? How many squirrels live in a tree? Do they have extended families? Heck, people are all around us and we don't know a thing about them, let alone rodents. How many people in an apartment building of 50 units knows a single neighbor? Roger realized he hadn't heard a word Emma was saying and was pleased she didn't notice his daydreaming any more than she'd noticed the demise of the squirrel.

 Up the road the traffic was backed up inexplicably. With no shortcut or even long-cut around the jam, Roger got in line and waited for it to clear. He inched slowly towards the intersection and was able to merge gently around an SUV and into the right turn lane. At that point the cars came to a complete stop and failed to move even though the traffic lights appeared to be functioning. He glanced over at the female driver of the SUV as one always does at stoplights. From his position slightly behind her car at the rear quarter panel, he wasn't able to see her face. She had a look that said "money." Her hair was highlighted the perfect shade of blonde, pulled back to a businesslike ponytail to reveal enormous diamond stud earrings, easily 2 carats. Her silk blouse was blinding white and the blue suitcoat must have been some impractical cut and weight of designer fabric. He could see the sleeve of her right arm, the French-manicured hand resting on the passenger seat headrest. The driver began to caress the headrest of the bucket seat. She delicately swirled her sharp nails in the upholstered fabric, first lazy circles, then figure eights, extending and flexing her narrow fingers. Was she daydreaming of a recent lover? What a wonderful way to pass the time of a traffic jam, Roger thought. The way she fondled the passenger seat was identical to the way one would caress a lover's head during a deep, wet, sloppy, French kiss.

Then she did something even more curious. She started to spell letters in sign language. This headrest maneuver was no idle tic or daydream. She was clearly signaling someone. Since he was with Emma, Roger thought she might at first be spelling words to a child in the back seat, out of his view, possibly in a car seat. He knew a few letters but was she was spelling too fast for him to piece together the sentences. He glanced at the car stopped behind hers and was unable to penetrate the tinted windows, or see if the other driver was responding. Roger almost got out of his car to look in her backseat, when the traffic started to move. She stopped her signing, merged into the left turn lane and was gone forever along with her story.

Roger turned right and got in line with another crowd, this one inching slowly around the cause of the backup. How many times do we wait while driving only to pass the spot of the bottleneck with no payoff? This time Roger wasn't disappointed. A full-sized school bus was lying on its side, the driver and a police officer having a conversation with no animation whatsoever. One would have thought there would be pointing, shouting, the cop writing out a lengthy ticket, but no, they could have been discussing their favorite fruits, the way they ignored the overturned bus. It's odd enough to see a school bus on a weekend, but one exposing its undercarriage with seemingly no other damage was a curiosity worth stopping for.

Emma raised her head from her knitting and said, "That's Miss Marcie, my bus driver," as calm as if they were passing her in the supermarket. She looked down at the clock on the dashboard, satisfied that she'd still have time for warmups, and went back to her knitting. Roger couldn't help but wonder how this child had become so jaded in 12 short years. Maybe the opposite was true, since she had zero life experience, knew only this small-town world, perhaps she had no perspective from which to realize how phenomenal this drive to the soccer game actually was.

At the field, Roger parked at the first spot he saw, not the one closest to their destination. He got out with Emma and arranged their gear so they could hold hands on the way. He exchanged pleasantries with the other parents and ensured she was set up for the party with her change of clothes, gift for the birthday girl, and full sleepover gear. The pile of little girl accessories near the coach's bench looked like they were preparing for an invasion of France, albeit a colorful one, and all the armaments were gift-wrapped.

Roger managed to beg off watching the entire game with a kiss for Emma at halftime and an excuse about housework to do, papers to grade or some such half-truth. In reality, he couldn't wait to get to pen and paper and write down the impressions he'd had of his morning. With no clue how they might later fit into a story, if at all, he knew he didn't want to forget the squirrel, the lady or the bus. Back at the house he jotted down the essentials in his study. One entire shelf of the home office was dedicated to story ideas, dated and filed according to topics with categories like "Unusual Characters," "Funny Moments," or "Weather and Plot." From time to time, when not revising earlier chapters or writing new ones, he'd pull out a folder at random and see what ideas began to overlap. Then he'd start a new folder with potential scenes, graduate those to another shelf, and if they were deemed worthy, they would end up in the "First Draft" file. Roger was living proof of the perspiration over inspiration cliche.

The rest of the afternoon passed with deliciously mundane chores. It was rare that Roger had such free time so he lingered over every event, savoring his grilled cheese sandwich and pear lunch, the folding and putting away of the laundry. He even tried to take a nap, but was too energized by all his freedom to sleep. He then felt guilty about it so got up and returned to the study to try to write some more. A few story ideas started to come together and he began to type more feverishly. Before he knew it, he was awakened from his artistic frenzy by an audible growling of his stomach. It was dark outside. A look at the clock confirmed it was time to make for the Diner, throw down some comfort food and knock about a few ideas with the Club. In all, it was just about a perfect day.

Josh couldn't help himself. "Well, it's official," he said. "You two are tied for the title of Most Boring Person I've Ever Met."

"You redefine what it means to be an asshole," Danny said. "How is it that you can so consistently make all those around you exist in a constant state of discomfort?" To answer her own question she added, "You're like a hug from the relative that nobody likes."

Will added, "Or a handshake that's too strong." There were nods around the table and everyone joined in the verbal beating.

"You're a bowl of soup that's too hot, then instantly too cold," Paul said.

Even Courtney joined in the fun with, "…a forced laugh that's too loud and too long."

"Rain at an amusement park."

"A limousine with a flat tire."

"The last bite of a hot dog."

"Oversleeping for an interview."

"You're a short, white coffin."

Josh raised his hands to stop the bleeding. "Geez, guys. I meant it as a compliment. Just look at 'em. They're a perfect match." All eyes went from Josh to the counter where June and Roger looked to be in the middle of an intense staring contest. Their faces were a foot apart and held mutual expressions of admiration. There was no competition, no anger, no regret, no inequality, no disappointment, no animosity, no expectation. They shared a relaxed contentment.

25

Company Loves Misery

June found herself in Roger's office with increasing frequency after the Xmas break. She was amazed to have made it through her first semester as an English teacher, yet wrongly assumed it would get easier as time passed. In the new year and with all new students she thought she could start fresh but only found herself feeling intimidated and inadequate all over again. Her various classroom disasters were legendary. Not a week went by that something didn't go either comically or painfully wrong. Often times it was both.

Roger had actually started enjoying her little crying fits and was becoming more skilled at calming her down. It gave him a boost to have someone depend on him even for something so simple as a sympathetic ear. He set aside Friday afternoons both hoping and knowing she'd show with another week's worth of lamentations. When they parted from these sessions, she began giving him friendly hugs which was more than he could say for any contact from his increasingly distant wife. The brief, professional contact from June, whatever form it took—a smile, a hug, a handshake—seemed all at once more genuine, more warm, and more intimate than any he could recall from Sharon.

This particular Friday in January, Roger was seated at his desk, staring at nothing out the window. He was wearing his version of casual Friday, khakis and a long-sleeved dress shirt, no tie. There was a soft knock at the office door. Normally it would be open to allow a passing colleague or student the chance to shout out a hello, but there was only one person Roger wanted to see. He was trying to discourage all others. "Who is it?" he said firmly, more as a statement than a question. Roger was prepared to act busy and make excuses if needed.

"It's June. Alright if I come in?" He felt instant relief. Roger spun around and leaned forward in his chair. He recognized the blue suit she'd worn on her first day and mentally noted it was a better choice for January than August.

"Sure, your company is always welcome. Sorry if I sounded short." Then, when she'd entered, "Close the door if you don't mind. I'm not in the mood for stray visitors. Present company excepted, naturally."

"Yea, I heard about your son drowning." June demonstrated her complete lack of tact. "That's shitty. I never know what to say when something like that happens and it bugs me when people ask how you're doing. As if you'll get over it just by them asking and acting concerned for you. As if you *could* get over it. I guess you don't want to hear about my problems," she said.

"That pretty much sums it up," agreed Roger. Oddly enough her frank and succinct statement of his condition was a welcome change from all the predictable expressions of sympathy. Coming from June, it felt better than any basket of flowers or casserole.

"Should I go?" she asked.

"No, no. It's alright. You're about the only person who doesn't annoy me right now. I could use a little chat about something other than death, funerals, regret and the like." June sat on the new love seat Roger had stuffed along side his desk.

"Thanks," she said only then realizing the new furniture and adding, "Hey, this is new, isn't it? Comfy."

"Uh, huh. I call it the Wailing Sofa." She looked at him with her eyebrows up. "It's for when the crying fits won't stop. I unplug the phone and bury my head in the throw pillow. After an hour or so I can go home and face that thing I call a wife. I swear she's making my life a living hell since RJ died."

"Aw, geez, Roger," she said with genuine concern, "I thought you guys were okay."

"Nah, we might have been putting up a good show before he died, but when I look back, maybe our son was the only thing we had in common. Now she openly disagrees with me about everything I thought we shared. I don't know, maybe she's just as hurt and scared and pissed off as I am but it's coming out in the wrong way. As if I'm not feeling guilty enough about the whole thing she blames me for his death. When I try to suggest we have another child she accuses me of trying to replace him like a broken lamp. I figured going back to work would help me get on with things. She sees it as me trying to escape the tragedy. I ask you, what the hell am I supposed to do? She acts like there's a script for this pain that I'm supposed to be following. She actually told me I should write about it, that's what a Great Writer would do. Can you believe that?"

June just nodded. Her mind was a blank. Then she started to sympathize with Roger. He was a good father after all. He was a great teacher. She hadn't read any of his writing but she assumed there must be some promise there as well. Compared to her current lover, he was a catch and a half. Despite the money, power, and prestige Chuck really didn't have much to recommend himself as a life partner. She began to feel ashamed and realized she was staring at her own feet. When she looked up Roger was rubbing his left shoulder with his right hand. His head was thrown back, his face in a grimace and tears were running down both cheeks. She couldn't tell if it was pain or sadness. The tracheotomy scar was an angry red gash across his throat. On the right side of his neck was a scar from the central lines. "Are you all right?" she asked.

"Oh, I'm such a baby. I wish you hadn't seen me like this. It's just this neck pain I've been getting. When I got out of the hospital I couldn't turn my neck to the right for a week. Apparently I spent a lot of time looking left with the IV and the ventilator. It still gets me from time to time."

"Come here," June commanded. She wasn't asking. "Let me see if I can work that out for you." Roger looked out of the corner of his eye and realized she was serious. He wiped away the tears and sat next to her on the love seat. June handed him the pillow and told him to lean away from her over the arm of the sofa. He did as he was told, crossed his arms, buried his head in the pillow and starting sobbing. June touched his aching neck at the spot he was just rubbing, lightly at first. "Roger, your neck muscles are like rocks."

It took a few minutes but June began to work out the kinks. Roger's breathing slowed and he started to relax. He took a final, deep, sighing breath and all of the physical tension melted away. She thought he might have fallen asleep but inside Roger's mind his thoughts began to race, but in a new, more pleasant direction. Sharon had never, in all their time together, even when they were dating, touched him the way

June did. It was obvious she wasn't a trained masseuse and that seemed to add to his pleasure and release. Her touch wasn't clinical with the single goal of removing the knots. No, her touch was surprisingly tender. His writer's mind started to wander. She understood his emotion and didn't judge him or expect anything of him. Her rubbing was the physical expression of the fact that she really cared for him. Maybe not as a wife or in a sexual way, but as a part of the human family. Roger wondered if one person out of 10, out of 100, ever experienced such a connection. Could he just be imagining it in his fragile emotional state?

If there was any doubt about her true feelings for him, what June did next removed any doubts. She finished with his back and gave him a hug from behind. Before she reached around him though, she hiked up her skirt in order to put her bent leg beside him on the sofa and face him square. She removed her blazer, blouse and bra and tossed them on the floor. She lifted Roger's shirt and pressed her breasts squarely into his back, squeezing him from behind with her hands under his shirt in front. She held him that way without a word for a full 5 minutes. Soon, there was only one part of Roger which wasn't exceedingly relaxed.

It's often said that Misery loves Company. In this case it was Company that was on top. June made love to Roger with real affection. Neither was under the illusion that their meeting was evidence of deep, true love, but it wasn't mere lust either. June's act was one of kindness and in recognition of Roger's need for a connection. He accepted the gift graciously.

Afterwards, June unbuttoned Roger's shirt, and leaned forward to press her skin to him once again. She held him in this way for another full 5 minutes. He was glad to be able to hug her in return. When she sat back up and gave him a pleasant smile, she saw that he was crying again, but with a smile more of hope than resignation.

Showing complete confidence and not a tinge of regret or embarrassment, June left her top bare while she helped Roger dress himself. Only then did she recovered her bra from the floor. She put her arms through, assembled her front, then turned her back to Roger and held up her hair. He understood and hooked the clasp for her. When her blouse and blazer were back on she did something that surprised him most of all. She stayed.

June sat on the love seat, patted the cushion next to her and Roger sat down as well. She put an arm over his shoulder, turning him so his back was to her and they stared out the window together at the passing clouds. After a moment Roger broke the silence. "Thank you, June," he managed to say weakly.

"You're welcome, Roger," she answered simply. For both of them it was the most adult interaction they had ever had. The reason was not its intimacy but in its honesty. Neither was there to take advantage of the other. They both understood the implications of their act, yet neither would make new demands. June would still be the associate professor, Roger the Department Chief.

26

June's Diner

When her last class was done for the week prior to Spring Break, June made sure to stop by Roger's office to say goodbye. She wasn't going to be keeping their usual counseling session. Roger was the one bright spot in her academic life and she'd been careful not to ruin that relationship by continuing to have sex with him or to take him for granted. She peeked her head into his office, not intending to stay, and said, "Hey Roger, have a good break." Seeing his disappointment she added, "Uh, you and Sharon getting out of town?"

"Hi, June. No. I don't think either of us could handle a trip together," Roger said. "You know, it'd be impossible not to think about Mexico."

"Well, maybe you can have a nice dinner in town or something. Rent a movie," June said, fully realizing how lame it sounded.

"Yea, last week we went out. I told the hostess to give us a table for 3 and a booster seat. Did I tell you the airline delivered Roger Junior's suitcase?" Roger said. June nodded, she'd heard the story. "Uh huh, apparently the hotel thought we'd left it by accident, so they made sure we got it back. Couldn't have been worse timing either."

"What do you mean?" she said.

"Well, you know, we were doing okay for a while there. With the remodeling we were a team, now that it's done, she's acting distant again," Roger said. "Makes me wonder what she's thinking."

"I'm sure she's just sad," June said. "It's gonna take some time. You keep working on that adoption angle, she'll come around. See ya later." She felt bad for leaving Roger hanging considering all the time he'd spent supporting her. June didn't want to miss Chuck before he left for the East Coast.

Chuck wasn't a complete disaster but he was beginning to wear out his welcome. On her drive to the Dean's mansion she wondered which was worse: that he'd been coming to her office only when it suited him, or that in the past month, he'd visited her only once, and not for sex. He'd been a fun diversion at times. They'd kept completely out of the public eye which she knew suited his needs for discretion. She'd even parked her car out of sight to visit him at the mansion on a few occasions. Lately he'd begun making excuses. She thought the toilet paper in the trees would get his attention, or at least a response of some sort. In a way, June thought it was even a touch romantic, like a lover's quarrel. Her gesture went completely disregarded.

She parked boldly in the circle drive and walked right in the front door. The house was quiet and she stealthily searched the first floor for Chuck. She stopped at the open door of the study when she heard a woman's voice. At first she thought he might be with someone else, but the voice was thin and metallic. Her fears dissipated when she heard the voice call him "Charles."

June slid through the doorway and leaned against the wall to eavesdrop. She found Chuck at his desk staring into the speaker phone with a frown on his face. "...but I've told you Charles, we aren't looking to expand to the Southwest. Our delivery routes don't reach South of Tennessee, let alone across the Mississippi."

"But mother, that's my point. They don't need to. I've done the analysis, it'd be cheaper to get West Coast support. Have you looked at a map lately? The country has expanded beyond the 13 Colonies," Chuck said. June was amused to witness this exchange. She didn't know what it was about but she could tell he was losing the argument. No doubt he regretted insulting his mother. Any hope of getting what he wanted was shot to hell.

"I'm well aware of that, Charles. Never mind about the family's business interests, we're doing just fine. Just continue to keep your nose clean and we'll see. It's always good to talk to you son. I look forward to seeing you when you arrive," she said. June heard Chuck's mother end the call and gave him a look. June cleared her throat to announce her presence.

"I saw you there," Chuck lied. "What do you want, June?" He sat down heavily in defeat.

"What was that all about?" June said. She took a seat of her own in one of the interview chairs.

"Nothing," he said. "I don't really want to talk about it. At least not with you."

"Southwest expansion? Delivery routes? Have you been working again? I told you that's not good for someone like you. It might lead to responsibility," she said.

"Cute. But it's none of your business," Chuck said.

"I'm not saying it is. I'm just interested. I never you knew you had any skills. I might just want to start having sex with you again," June said. Putting Chuck on the defensive was likely to open him up.

"I wasn't completely comatose during business school. Besides, it's all anyone talks about at family gatherings for the past two years. They're trying to get this restaurant thing going nationwide. I suggested a niche market, these retro Diners. We had a bunch of defunct railcars from the shipping company holdings. They were going to scrap 'em all until I suggested the restaurant idea," he said.

"Ooh, clever boy," June said.

"Yea, well, it turned out to be cheaper to build 'em new from scratch than refinish the cars," Chuck said. "They stole my idea anyway. Now they're churning them out cheaper than mobile homes. I just can't get my foot in the business. They wouldn't let me in sales, regional management, or distribution. I'm beginning to think the only way into the business will be to buy one and open my own diner."

"Well, sorry to hear about your problems. I'm sure it'll all work out for you, it always does," she said. "So, how come you haven't been coming around lately?"

"Um, what? How long's it been? What do you care?" Chuck said. "Oh, you're upset like some high school crush. That would explain my trees. I watched you do that, you know. If I find out who that rent-a-cop was I'll have him fired." Despite his show of strength and indifference, June saw Chuck start to fidget. He leaned forward, acted like he was reviewing figures, then shuffled the papers on his desk. When he straightened the pile and started tapping a pencil she knew he was hiding something.

"What's going on Chuck?" June said. "And don't tell me you're so preoccupied with work you've haven't thought about guilt-free sex for a month."

"I'm seeing someone else," Chuck said.

June was unfazed. No doubt his abrupt language was a dismissal of some sort. Well, she had her own bomb to drop. "I'm late," June said. It was as good a time as any to bring it up, she thought.

"Late for what? Then go. I didn't ask you to come here and interrupt me. Look, I told you, there's another woman," he said. "I thought we were going to act like adults here. No strings, no whining."

"Pregnant, Chuck. With your baby. Remember how you said you could do something for me? Now's your chance to be a man," June said.

"What? I don't owe you anything. Get rid of it. I don't care." he said. June waited. She'd counted on him getting hysterical. "Did you think I was going to propose to you? You're a bigger fool than I thought," he said.

June had an idea. "I'm sorry you feel that way," she said. "Any idea what your mom might think? Never mind about Sharon, I just don't want Roger to get hurt worse than he already is."

"What? How did you know about Sharon? We haven't even had sex yet. I haven't done anything wrong," Chuck lied.

"Yea, you're a regular saint, Chuck. By the way, I didn't know about Sharon. Until now," June said. "Roger and I talk, he is my boss you know. He told me the marriage was doing pretty well considering they lost their boy. Until recently, that is. I'm guessing you got a little bored with me, saw a chance for some excitement and started oozing that considerable charm of yours all over my friend's wife."

She got up and in two quick strides was at his desk. The weakling sat back in his chair. She spun the phone around, hit speaker, redial, and waited. "Hey!" Chuck said. "What the hell are you doing?"

"Yes, Charles. Was there something else?" the speaker said.

June spoke before Chuck could protest, hang up, or invent an explanation. "Hello, my name is June. I'm one of the English teachers here at the college and Chuck and I just wanted to let you know we're having a baby."

Silence.

"Charles? Are you there?" she said. "If this is some kind of a joke, it's a poor attempt and I don't appreciate it."

"No, mother. Sorry, it's nothing, I'll handle it," Chuck said.

"Actually, Chuck's not handling it," June said. "That's why I called you Ma'am. I thought maybe you could convince him to accept some responsibility. With all due respect, I didn't get in this condition by myself."

"Charles? Is this true?" she said.

"Well, more or less," he said. "Maybe. Probably."

"Young lady," the speaker said. "Is there any chance there's another man? Are we sure my son is the father? Forgive me for my bluntness. I'm a woman of action and not one to mince words."

"On the contrary, I appreciate your coming to the point," June said. "To answer your question, no, there's no chance it's another man." Thank goodness for the 2,000 miles between us, June thought.

"Well, then we are at an impasse," Chuck's mother said. "What do you propose? I take it you understand the delicate nature of this situation. You also know my son. He'd likely make an unacceptable husband and father under the best of circumstances. Forgive me son, but I don't wish you on any woman. In this situation, our need for discretion puts us at your clemency."

June couldn't resist the opportunity to score points with the old bat.

"Clemency? I'm sure you don't require my leniency or mercy. Perhaps a careful measure of politic would suit you better?" June said.

"We read each other loud and clear," the speaker said. June was sure Chuck was completely baffled at this point.

"Ma'am, these circumstances are as much a surprise to me as they must be to you," June said. "With your permission, I'd like to discuss our options with the father. While the best solution may not be readily apparent, I'm sure in time we can reach a conclusion which will be beneficial to us all. Would that work for you?" June was beginning to enjoy this charade.

"Yes, thank you young lady. Charles? I know you're still there. Give this woman what she wants and don't make this more difficult for us than it needs to be. You know what to do. For once, don't make me have to fix your problems for you. Say goodbye, Charles."

"Goodbye, mother," Chuck said.

June couldn't believe her good fortune. She didn't want a child any more than Chuck did. But she was able to play the game as well as Chuck's mother. He was hobbled by his history and his mother was constricted by her sense of propriety. She had to be sure not to sound over-anxious. Blurting out her solution would make it look like she planned it all along. Then again, what did she have to lose? He'd likely be happy just to have an out that satisfied his mother and guaranteed her silence. Still, she started innocently enough. "Any brilliant ideas besides abortion, Chuck?" she said.

"I don't see what the big deal is," Chuck said.

"You know your mother would never go for that," June said. "Plus, I may not be religious but I have always thought I'd be a mother someday. I just hoped for a proper father to do it with. I'm willing to put it up for adoption, but I ask you, what's in it for me? I have the ability to make this very uncomfortable for you, Chuck."

"Yea, you keep reminding me of that," he said. "I don't know. What do you want? Just tell me what you want and we'll get it done."

"Well, now you're talking sense. My first request is that you leave Sharon alone," she said. "I know, it's not what you expected, but let them be. If Roger can work it out, I want him to be happy. If they end up divorced, then do whatever you want. But for now, leave her be, make up some excuse, tell her you have business out East and take a long vacation. Agreed?" She wanted to go slowly to be sure his reptilian brain retained all the facts. He nodded.

"Good," she said. "Next, we can't exactly hide my huge belly come next fall. I can't be teaching when I'm 8 and 9 months pregnant, without lots of questions. I'll need a source of income." She saw his look. "No, I don't want just money. I want one of those Diners you've been talking about. I can run a restaurant. Especially if I don't have to worry about a mortgage, if you know what I mean. I've been a waitress, managed a bar through grad school. I can handle it if I'm not worried about a liquor license or the bottom line. Can you make that happen?" He shrugged and nodded again.

"Great," June said. "We're making some progress here. Next, I want the house I'm currently renting. It's come up for sale and its probably cheaper than one of those diners. I don't want to have to sleep in the restaurant. I can rent out a room or two if money gets tight. But that shouldn't be a problem considering I expect a small monthly stipend for, shall we call it child support? For the next 18 years or so. Associate professor salary would work out well. Inflation included, of course."

"Whatever," Chuck said. "Do you want it monthly or in a lump sum? Just make that kid disappear. Mother can make that happen like a blink. But what's our guarantee you'll keep quiet about this?"

"I guess you'll just have to trust me," June said. "I've got a certain police officer on my side that you've failed to identify. He happens to know of my condition and would start asking some embarrassing questions if anything should happen to me. I guess you don't even need to trust me. You just need to make sure I don't get hit by a bus or struck by lightning."

"You bitch," Chuck said.

"You should be a little more kind to me, Chuck," June said. "Who knows? If you play your cards right, you may end up with Sharon. Apparently she's not too excited about having kids either."

Spring break was more productive than June could have imagined. She graded all the mid-term papers in the first weekend. When Chuck came back from the East coast, he had Carl deliver the good news. In a fat manilla envelope she received 3 property deeds. One to the house she was currently renting, another to a Chuck family diner, and a third, to 5 acres of old farmland, just outside of town.

It was the perfect location. Chuck probably thought he was setting up the Diner for failure, putting it so far off the beaten path. He couldn't have been more wrong. The last thing June wanted was an all-consuming, booming business. She planned to run it herself, keeping it just busy enough to cover her measly expenses and justify the occasional vacation. There was room for a parking lot with a nice view of the woods. Eighteen years of associate professor's salary was not quite what she imagined it would be but she was glad to have the lump sum all at once. She figured she could invest it better than that idiot Chuck.

27

Paul and the Suburban Terrorist

Prior to the completion of her first and only academic year, June made sure the word "asshole" slowly appeared in the lawn of the Dean of the College. The image in dying grass was faint in late Spring. By the time graduation rolled around, it was clear that this image was not by chance. The letters were at least 6 feet high and properly angled so as to be read most clearly from the quadrangle. The effect was similar to the way traffic signs are painted on streets so that drivers can read them. Up close, the letters were enormous.

The Dean's mansion sat on a hill, high over the campus and was fronted by a large and luxurious green lawn. In the desert climate nothing says success like a ridiculously wide yard of Kentucky Bluegrass. Installing it was one of Chuck's first moves as Dean and no small matter of pride. Having to choose between his sports car and the lawn would have been difficult. The velvet expanse extended down the hill so that it looked more like a golf course fairway than a residential yard. At the time the College was founded the Dean's mansion was situated in such a way as to afford the occupants a clear view of the quadrangle. Unfortunately for Chuck, the view of his front lawn was equally clear to all the students walking between classes.

This particular act of suburban terrorism was her masterpiece and personal favorite. An abundance of fertilizer was all it took and in a couple of weeks, the letters began to take shape in light brown, dead grass. Even though she'd gotten what she wanted from ending her relationship with Chuck, she felt he needed a goodbye present. Security around the mansion had been tightened after the graffiti, the slashed tires, the broken windows, the toilet paper, the dog shit, and of course, the eggs. What she lacked in originality up to this point, June made up for in persistence. Her arrangement with Paul eliminated the risk of any repercussions by this time.

The best part of the plan worked to perfection. Naturally, the lawn had to be replaced prior to graduation ceremonies. What Charles didn't anticipate was a slight mismatch in the color of his mature grass and the newer, brighter sod. During his graduation day speech it was impossible for the audience not to look over his shoulder, up the hill to the mansion and read the giant, bright green word, "asshole." Paul failed to stifle a chuckle as he stood in uniform at the back of the crowd. He was being paid to enjoy this spectacle.

They say, if you're not a part of the solution, you're part of the problem. Paul was a willing and enthusiastic part of the problem. As a member of the campus security staff, he was well aware of who was performing these dastardly deeds. He just didn't know why.

About 4 months after he'd stumbled upon June and Chuck on the desk in her office and a week prior to Spring Break, Paul drove up the hill to the mansion on one of his usual night shift security rounds. June was busy draping Chuck's front pine trees with toilet paper. She had some trouble getting the rolls completely over the tops of the taller trees. The effect was something like the way a toddler puts all the ornaments on the bottom 3 feet of the Christmas tree. Paul turned his squad car into the long circle drive. As his headlights swept the lawn, June was highlighted like the classic prison escapee, outlined making an overhand shot. When the missile failed to come down out of the tree, she simply bent down to a pile of twenty or so rolls, picked up another, unrolled a 6-foot tail, anchored it under her tennis shoe and heaved again, this time angling it to be sure it would come down over a side branch.

Paul backed up the car to capture her in his headlights again. At first he thought it must be some disgruntled student or other local punks. June shielded her eyes with her left hand and looked in the direction of the car. She neither dropped the roll, nor ran, but hoisted another bomb to the upper reaches. When Paul had a better look, it didn't take long to recognize June. It was not just the way her sweat pants failed to disguise her womanly figure. It was her insolent attitude that Paul recognized so readily. He left the car and approached her, figuring he had the upper hand. However, June recognized Paul as the officer who had nearly interrupted she and Chuck during one of their trysts earlier in the school year.

"Excuse me. Professor Turner, is it?" he inquired politely. "I'm Officer Paul Romero. Would you mind stopping this vandalism?"

"Yes, I would mind. This bastard's a complete asshole," and she flung another paper snow ball over the apple tree.

A thousand possibilities raced through Paul's mind. He was relatively certain the rookie associate professor and the Dean were still having sex. Had they broken up? Were they ever really a couple? He decided to take a chance. Fining, ticketing, or arresting her would not be the most likely way to get a date. He'd have to gain her confidence by making up that they had something in common. "Look. We all the know the Dean's lacking a few IQ points. But it is my job to protect the grounds, if not the man directly. If this kind of damage occurs on my shifts it's going to affect my job."

Hearing this fact brought June to a halt. She stopped with a roll in each hand and turned to face Paul. "Look, sorry. I've got a little grudge here, shall we say, and I'm trying to get this prick's attention. He's not answering my calls or mail. I figured a little public humiliation might get him to wake up. Plus, it's fun. What do you propose?"

Far from turning him off, her crude language and open emotion excited Paul even more. He decided to change tactics. He had nothing to lose being direct and honest. "Look, I've been watching you for a few months and didn't know how to ask, but I'd like to get to know you better. And gee, what better time or place than the front lawn of the Dean's mansion at 3:30 in the morning?" When she smiled at his joke he rightly assumed he had permission to continue. "So here's the deal. I won't arrest or fine you on the condition that you don't perpetrate any more of these heinous crimes on my shifts. I'll provide you with my schedule and the usual routines of my colleagues so you don't get caught by someone less understanding than me. Plus, that will allow you to pick one night a week when you let me take you to dinner."

June was following up until the last bit about the weekly dates. "How long do I have to date you? That seems like a lot of dinners. You're not suggesting anything unseemly, I hope." If Paul knew of her condition and situation, he'd likely not be propositioning the pregnant, soon-to-be unemployed teacher.

"Only until we get to know each other." She stared at him out of the corner of her eye with a suspicious glance. Realizing he'd asked for too much, Paul retreated. "Hey, imagine we're real people. If you're completely repulsed by me on our first night out, I'll give you your freedom. But you still have to stick to the other cops' shifts. Deal?"

"It's a deal. So are you going to help me with this toilet paper or what?"

Paul had a wonderful time with a guilty pleasure he hadn't known since high school. Looking back, he would mark this night as their first official date.

Their second date was somewhat less successful. Paul chose a nice restaurant, wore a nice suit, picked June up in his nice car, and was careful to be nice the entire night. At dinner, June thought to herself as she yawned openly, he's certainly nice. He was a welcome change from the unfiltered ego and testosterone of Chuck. Still, considering the origins of their acquaintance, she quickly thought of him only as a potential confidant. Paul was more than just a friend but less than a possible lover. No chance he was a life partner.

The death knell of any romantic overture is the statement by one or the other interloper, "I feel like I've known you all my life." It was June who had the opportunity on their first date to let Paul off easy. After dinner and skipping dessert they chatted easily and comfortably over coffee. Then, without warning or intent, she delivered the blow, "This has been more fun than I expected, Paul. You're like the brother I never had."

Ugh. Paul died inside. What now? He couldn't avoid seeing her, he'd invariably be assigned the security detail at countless college functions and she'd be required to attend. He knew he wasn't likely to sway her first impression. If he'd had other opportunities, perhaps he could give up the quest for her companionship. He knew he had nothing in common with the female undergraduates. Given his job they thought of him as a threatening authority figure. He thought for a moment just how much he had in common with the Dean in this regard.

No, in the space of downing his after-dinner coffee, Paul resolved to simply be there for June. Maybe she'd finally be persuaded to give him another try based on his fidelity and devotion alone. Maybe he'd go to college, yea, that was it, take some of her classes. Then he'd have an excuse to contact her about assignments, the fine points of his literature studies. Little did he know that June was 2 months and one baby from retiring. His plans for an undergraduate degree wouldn't be realized until years later and then only as an inevitable consequence of his intellectual curiosity, not any attempt to win her over.

28

Labor and Deliverance

June waltzed into Roger's office as if it were any other Friday. She handed him a single sheet of paper. "Hi Roger."

"What's this?"

"Only a couple of weeks 'til graduation, huh?" she said by way of avoiding his question. He took a moment to read the two-line memorandum.

"You're quitting? You can't just quit. You've come this far…" and his voice trailed off. "Can we talk about this?" He motioned to the love seat but instead she settled in the armchair set aside his desk for tutoring and counseling sessions.

"Don't act as if you didn't see it coming," June said. She'd been visiting much less frequently. It never occurred to her that his interpretation of her absence would be a newfound professional success. Roger must have thought she was finally getting some control over her classroom. On the contrary, since Spring Break and her decision to retire, the classes had become downright unruly. The little beasts sensed her indifference and were unforgiving. She liked it better when they enjoyed making her suffer. The lions were finished, now the vultures were having their way with her academic carcass.

"Give it a chance, June. It's only your first year. Really. Trust me, it'll come."

"Easy for you to say, you're a natural Roger. You can't help but be a great teacher. I'm a fish on a bicycle in front of those kids. They're sharks and they smell the blood in the water." It was a convenient excuse, her lack of classroom expertise. There was no way she could tell him her real reasons for leaving. She did like Roger and wanted to please him. Short of that, she could at least let him know he wasn't the problem, but saying they'd "still be friends" sounded more weak and pathetic than June could have imagined.

It wasn't just a courtesy that June hung around to chat. Their conversation flowed as easily as ever considering the circumstances. Roger allowed that his marriage was at least stable, much the same way the La Brea tar pits are stable. Sharon was currently neutral on the topic of children and Roger failed to share that adoption was their only chance to resume having a family together.

Chuck had been keeping up his end of the bargain by staying out of the way, though June didn't educate Roger on that point. He didn't seem to know he had competition and June rightly guessed it wasn't her place to break the news. Once they'd settled the issue of children, he would go about trying to rekindle some romance with Sharon. Summer break would allow time for getting their married life in order.

"So, what's next on the career track, June? I'll bet you're going back to school, getting your Doctorate," Roger said.

"Ha. I may be a masochist but I'm not insane."

"Oh, it's not such a stretch. You know your stuff, it's just a matter of finding a niche." June admitted it would be an easy way to make some contacts, do some networking, if she had any interest in remaining in academia. She also knew what he was really asking and answered his unspoken question.

"If you're worried about me skipping out of town, that's not in the cards. I'm going to stay on in the house I'm in now. You know I bought the old shithole, didn't you?" she said. Roger shook his head. "Well, as a last resort, I could just be a landlord for college students. Probably make ends meet that way. In the summer, do the Bed & Breakfast thing. I don't know. Anything but teaching.

"You won't see me around this summer, though. I've got some money saved up and I'm going to take a vacation," she lied. "Come back in the Fall and figure it out then."

"Well, if you ever consider teaching again, let me know. I heard there's an opening in the English department." They both chuckled at his lame joke and the conversation came to a natural conclusion. They rose to say goodbye and June was happy the desk was between them. It reduced the contact to a handshake and Roger would be less likely to notice the change in her figure than with their customary hug.

"It's not goodbye," she said, "just see you later." Roger nodded and turned away so as to not see her leave. Even though there were still a few weeks left in the school year, his voice was cracking when he gave a weak "see you later, then." The air left the room and a lonely melancholy took its place. So much for a strictly business-like resignation.

For the last few weeks of school and just as the weather was becoming more unbearably seasonal, June found it necessary to wear increasing amounts of clothing. Hiding her ample bosom had been a lifetime chore she'd learned to conquer. Now that she was paid a visit by the Hormone Fairy the challenge was becoming comical. She had a ravenous appetite and her wardrobe was at its limit. Her goal was to let Chuck think she'd had an abortion, end the school year blaming her fat ass and ankles on the Freshman Fifteen, and have the baby just to spite him.

She didn't bother telling her few loyal students she was leaving. They wouldn't have the pleasure of her unique teaching skills in their sophomore year even if she did stick around. She cleaned out her office over the final days and made only a half-hearted attempt to grade her final exams and term papers. By not spreading the word of her resignation, it was no trouble to walk right off campus after graduation to her new house. No need to say goodbye to Chuck, he'd no doubt gotten his message on the front lawn of the Dean's mansion.

June attacked the remainder of her pregnancy the same way she approached everything in her life. She read about it obsessively from all angles. She started with her own collection, reading every piece of fiction she could recall which had a pregnant character. Given the high number of deaths in childbirth reported, she gave herself a 50% chance of surviving. She decided as good a plot device as maternal/fetal demise could be, it made for lousy science. When her library was exhausted of choices, she took a trip to the nearest mega-chain book warehouse and gathered everything she could carry from teen pregnancy through post-menopausal in-vitro fertilization. At the counter, she nearly paid by credit card, but instead, laid out a pile of cash not wanting to leave any paper trail that might arouse suspicion. One might never know what Chuck's mother was monitoring. She read medical textbooks, treatises on mid-wifery, delivery methods in Third World Countries and her favorite oxymoron, natural childbirth. The more she learned, the more she decided there was nothing "natural" about producing 7 or 8 pounds of flesh from an area with no business passing anything but liquids.

In June, she calculated she was exactly ½ way done, 20 weeks out of 40. Everything went downhill from there. June woke up in an unpleasant sheen of greasy sweat. Parts of her body were touching each other when they shouldn't have been. Her belly was rubbing her thighs, which in turn were making gross contact over far too large a surface area. Her breasts were downright absurd she thought, not only in blocking her view of her feet to the south, but rudely pushing against her arms east and west. At every new and larger point of contact, drops of water formed and flowed, following the creases to her mattress. She was repulsed by the sensation of her own body, like an actor trapped in one of those Hollywood fat suits. Even sleeping atop the sheet in the same skimpy undershorts she wore before she got knocked up, June was unable to escape the heat she was generating.

She took a cold shower just to rinse off and played a game with her reflection while drying. She covered the view of her body with the over-sized beach towel and imagined nothing had changed. She had a handsome face, radiant hair, and clear vibrant skin. Attractive, by any definition, she was. When she raised the towel to block her face, yet uncover the view of her ballooning body, she felt like a voyeur. It was like peeking into another house, she had no idea whose body that was.

Her first chore was a quick trip to the mailbox, to get the previous day's junk mail and bills. As ravenous for a lumberjack breakfast as she was each morning, going out in the heat of the day was unthinkable, even the twenty steps back and forth to the curb. She dressed in shorts and a tank top but covered up with a robe in case any neighbors saw her. She scanned the street from behind the front window. In her condition there was no sense making idle chat with nosy neighbors starved for gossip.

Hair still dripping, she popped out the door barefoot and in less than 20 seconds was back, to sort the pile in the kitchen. Even in her hunger for knowledge and sources to pass the time, she avoided subscribing to any magazines. What she dreaded most each day was a jury summons.

In the kitchen she cranked out a huge breakfast, well over 2,000 calories: 4 strips of thick-sliced bacon, 4 large scrambled egg whites with butter and milk, into which she folded a pile of whatever vegetables were in the crisper, all hemmed in by a silly number of silver dollar pancakes. She was delighted to learn firsthand that the cliche about food cravings was true. While she hadn't yet gone out after midnight for pickles and ice cream, June had found that everything tasted better, especially in larger portion sizes.

She waddled to the front room with her meal on a turkey platter. She made another trip to retrieve an over-sized salad fork, a pint of whole milk, and the remains of the real maple syrup. Once seated, she balanced the tray on her belly and drizzled syrup over the entire concoction. She ate like a linebacker during training camp 2-a-days, smiling to herself while barely chewing the sticky mess, smiling at how clever she was to think of using the salad fork for faster service.

Satisfied, she leaned back in the recliner and stifled the sensation to let out an enormous burp. Downing the milk in one breath put out the heartburn fire. Then June felt a new and odd rumbling. This thrill wasn't stomach acid, nor was it the other end. She held her breath to see if it would come again. There was an audible bump on the underside of her breakfast platter. June stared at the plate, eyes wide, still not breathing. The next kick was more violent and toppled the platter clear off the recliner, spilling bacon shards, soggy pancake dregs and splattering her stack of textbooks. It was no longer a mystery to her why people said the baby "kicked." This phenomenon was no gentle love tap and her baby was only half-grown. What would it be like at the end?

June cleaned up the mess as best she could and carried the dish to the sink. She couldn't reach the faucets to rinse the platter without bumping her belly into the counter. June looked down, rested her hand on the bump, and her baby kicked back. June gasped and giggled and immediately felt horrible. She was mad at Chuck all over again for being such a jerk, angrier still at herself for the same failing of character. Now this thing that was just an idea in books alone, was reaching out from inside and forcing June into a relationship. She wandered back to the front room, with a glass of water, sat down heavily, picked up a textbook and proceeded to calculate her risk of Down's Syndrome.

In mid-September, one month before her calculated due date, June drove to Albuquerque and checked into a motel with weekly rates and a kitchenette. Four weeks' rent up front and in cash was enough to silence any questions from the bored clerk at the desk. The motel was within walking distance to the largest hospital she could find with the word "Saint" in the name. This proximity was chosen intentionally, assuming she could walk in as "Jane Doe," have the baby, leave it for adoption, pay cash and exit. A healthy Anglo-boy with Chuck's good looks should be snapped up in no time, she figured. She had a suitcase full of books to keep her entertained and was able to keep to the same routine as over the summer. She got to know the local grocery store, aisle by aisle, but avoided making any close contacts. Whenever she felt a twinge, June got up and walked around trying to stimulate labor, mostly by doing laps around the hospital grounds.

As some of her contractions increased in intensity, frequency, and duration, she was tempted to go to the hospital more than once, but resisted. She reviewed her books, but found no consistent guidance as to when she was to know she was really in labor. How long, how painful, how far apart, none of the self-proclaimed experts agreed. All they said was Braxton-Hicks contractions weren't real labor, just a warm-up. It was worse in the medical literature. All the definitions were circular. If contractions led to having a baby, then it was true labor. Another said if there was dilation and effacement, then those were meaningful contractions. How the heck was she supposed to check for dilation? The last thing she wanted was a prolonged hospital stay, or worse to have to give information that would leave a paper trail. She decided to go only after it was obvious her water broke and call a taxi.

One early September night, after a double helping of spicy Thai food, washed down with a quart of raspberry tea, June went for a walk. While far from cool, the hint of Fall was in the air, some stars already showing in the East. After two laps around the hospital and ignoring the frequent twinges in her belly, June headed back to the apartment for a rinse. Even with the cooler weather and the mild exertion, she was sweating profusely, wetness and sticky spots were everywhere, most unpleasantly, between her legs. She dried off in the bedroom rather than the bathroom, so she could play the towel game again in the mirror over the dresser. The enormous body was becoming familiar, but a new tragedy was becoming apparent: her posture. She stood like a bag lady waiting for a bus, pelvis thrust forward, legs splayed for stability, in an inadequate attempt to counter-balance the medicine ball attached to her bladder. She reached forward and dabbed at a wet spot where her thighs were touching and was dismayed to see it reappear in the mirror. How depressing, to now have creases full of water that were supplying her with fresh moisture. She'd have to worry about chapped skin. There it was again. Was she peeing herself? How gross to lose control all for a baby. First her body went larger and south, then her once regal and voluptuous posture vanished, now her bladder had betrayed her.

June waddled into the bathroom, sat down in a depressed huff on the toilet and produced nothing but a bloody wad of mucous. Her months of reading allowed a light to go on and all her depression vanished. This fluid wasn't sweat, shower water from her behind, or urine, but amniotic fluid. Her water had broken. She dabbed at the spot with her hand wrapped in toilet paper and held it to her nose. The smell was like nothing she'd ever experienced and memories she'd never had flooded her brain from the primordial past. She closed her eyes and saw the beginning of life on Earth, seawater teeming with living fossils, jungles of steaming vegetation overrun by a ridiculous proliferation of new species. The smell had a salty warmth, neither fishy nor of yeasty breads, but the ultimate perfume. If the odor were introduced in high school health classes, there would be no crime, marriage would be allowed at age 15 and the divorce rate would be zero. June shook herself awake from her reverie. It was no time to wax rhapsodic, she had a baby to deliver.

She returned to the bedroom and dressed in a loose peasant skirt with no underpants, leaking all the while. An invisible monster clamped its jaws around her from navel to knees when she tried to dress. At 30 seconds per contraction with barely a minute to rest between, it took her 20 minutes to get dressed and call a cab. She tucked her breasts in a circus tent brassiere, covered that with a long-sleeved turtleneck and a loose blouse over the whole ensemble. She stuffed the envelope with a stack of $100's in her shirt pocket and a motel towel between her legs. She planned to refuse a hospital gown and try to avoid any poking of her arms with intravenous needles, all the better to make her escape.

June waited inside the motel room for her ride somewhere between 3 and 4 days, breathing and counting out contractions the entire time. Out of impatience and in a false belief the taxi would arrive sooner if she was ready outside, she moved to the curb and waited there for about a week. Hard as it was to think between kicks to the back and groin, she reviewed the plan in her mind. Cab ride, frantic ER delivery, 20 minute nap, beg off paperwork with excuses about resting and sneak out with excuses to leave for a potty break. She'd written the adoption note and had money ready for the bill and a small endowment for her unborn child. The evening delivery time would be perfect. A shift change for the staff would be ideal.

Sometime a decade later her cab arrived. June was staring at the pavement breathing in heavy, purse-lipped pants when Miguel pulled up and waited. She looked up when the contraction ended and was surprised to see a friendly face staring out from the yellow cab. She rose up from the curb in decidedly pregnant fashion, one arm back, legs ajar, enormous belly first. Seeing her condition, Miguel jumped out, and grabbed her free hand, opening the driver-side passenger door in one graceful balletic movement. "No luggage, senora?"

"Just get me to the hospital. I'll give you $100 if you can manage to not ask me any questions."

Miguel couldn't resist talking but he was careful not to pry. "There's a hospital right around the corner, lady. I can get you there in 30 seconds. I've got 5 kids of my own, you know, that's why I drive the cab. But this ride, I give you for free. Nothing more magic than a baby. If you'll pardon me saying, I recognize a certain smell, so it won't be long for you."

June closed her eyes and grunted through a contraction, Miguel's words barely registering in her endorphin-laced brain. She opened her eyes and felt instant panic. She was at the Emergency entrance but her driver was nowhere to be seen. June tried to reach for the door handle but grabbed only air as another kick to the belly overtook her. When her eyes opened again, Miguel was at her door with a wheelchair. His hands were rough in texture but his firm grip was reassuring as he guided her gently to her seat and placed her feet delicately on each footrest. He wheeled her through the automatic double doors and directly to an empty station in the Emergency room. He helped her onto the gurney, drew the curtain closed and went to the nurses station to return the wheelchair. June overheard him speaking in rapid-fire Spanglish to the receptionist and that was the last she heard of him.

Over the next hour June was assaulted by all manner of attendants from candy stripers and interns, to an endless parade of nurses. She refused every protocol, some through obstinate glaring, and others by being in intense pain. No, she didn't have a doctor. Name: Jane Doe, no insurance. No, there was no father to be present or family to contact. A nun was not necessary to hold her hand, let alone be her "labor partner." She would not be changing out of her street clothes, despite the obvious mess that was about to happen. A strap to measure her contractions? Were they idiots? When the mother-to-be is panting like a horse at the finish line of the Kentucky Derby, THAT's a contraction. No, an IV wasn't going to be necessary as she wasn't going to be having a Caesarian section, medications, fluids or a heart attack. She finally convinced them she wouldn't hold the hospital or its employees responsible for any unfortunate outcomes or refusal of service. She scratched a wiggly "Jane Doe" on some form she never read and left someone else to fill in the date. Couldn't they see from the puddle on the gurney that there was a baby coming?

She finally consented to allow the Chief to check her progress. Dr. Ramirez entered her curtained room with an expression both annoyed and condescending. Upon seeing June his expression changed to one of amusement. "Hello, I'm Dr. Ramirez but you can call…"

"Ungh," said Jane.

"Oh, pardon me. I see we're about to have a baby. You're probably much further along than I was told." He sat down on the edge of the bed without asking for permission and placed his large hand firmly on June's belly. He felt it was rock hard and looked up to meet June's eyes, her face turning red with effort. "Best not to hold your breath, difficult as that may be. May I check you?" June nodded and Dr. Ramirez went to the bedside table to retrieve a pair of sterile gloves.

If he'd been any cuter she might have fallen off the gurney. He was wearing baby blue scrubs, which matched his bright eyes, had a 36-hour beard and smelled of honest exertion. It was a fairy tale odor like that of a hard-working farmhand who spent his days with large animals and hay, not bench press machines and sports drinks. Hollywood hairdressers would die in order to bottle the quality that made his tousled crew cut look so adorable. While he put the gloves over his slender fingers June couldn't keep herself from staring at his hands and her mind from lascivious thoughts of his touch. Her hormones were way out of control. Between contractions she tried to restore her frame of mind to something more familiar. "You don't look like a Ramirez, blue eyes and all," she said.

"Funny. Jane is a pretty name, but you don't look like a Doe," he said. He unfolded a heavy warmed blanket over her belly and legs, which despite her exertion and sweating, felt heavenly, a warm hug. Dr. Ramirez instructed her to sit frog-legged with her ankles together and he'd check her progress. The lubricant gel was cold but welcome at the same time. June kept her eyes on the doctor but he was careful not to reveal anything by his expression. "Ramirez is a married name. It's complicated but I'm actually German. From Baltimore, originally. Dad's name was Mittelschmerz."

Before she could help herself, June blurted out, "Oh, like the ovulation pain?" Then she knew she'd been discovered. All her reading had been so helpful up to that point.

"I'm guessing you're not the usual un-attached mother, coming to have a baby out of wedlock, Jane," said Dr. Ramirez. "Don't worry, I won't rat you out. Plus, there's not an OB doc upstairs who would have you anyway, so it's just you and me 'til this baby is born. Frankly, I'm glad for the opportunity to deliver. We don't get many women having babies in the ER who are conscious. The drug withdrawal is a real struggle for the kids."

"Thanks." said June, followed by another grunt.

"Oh, by the way, we don't need any ultrasound. That pressure you're feeling in your backside is a baby's head. You can start pushing now. I'll get a nurse to give us a hand."

"No, don't leave me…" she whimpered. Before the contraction

was over, he'd returned with a nurse, some instruments wrapped in a sterile procedure kit the size of a large toolbox "just in case" and half a dozen pillows. The nurse's name tag said "Cindy" and she was rotund as she was efficient. She propped up June from all angles with pillows including two under her bum and raised the head of the gurney. The new posture intensified the burning pressure to June's groin area but Cindy was immune to all complaints. She'd had a few kids of her own, not to mention the stint on Labor & Delivery a few decades back, so there would be no arguing at this point. Perhaps June could have been a little more accommodating about the paperwork earlier.

June's delivery was the most silent affair in the history of the hospital. There were no beeping machines, no spouse yelling encouragement, no television or radio, no one counting out her effort with each push, no junior director-in-training trying to get just the right shot with his new digital video camera. When it felt better to push she held her breath and did so with all her might. Cindy helped her into position: one hand behind each knee, chin down, all business. In between, Dr. Ramirez smiled pleasantly from between her legs as if there were no place he'd rather be. He couldn't leave at this point, other patients would just have to wait and they'd be talking about this day in the ER for weeks to come. Cindy stood by for instructions, making no comments about the strength of the contractions, the quality of June's pushing, or inane observations about pink and blue.

At the moment of delivery, June's joy and agony were total and equal. He physical pain was matched only by her emotional misery. She'd come to see the fetus as a companion. Instead of a symbolic object with which to punish Chuck, she now had a friend with whom she had to part ways. There would be no more angry kicks after meals containing garlic. June was never the sentimental type, but now realized why babies were so important to everyone else. It wasn't a rational argument she'd had with herself somewhere between meeting Miguel and Dr. Ramirez. It wasn't the physical change she'd been through or anything she'd read. It was all of those and none of those. The change came in her emotional state only. There was no why. None of the adults in attendance at her birth said a word, but they all could see, "it's a girl."

June had been alone much of her adult life, but she'd never been so lonely as after the delivery of her baby girl. Dr. Ramirez made some offhand comment about the baby being only about 5 pounds and "were you sure of your due date?" The comment failed to register with June in her delirium. With the placenta out safely, she just wanted to sleep. He went off to attend to the paperwork. Cindy made a random and unmemorable comment about breast-feeding and whisked off the baby "to the nursery."

When June woke from a nap of indeterminate length, she could hear behind the curtain that the ER was awash with activity. Noone was paying her station any mind. She checked that all her clothing was in order and stepped gingerly to the floor. Satisfied that she had the strength to support her own weight, she peeked around the curtain of her stall to be sure noone was looking in her direction. On the gurney she left an envelope with her adoption note and $10,000 in cash. The note said to give her baby to a "good family" along with whatever money was left over after paying her bill.

June was careful not to make eye contact with anyone from either the nurses' station or the waiting room as she slipped out the automatic doors. She was right that a shift change was to her advantage. Cindy's replacement had checked on her once and found her sleeping. The nurse had done a set of routine vital signs, pushed on her belly to see that the uterus was small and firm, then left her to sleep.

Outside it was still dark, but the pavement was no longer warm from the previous day. She walked very gingerly to the motel, which seemed miles away. At the room, she found her suitcase too heavy to lift and had to make multiple trips with all her books in order to pack. With a last look at her room and satisfied that this chapter was over, she drove to the hotel she'd picked out months before, well-known for its high-quality room service. More importantly, it was the only one not insisting on reservations or a credit card for room security deposit. She checked in with the lonely night attendant as Cindy Ramirez, paid cash for a week, and let herself be led to the elevator bank.

Once in her room, she over-tipped the porter, took a shower, dried off without playing the towel game, put a giant maxi-pad in her panties and sat on the edge of the bed. From a side pocket of her luggage she removed a gift from Roger, still in its wrapping. Her guess was right. A bottle of expensive tequila was inside with a note of congratulations about successfully finishing her first year, anticipating missing her over the summer, cherishing her friendship and looking forward to working together in the fall. It was all very chaste and the sincerity of his heartfelt note made her feel even worse about what she'd just done.

June took four belts of the tequila straight from the bottle and got under the covers. She cried herself to sleep and slept through the next day without dreaming.

29

Take a Penny, Leave a Penny

"Honey, I'm home!" Roger stepped gingerly into the new foyer and called to his wife as loudly as he dared. He placed his bundle gently on the couch in the living room.

"I'm up here," Sharon yelled from the second floor bathroom. Roger bounced up the stairs like a kid on Christmas morning in reverse.

"I've got something for you. For us," he corrected himself. He was sure this gesture would repair the growing rend in their marriage in one grand act of love.

He'd stumbled through the summer in a daze after June resigned. The Fall semester he got by on fumes. The anniversary of RJ's death was torture. The only things keeping Roger afloat were his wife's constant tinkering with the house and his work to adopt a baby. Denial has its uses.

Sharon's desire for upgrading was encouraging to Roger. It must have meant she was moving forward, getting beyond the pain. She hadn't yet shot down his ideas about adoption. He even deluded himself that she did the remodeling all out of love, she cared that much. Roger Junior's room remained untouched but there was an extra bedroom that could easily be converted to a baby's room. Still, doubts remained.

He was beginning to suspect the master bedroom remodeling was an excuse to avoid him physically. Sure at first, it was all about creating a larger, more romantic space, an escape. After 6 months with shards of drywall littering her side of the bed, he had to admit any casual observer could see she was avoiding him. Her sleeping on the living room couch wasn't just for convenience.

"What is it, Roger," Sharon said. It was a statement, not a question. Roger couldn't answer. Upon entering the remains of the bedroom, he found a scene that failed to register. Instead of her usual dusty overalls, Sharon was dressed in a little black cocktail dress and pumps. On the bed was a suitcase with towering stacks of shirts, pants, bras, undershorts. "You're home early, I was hoping to be gone. I didn't want to make this harder than it already is."

"What?" Roger said, a mix of shock and confusion. The dress, the remodeling, none of it was for him at all. Glaciers move faster than the time it took Roger to realize his miscalculation.

"You took your little vacation, now I'm taking mine. For good," Sharon said.

"But I was only gone two days. Your suitcase looks like you're packing to invade France." His joke landed with a thud. He recoiled from the exasperated look Sharon fired at him. He'd come to know that look all too well. Her sneer summarized his complete failure as a man, husband, lover, author, and all around useless human being. "Plus, I went for us. Your surprise is downstairs," he finished lamely.

"Whatever." Sharon went to the bed and slammed the huge suitcase shut, trapping flaps of clothing in the gap. It was too heavy and clunked loudly to the floor when she tried to lift it and go.

"Here. Let me help you," Roger said, his kindness like a reflex.

Then, his common sense invaded. "What a minute. Why am I helping you? Where are you going? Why are you dressed like that?"

"Are you really that dense," Sharon said. She placed a condescending hand on his cheek. "I'm not just leaving. I'm leaving you, Roger. It's over. I'll have my lawyer send over the papers." Before he could protest she blurted out the entire story of her affair with Chuck. How he'd seduced her soon after his arrival to the campus. How her idea for the trip to Mexico was an attempt to distance herself, break it off clean. At that point, with Roger Junior approaching school age, the affair was in full swing. Then Roger Junior died eliminating any reason to continue the charade with Roger. With his family connections, his money, Chuck was what Sharon had wanted all along, kids or not. The part-time secretary job at the college wasn't to make a little extra money for remodeling or romantic vacations or to help adopt a baby. It wasn't even to be closer to Roger at work. She took the minimum-wage position only to further disguise her affair with Chuck.

She hoisted the suitcase with renewed determination and started to the stairs. Roger didn't have the strength to follow and sat on the bed, his head in his hands. At that moment, from the living room, came a sound that could only be described as a baby giggling. There's nothing like it. No animal makes such a noise. Sharon froze at the top of the stairs. "What the hell was that?"

"Oh, nothing. Just our daughter," Roger said to the open bedroom door.

"You've got to be out of your mind." Sharon returned to the bedroom to glare at Roger with her hands on her hips. The toe-tapping came naturally as she waited for an explanation.

"It's not like I've been the only one who's been oblivious," Roger said. "I've been talking about adoption since we got back from Mexico. Where'd you think I was going every other month for the last year?"

"I thought you were having an affair. At least I hoped you were," Sharon said. "And how the hell do you adopt a baby on your own?" Roger saw a ray of hope. At least she was talking to him. Maybe she'd listen to reason.

Roger launched into his story of the past 18 months as if the details might change things. Like Sharon and her remodeling distraction, he poured himself into the process of adoption with every spare minute of his time and even some hours that should have been devoted to his students. He considered overseas adoptions, different local and national agencies. He tapped the last of RJ's college fund and then started borrowing from his own retirement. After exhausting or ruling out most of his options he was ready to give up. The turning point came when he met a sympathetic nurse who heard his story of RJ. She guided him through the process at a Catholic hospital in Albuquerque. He agreed to a "first available" philosophy rather than worrying about getting a boy of a certain age with a particular lineage. That compromise put him "to the front of the list," she claimed. He suspected the nurse pulled some strings, moved as she was by his account of RJ's death in Mexico. The ropey scar on his neck helped convince her of the truth and horror of his ordeal. They shared a tear in the hospital ER waiting room. "All the nurse was able to tell me was that the mother was unmarried. She had Emma right there in the ER and just left, no explanation."

"Emma?" said Sharon. "She's got a name?"

"Well, of course. You can't just called her 'girl.'"

"Didn't you think I might want…" Sharon started. Her instinct was no longer to think of herself as married to Roger. She didn't care what he named the brat. "You've committed fraud. I didn't sign any adoption papers. You'll have to take her back." Roger didn't answer. One doesn't adopt a child lightly. His commitment to Emma was arguably more intense than to his own son. You don't exchange a child like pennies at a convenience store register. He watched her face change as she considered the implications of the immense choice before her. Roger knew a part of her would always love him, want his children, their grandchildren. He looked at her with as much love and pleading as he could muster. The pain of losing Roger Junior and the dreams of what she thought her marriage should have been, must have been too much for her to bear. She looked away and spoke to the floor.

"I'm not raising a child. Another child," Sharon said. "Besides, I'm not even sure Roger Junior was yours." She turned without meeting his eyes and left the room.

Roger was rendered speechless. RJ wasn't his? It didn't make sense. RJ was already 4 years old when Chuck arrived at the College. What did she mean? Was she just being cruel or were there other affairs? His stomach and brain were twisted in similar knots of confusion and pain. He yelled after her over the noise of her suitcase bouncing down the stairs. "I didn't sign your name I didn't lie " He almost added that it wasn't him who had the affair, then thought better of it, not wanting to call the kettle black.

Sharon stormed out the front door with not even a glance at Emma, snug in her car seat on the couch, still cooing and babbling happily. Sharon sat on the curb with her suitcase still trailing the bits of clothing and stared at her pumps until the taxi came to take her away.

Roger heard the taxi come and go. The house was quiet for a

moment until Emma sang out with another giggle. At the sound of her voice, Roger felt himself in tremendous spirits as if an enormous weight had been removed. He bounded back down the stairs two at a time to pick up Emma.

"I should have named you Penny," he said. "But I can't recall ever reading a book with a Penny in it. You, you're my lucky penny, not just some spare change. Are you hungry? Let's get you a bottle."

He carried her to the kitchen in one arm, the diaper bag in tow as well. He set about the task of mixing the formula one-handed with the full dexterity one would expect of a veteran father. Roger hadn't made a bottle in years, but some skills you never lose. "Did you know your dad's a writer?" Emma just smiled up at him, the embodiment of ease. "Oh, you're speechless, huh? Despite what Sharon might think, I've written a good amount, some worthwhile, and I'll admit, some tripe. Would you like to hear a story?" Her response was more smiling. "I'll take your silence as implied consent."

Roger sat on the couch with Emma in his arms as comfortably as if he'd been doing it since she was born. He tested the temperature of the formula by taking a shot of it himself. "Perfect. As always. Let's start with 'Vertigo.' Once upon a time there was a community on stilts, living fifty feet above a flat and dry plain."

Emma was asleep long before he'd finished telling the short story, imprinted by his sonorous voice and soothing scent of fresh coffee and faint musk.

30

A New Complaint

"All I'm saying is, I don't think Jesus came here to start a cult," Josh said. It was a rare moment of earnest dialogue for him. The topic of religion never got the Diner's Club into heated debate. Each member of the Club had long ago decided what he or she believed. The discussion was not about changing anyone's mind. It was all about the fun of hammering out just how long God's grey beard really was. June didn't care what they talked about, she was just happy for the company. She hadn't planned a summer vacation yet and was reluctant to make her annual trip given how well things were going with Roger. She had to admit, if her biggest complaint was deciding whether to take a month-long vacation to somewhere exotic or spend the time with her boyfriend, things must be going pretty well.

"You're not Jewish," Courtney said. "Plus, you hate talking about religion. What's your point?"

"Think about it," Josh said. "We all know Jesus was a Jew. It just occurred to me, if he was coming to save the ancients from their sins, all he succeeded in doing was starting a new religion. One based on him and his life, not God the Father. Bummer, huh?" The Club gave out reluctant murmurs of assent. Will and Danny couldn't have cared much less. They were holding hands under the table. Paul was just happy to be off work and done with his final exams and papers. June came around with a pitcher of soda and one of coffee to freshen everyone's glasses and mugs.

"Well done, Josh," June said. "None of us will need sedatives to get a good night's rest." Seeing the hurt look on Josh's face, June changed tack. "But I see your point. Imagine, you give your life to show people the way to heaven and all they do is worship you. It's like a dog that looks at your finger, instead of the bird you're pointing to." She made another lap to the table with two baskets of fries, 5 small plates, and a fresh dispenser each of mustard and ketchup. The snacks acted like a mental sorbet, to cleanse the palette for further insights the way a professor might chew the pipe which he never lights in class.

It was the end of the school year and hence, the meetings of the Club until next fall. Every member had thoughts they wanted to share. Paul started by asking everyone if they had ever tried doing something "with the other hand." He had in mind an activity like brushing one's teeth or writing out a check. Josh added, "or wiping." From there, Danny added clumsy foot moves like pushing the car accelerator with you left foot. That one felt weird even if you were left-handed. Will asked about activities that could only be done with two hands, like clapping, raking leaves, or changing a diaper.

"What about praying?" Courtney said. "It doesn't require either hand, but everyone does it with two hands."

"Unless of course, you're hanging off a cliff," said Paul.

"…from a small tree with shallow roots," Danny said.

"…and fire ants are crawling down your arms," Will said. From there it was a hop and skip to Josh's comments about the Son of God's attempts at salesmanship.

Roger pulled up in his Professormobile, a forgettable beige wagon from another decade. His headlights swept across the Club as he cornered into a muddy spot by the door. A brief thunderstorm had doused the dusty parking lot and dropped the temperature back to comfortable levels. It was going to be a lovely summer evening. June looked up from her stool at the counter and saw he had a passenger with him across the bench seat. June saw him turn to the young lady and say something, then they both got out, Roger walking around the small puddles to help her with her door. He had a school folder in one hand and held her hand with the other, guiding her around the puddles. They came up the steps to enter the diner. "Hey," June said. "You can't park there. That's a handicapped spot." She had no such sign in her parking lot. She also knew Roger would never commit such a crime.

"Well, I am crippled with love for you," Roger said. A collective groan came from the Club. If eye-rolling were raindrops, there would have been a hurricane in the room.

"Hi, Miss June," Emma said.

"To what do I owe this special visit?"

"Emma finished 6th grade yesterday. All A's, Honor Roll. You know, the usual," Roger said. "We're here to celebrate. I thought I'd take her to her favorite restaurant."

"Dad," Emma whined at his flattery. "It's no big deal." She shared his skill at self-deprecation, modesty, and the complete lack of ability to take a compliment. They wiped their shoes on the mat by the door, and only stopped holding hands when they were seated at the counter and picked up their menus. It was a ritual gesture, since Emma always ordered the chicken strips and fries, no matter what the occasion. Roger had the menu memorized. June never brought what he ordered anyway. She always made him something unexpected and better than what he had in mind. After the charade of ordering, Roger pulled a packet of maps and brochures from his school folder. On top was a map of the United States from the National Park Service.

"Have you ever noticed how close all these Parks are to each other?" he said to noone in particular. "I think people see them in their minds like the planets. Really cool, different from each other, all worth a visit, but ultimately isolated."

"Sure, Roger," Josh said with his usual sarcasm. "Like the way American Samoa is near the Everglades."

"Or your internal organs," Paul said. "You never think of your aorta running next to your spine and esophagus."

"Did you know you have to go south from Detroit, Michigan to get to Windsor, Canada?" Danny said.

Will finished off the first round of interruptions. He couldn't resist. "You mean how Brazil is right next to Nigeria?" When all he got was quizzical looks, Will held up his hands mimicking the continents drifting apart. "Get it? On a geological time scale? Right next to each other? Oh, come on, mine was at least as good as the anatomy lesson." He gave up when they all said, "whatever." June failed to suppress a giggle. As a group, they were too quick and clever for Roger to get a word in edgewise. One at a time, she knew he could best them all.

"I was thinking more the way Bryce is right near Zion, which is right near Canyonlands and the Grand Canyon," Roger said. "And how did you know there's a National Park in Samoa, Josh?"

"Well, you know, Spring Break in Mexico is so last decade," Josh said. "Like your car."

June returned the coffee pot to the percolator stand to keep it warm and set the soft drink pitcher near the soda fountain. She strolled over to the counter opposite Roger and bent over his map. She folded her arms and leaned in as if to sprinkle magic cleavage dust all over his map. "So tell me Professor, just how many of those great, big, National Parks are there?"

June's decolletage was like a 9th person on the room and her flirting was not lost on Roger. He pointed to the map, eyes on her straining top button. "Well, uh," he stammered. "If one had a mind to, he, uh or she, could drive over the mountains here" he pointed to the map "and through this valley and visit 5 Parks in two days. More or less."

"Umm," June purred.

"In fact, you could continue into California, up the West Coast, over to Wyoming and back down the Front Range, in one grand tour."

"Are you asking me on a date, mister?" Another strangled groan came from the Club. If eye-rolling was snowflakes, there would have been an avalanche in the diner. June batted her eyelashes at Roger and gave Emma a wink. Roger cleared his throat and took a sip of diet soda.

"I'm just pointing out something I noticed," he said.

"Yeah. Well I noticed you'll have nothing to do once your final exams are graded next week. You know I close the diner every year after graduation and go on a vacation. A little bird told me Emma is spending two weeks at summer camp, then another week with her grandparents. You're running out of excuses, buddy. Don't try and tell me you don't have a tent and sleeping bag."

The fryer alarm beeped and June left the counter to retrieve

Emma's chicken and fries. She set them on clean paper next to the grill to drain and cool. Next, she bent over the adjacent freezer, knees straight, to retrieve the vanilla ice cream and whip up a homemade milkshake. The whole milk was on the bottom shelf of the refrigerator. June made sure Roger was watching her every move and her every curve. Into the blender went the ice cream, milk, chocolate syrup, and two extra scoops of sugar. With her back to Emma at the prep station, she snuck in a single malted milk ball and one square of English toffee. While it was mixing, June returned to the freezer to retrieve a chilled mug for Emma and once again show Roger the ample bottom he'd be missing should he pass on the National Parks Tour. At the counter, she poured the shake which Emma attacked with spoon and straw. She plated the chicken and fries, delivered them to Emma's station, then nudged the ketchup and mustard closer out of habit, knowing Emma would eat them unadorned. For Roger she scooped a mound of rice into a bowl 3 times the size he could eat, went to the stove and drenched the pile in four ladles of shrimp gumbo. The volcano of comfort food in front of him, she leaned in once again, smothering his food with cleavage and asked, "Well?"

"Is this your idea of a burger and fries?" was all he could say.

Roger did a poor job of averting his eyes. Instead, he grabbed his spoon from beside the bowl where June had left it, all the while his gaze riveted on her chest. Trying to compose his thoughts, Roger took a mouthful. As usual at the diner, his eyes closed involuntarily as the waves of exotic flavors washed over his tongue and psyche. The bell pepper, shrimp, onion, and even the celery were perfectly balanced. No flavor overwhelmed the other. The concoction made him nostalgic for a life he'd never had, a life in the deep South, oak trees covered in

JUNE'S DINER

Spanish moss, the sound of cicadas at dusk, alligators crossing dirt roads, long porches, sweet tea, and a perverse love of mosquitos. When Roger opened his eyes, June was gazing into his with the satisfied look of a foregone conclusion. "C-can, you do this off the t-tailgate of the Professormobile with a propane stove?" he stammered.

"Yeah. Not a problem. Have you ever seen Heceta lighthouse from the 101 at sunset?"

"Sure. Who hasn't? Isn't it perfect?" he answered, not bragging in the least.

"What about the sunset from Key West?" June challenged him. It was a sunset showdown.

"Can you believe they have a parade every night?" He scooped up another mouthful of the gumbo, this one from the side of the bowl, mostly rice and sauce.

"Eiffel tower?"

"The pollution makes it gorgeous shades of red."

"Ipanema?" June figured she had the champ on the ropes with that one.

"Uh-huh. I'd say the Two Brothers rival a Waikiki, Diamond Head sunrise any day." Now Roger was just showing off. June wasn't beaten yet, but she was surprised by his answer. She didn't know he'd been to Hawai'i, let alone Brazil. Even people who'd been to those once-in-a-lifetime locations to ogle the skimpy bathing suits and sample the local rum drinks weren't aware the famous mountain formations had a name. She wound up for a haymaker, her best punch.

"Skydiving?"

"Does tandem count?"

"Geez," June said, "it's like playing Stump the Professor. Is there anywhere you haven't been or anything you haven't done? No wonder you don't want to drive around the National Parks with me. It must sound as boring as a trip to the mall."

"No, no, no. That's not it. I thought I'd use the time after graduation to get a little writing done." Roger said.

"Yea, so what's the big deal? What're you working on that you can't take a little drive?"

"Not tellin'. That's a sure way to ruin the creative process, let alone the surprise when you break into my house and read it without my permission." June wasn't the least bit apologetic about that minor felony.

"Oh, nonsense. I never broke in, Emma invited me, didn't you? High five." Emma looked up from her chicken and gave a nod. June held up her hand and they slapped palms. "But I'm not letting you change the subject. What are you writing? Spill." Roger lifted another spoonful of gumbo, but before he could get it to his mouth, June plucked out the shrimp with her bare fingers and popped it into her mouth.

Roger considered his response for a beat. It was a tough crowd. Josh could be funny at times, but it was easy to ridicule. The subject, the theme of his writing, if not the content, had been on his mind for some time and he decided to take a chance. "I want to write a story with no irony. Something genuine. Something that makes people sigh when they finish it. A story a reader wants to keep for herself, like it's our secret. I want to make people ache with nostalgia, like the memory of their first kiss, crunchy leaves underfoot and holding warm, sweaty, nervous hands on crisp fall days, to a soundtrack of distant football crowds. That's what I'm working on. An authentic recreation of life in the written word."

JUNE'S DINER

"Pretentious much?" June said. Then regretted it immediately. She loved what he'd said but couldn't bring herself to say as much.

"That's exactly what I'm talking about. Noone takes anything at face value any more. It's all irony and sarcasm. We're all too jaded. Blame it on the media, our fallen heroes when we find out they're all too human, just like the rest of us. But I wish for a time when we could be honest and mean it." Josh slunk down in his booth seat. Roger's comments weren't meant for him directly, but the sincerity of the sentiment hit home.

June leaned in and grabbed Roger's face in both hands. "Marry me," she said with all the sobriety she could muster, but it came out as scorn. Another derisive insult, however unintended, when Roger didn't have a false bone in his body. She agreed with what he had said, she just lacked the skill to acknowledge it.

"Very funny. But you see, Sharon used to drag me all over the place. I've been resort diving to see coral and whale sharks. Had dinner on countless dirt floors, ate bugs and fruits with names I can't pronounce. I've been to rivers, lakes, oceans, on rowboats, canoes, kayaks all the way up to massive cruise ships. Heck, sometimes on the same trip. Yea, I've done the jungle zip lines, seen the Australian Outback, ridden camels and elephants. Cool stuff, all of it. But none of it made me want to write a story."

"Sorry, Captain Buzzkill. You're not ignoring me. The proposal stands and I don't just mean the National Parks Tour." June leaned forward to whisper something in Roger's ear about the fringe benefits of camping on the beach. Roger's face turned 5 shades of red. "…and besides that, I can drive while you write. Those Parks you're listing may look close on a map, but you're looking at a 7,000 mile road trip there. Truly epic, Roger."

"Hmmm." Roger put his thumb on the map at the mileage legend. One inch was equal to nearly 200 miles. He walked his thumb across Arizona, up the California coast, across the Canadian border to Montana, then south down the Front Range to New Mexico. "You've got a point there. Maybe I'm too old for this kind of adventure."

"Nonsense," June said. "Steinbeck was 58 when he made his trip. And all he had for company was a dog. You've got me to keep you feeling young." She gave him a wink.

"True, but it took him more than 3 months. You want to do it in 3 weeks."

"But you forget, he saw the whole country. You're looking at less than a third of the states." As a group, the Diner's Club could guess how this gentle argument would end. Josh got a suppressed giggle when he said under his breath that having only a poodle as Steinbeck had, would be easier than traveling with either June or Roger. Paul waved him down so as not to interrupt the fun. Roger went on listing his objections and June supplied a reasonable counter for each complaint. "I get car sick if I'm not driving."

"Okay. Fine. You drive, I'll take dictation, write down the stories for you."

"What if Emma needs to get in touch with us? She might get homesick, or injured at camp."

"We can set up a time to call daily. I'm sure the camp staff is prepared for any emergency. I doubt she'll get bored at Gramma's house. That woman is a one-person craft store, right Emma?" June looked to Emma who had a mouthful of french fries. Instead of swallowing to speak, she took a draw from her milkshake in order to mix the flavors. A chunk of toffee clogged the flow, so she inverted the straw, sucked out the candy and just nodded in agreement. Emma took the long spoon and probed the bottom of her cup, finding the frozen malted milk ball. She popped it in her mouth, then returned the straw to suck up the last of the shake making a loud slurping noise. On reflex, June dumped in the remains from the blender, this time topping it off with a squirt of cola. Emma took a sip without missing a beat and went back to the last of a massive pile of french fries.

"My hair's getting thin…I get sunburned up there."

"Wear a hat."

"I'm getting far-sighted, so I can't read maps very well. What if we get lost? My back hurts if I sit too long, too much sunlight gives me migraines, if I don't get enough fiber I get constipated and with my prostate problems I have to go twice an hour." At this last complaint the club could no longer keep silent and they broke out in a group howl of laughter. June, still trying to convince Roger of why he should make the trip, looked to the Club, then back at Roger. The laughter ceased, leaving the room quiet enough to hear the fluorescent lights buzzing. Roger kept a straight face through it all, then shrugged his shoulders as if to say he had no idea why they were laughing. Not to undermine his theme, but it was Roger's turn to have a little fun. June looked at Emma who was swirling a french fry around her plate and finally had to pretend to wipe her mouth with a napkin to keep from giggling.

"What?" said June to anyone who would answer.

Another round of laughter erupted from the table until Josh said, "You done been played like a banjo, June." She took a french fry from Emma's plate and winged it at Josh who caught it and popped it in his mouth. Then she looked to Roger and tried to pretend she was angry.

"Sorry for messing with you. Of course I'd love to go on vacation with you June," he said. "I'm actually working on a new short story about a guy with too many complaints." June relaxed and sat down on the stool on her side of the counter. When Josh turned back to the group, she quietly stole another french fry and beaned him in the back of the head, inciting a new round of squeals.

To Roger she said, "So tell me about this guy."

"You see, his life is fine by just about any standard, if a little dull…" he started.

"Sounds like someone we know," Josh said under his breath.

"…but he complains about every little thing. The neighborhood kids are too loud when they play in the street in front of his house. He hates to mow the lawn. The next door neighbor's new juniper hedge stinks to high heaven. The sun is too hot, the wind and rain too cold. You get the idea."

"Yeah, So far so good. So what happens to him?" June said.

"That's the part I haven't worked out yet. But I'm gonna slowly take all his complaints away and see how he handles it. He'll lose his hearing so the kids won't bother him. I'll give him a gout attack. His big toe will hurt so much he can't mow the lawn. Maybe a stroke will take his sense of smell. You know I love the science fiction angle, so I'll have to do something about the sun and elements." He spooned up a shrimp and shoved it in one cheek.

"Don't tell me it's going to be a genie in a bottle story," June said. "Careful what you wish for, and all that tired nonsense, huh?"

"Right," Roger said. "Now you see why I'm bogged down. The Story of Job has already been written if you know what I mean. Not every tragedy ends with redemption. Well, maybe this trip will help me think it through. I don't really get car sick, by the way. If the biggest of my problems is inventing a device for torturing my lead character, things must be going pretty well."

31

There's Too Much to Do

Life is too short. June Turner was looking at a map of the National Parks of the West. She took a rare turn in the passenger seat of the RV heading East on I-40. The 24-footer they rented was nothing too fancy since it was only the two of them, but it did have ample storage for food to minimize grocery store stops. It was the height of luxury compared to the Professormobile. There was a small bathroom with a tiny shower stall, comically low water pressure, and a commode they joked was for potty training. June had no trouble convincing Roger that the 6-gallon hot water tank would be plenty since they'd be saving water by sharing their bathing time. The RV also had a small refrigerator so they could enjoy treats they'd foregone on their first trip like Italian ice and cold drinks. The whipped cream never seemed to last very long in a cooler before spoiling to a runny mess or worse, taking on cheese and bologna-flavored water. If there was one thing they'd learned on their first trip, it was that ice doesn't last long in the summer in the West. "Pilot to navigator," Roger said into his cupped hand. "Request coordinate confirmation."

"Krrrrich." June made a static noise into her own palm. "Roger, Roger," said June. That joke never got old. "Hang a Louie at Albuquerque. North to RMNP."

Ten years earlier, she and her fiancé Roger Steadman had toured a good dozen and a ½ of the Parks on a whirlwind 19-day, 7,000-mile odyssey. Now, for their 10th anniversary, they were repeating the trek, this time in reverse order. Looking at the map, it was readily apparent there was too much to do and see. On the map between the Parks they'd visited there were as many they hadn't. On this, their first day on the road, they had already blown right past El Malpais National Monument. June saw on the map it had a feature called "Bandera Volcano & Ice Caves." The name alone was intriguing enough to warrant at least a side trip, but they reasoned it could be done in a day trip from home. Why bother to include it in a 10,000 mile journey, when it was only 100 miles from the College?

Truth be told, even the Parks they'd seen ten years prior were only given a cursory glance. Some days had been a grind of unrelenting miles and unremarkable gas stations, cold-cut sandwiches washed down with lukewarm tea, and Ranger Station arrivals after dark. They had often set up the tent by flashlight and fallen asleep with rocks under their heads and hips. Their reward came in the mornings when they would rise to inspiring mountain views, the smells of strange pines, and sometimes the cooking of other campers. To stay on schedule though, they would have to break camp immediately, having a cold breakfast of fruit, prepacked pudding and dry granola bars in the Professormobile. At least the tea would be colder in the mornings. It was the memory of rushed days and nights, of seeing the Great American West through the windshield that inspired them to repeat the trip. This time, they vowed to linger for days, maybe even weeks in each Park. Being voracious readers, they wanted to experience all they'd read, from the flora and fauna, to the geology and even the weather. Roger wanted to see a high altitude lightning storm. June advised him he should be happy to be pummeled by fist-sized hail rather than wish to be cooked through by lightning.

Now they were road-tripping north from Albuquerque on I-25. Roger continued his turn at the wheel, leaving June to prepare the sandwiches. Always the cook, she handed him a portable meal precisely contrary to what he had ordered. "I'd ask how and why you do it," Roger said, "but I don't think you know yourself." He grinned through a mouthful of bread and mystery ingredients. Instead of the usual drab bologna and mustard on white he had ordered, June flipped him a masterpiece without explanation or warning. She found a loaf of thick-sliced sourdough at the last gas stop. On it she placed the requested bologna but added a single sliced pepperoni which Roger found on his third bite. The mustard was the spicy brown variety with a smear of horseradish on one end. The cheese was pepper-laced Monterey Jack. Instead of lettuce or other greens she put in sour cream and onion potato chips "for texture." The concoction made Roger want to pull over and "make out like teenagers" and he told her so. She told him to wait until sunset, the anticipation being half the fun.

"The secret ingredient is love," June said. When he looked at her askance with mock confusion she added with too much emphasis, "Love. I made it with love. Get it? That's why it tastes so good." It was a ritual that had played out countless times in their marriage. Neither was good about expressing their feelings. Roger was too shy and June was too jaded and sarcastic. The marriage survived, flourished, and galvanized in shared moments of intentional stupidity.

Similar to their previous trip, Emma was busy with other projects. Having finished her studies at Southwestern Community College, she opted for an additional summer of graduate work in Mexico. Part of her undergraduate language studies and English degree required a semester abroad. It could be argued as June had, that a native of New Mexico was almost bi-lingual by birth. To spend time near a resort town teaching English to Mexican kids was cheating. Besides, June said, her tan was far too deep, suggesting she had spent more time on the beaches of the Pacific than in a classroom. Emma explained her deep color by the simple fact that she worked in an impoverished area that had no school. All the classes were outside. Wearing sunscreen, even if it were available, would have been an insult to her charges. Mazatlan was over 100 miles west over sketchy roads. It wasn't frequent beach trips that deepened her tan. Besides her teaching, she readily volunteered for extra work. Not a weekend passed that some local village didn't have a building to fix or raise, a well or sewer to be dug or a road to be repaired.

"Hey, Peaches. Any chance we'll be swinging by the Great Sand Dunes?" Roger said. "You know it got upgraded from Monument to National Park."

"Sorry, Fabric Softener. We've got more time than before, but we're still on a mission. Gotta move." The pet names were random. Roger favored fruits and vegetables, June usually went with inanimate objects and cleaning products.

"Okay, understood, it's a bit out of the way. What about Garden of the Gods? It's right off the highway," Roger said.

"Sure, but we'll have to be careful about time. We don't want to hit Denver smack dab in the middle of rush hour traffic," June said. Then she thought about his request. It didn't matter the official designation of the geological feature. They'd had that argument before in the Diner and agreed that the labels applied by humans to the earth and its natural attractions were arbitrary. They favored the idea that we are only borrowing the views. The previous trip as well as this one was about how they would reach the destinations and link them in some logical order. Those nearest the highways were by default more desirable. Garden of the Gods is only a city park but the Great Sand Dunes was at least 75 miles out of their way. Round-trip with exploring would add a full day to the itinerary. "You didn't really want to see the dunes, did you?" Roger shook his head no. "So you just talked me into making an unplanned stop in Colorado Springs."

"Yea, funny how that works, huh Cucumber?" Roger laughed.

"That's totally unfair," June said. "You fight like a woman." Roger let her have the last word. He popped the final corner of sourdough crust in his mouth and washed it down with diet soda. He brushed some crumbs off his lap and returned his eyes to the road. "Don't even think of stopping at the 'Welcome to Colorado' sign. You're on probation, Dust Mop." The pet name let Roger know all was forgiven, no harm done. Then June unbuckled her seatbelt and scooted over next to him on the bench seat. She put on the center belt letting him know she'd be there until the next gas stop. They listened to talk radio, random music stations and had a bubble blowing contest with the most offensive gum June could find, a putrid watermelon flavor that tasted like no real fruit on earth.

As promised, June agreed to the side trip in Colorado Springs. They needed gas anyway and it was a good time to air the rotten fruit smell out of the RV. "We need to come up with a name for our trusty, steel steed," Roger said as he filled the tank.

"Now you've gone and done it," June said from the front of the truck where she was wiping bugs from the windshield and headlamps. "It's like looking for an electron. If you shine a light on it, the thing disappears. Now we'll never come up with a good name."

Roger took a potty break and came back with some mints. "Here," he said to June back in the cab. "This will help get rid of that bubble gum taste." June waved him off, pointed to her bulging cheek and held up a bag of spiced beef jerky. "Suit yourself," said Roger as he put the truck in gear and pulled out of the lot. "But don't expect me to give you a kiss anytime soon."

At Garden of the Gods Visitor Center they pulled into a double-sized spot and went in to pick up a map. After a loop around the entire Park in the RV, they decided on a short hike to get out among the rocks. The path was wide, paved and relatively flat. They were able to walk side by side holding hands the entire loop. They marveled at the colors and shapes and talked about the geology and history of the area. Roger admitted the rocks looked artificial. Every zoo or amusement park he'd been to had similar formations. At any moment he said, he expected a polar bear or a roller coaster to come around the corner. Now he had to concede the fact that those architects did a pretty darn good job at recreating nature.

The next stop up the I-25 corridor was Rocky Mountain National Park. At Lyons, June couldn't resist commenting on the origins of all the tiny mountain towns. Roger said the same story could likely be told about nearly all of them. They start life near rivers as trading posts, then someone builds a grist mill. Silver or gold is discovered, or more likely, rumored to have been discovered nearby and the attendant supporting businesses spring up. If they're lucky, a major interstate goes through. If they're unlucky, the highway goes by instead of through, and no one stops anymore for provisions, the modern versions being gas, food, and lodging. A hot spring is helpful, a ski resort, even better. At some point the surrounding topography limits the growth and its done.

At Highway 7, Roger headed south up the canyon. "There's your river," June said. "There must be a whorehouse around here somewhere."

With each mile of winding road they gained hundreds of feet in elevation. They absorbed the ever-changing scenery without talking. Roger took a sharp curve a little too fast and June grabbed onto the dash and door handle with theatrical exaggeration. The van failed to get up on 2 wheels but there was a distinct squeal of complaint from the tires. Roger slowed down and lowered his window giving the excuse that he wanted to hear the river.

Close to the south entrance for the Park the canyon faded, the views opened up and the scenery became more grandiose and expansive. There was no indication that they were approaching a landmark visited by 3 million tourists a year. A squat brown sign announced "Long's Peak Ranger Station" and Roger slowed to make a lazy left turn. They went up a short winding road which soon became lined on both sides with cars leaning into the ditches, an ominous sign for their parking prospects. Echoing Roger's unspoken concerns, June said, "At least make a lap around the lot, Paint Brush. It's late. Maybe some people are leaving."

Sure enough, a few spots were scattered here and there in the parking lot, but none in pairs to accept the bulk of the RV. Roger found an end slot and backed in, cramming the last 7 feet of its tail into the bushes bordering the lot. During the long leg up from Denver, June had gathered extra clothes, dry foods and loaded a pair of backpacks. To those, she now added cold drinks and water from the fridge. Roger raided the glove box for the Park map from their previous trip. Their goal today was Chasm Lake, a high altitude tarn at the base of Long's famous east face, the Diamond. Reading of the destination had informed them they were woefully late to be starting this hike, not only missing the prime light of early morning Alpenglow, but risking the afternoon storms that promised rain at the least, deadly lightning and hail at the worst.

Undaunted, June and Roger grabbed their packs and headed up the well-worn trail. June had her usual shorts, tank top and hiking boots. Roger took the lead in his lumberjack shirt and worn out dress pants. Ironically enough the polyester made a good back country fabric, unfashionable though it was for the classroom setting. It wicked away any rain from the outside or sweat from the inside. They made a brief stop at the trail marker to enter their names, destination and time into a log book. It was the socially acceptable equivalent of carving their names into any nearby Aspen tree, they decided. As for safety, it was just as likely their carcasses would never be found if they were to leave the trail and perish for their hubris. Multiple warnings were posted about the dangers of high altitude foot travel. One would think the chances of survival were about even what with the lightning, dehydration, hypothermia, and wild animals. That's what made it worthwhile, June argued, otherwise you might as well sit home on the couch and watch it on television. Being in good physical condition, they kept a rapid, yet conversational pace. Despite the altitude, neither of them could shut up for two minutes and the conversation flowed freely.

The map showed a feature that didn't make much sense until they were in it. As it turned out, Goblins Forest couldn't have been more properly named. They were well below tree-line but the expected spruce and pine forest suddenly gave way without warning to a grove of dwarf pines of indeterminate species. They were probably related to the dominant spruce, but the overall effect of their mysteriously stunted growth was magical. Maybe the soil was poor in some way. Even the rocks poking through looked more polished than the typical granite outcroppings. They stopped mid-trail just to listen. The faint gurgle of a distant stream could be heard. The pungent odor of the evergreen forest still dominated, but the air and light were dreamlike. Overall the grove had the singular effect of an underwater scene. Uphill, at the terminus of the Forest, the trail cut sharply to the south and over a sizeable stream. There was a substantial bridge, constructed from a single log, cut lengthwise and laid open like a hotdog bun. The chainsaw marks were visible and provided traction at a 45 degree angle to the length of the sturdy halves. Midway across the stream and overcome with the magic and romance of the situation, Roger stopped and turned to face June, who was following him up the trail. "This is what I've wanted my entire life," Roger said. "I didn't know it, but this is it. I couldn't imagine sharing this with anyone else but you. Let's not tell anyone about this. It'll be our secret. More special than even our wedding vows. I love you."

"Yes." It took no effort for June to strip away her usual cynicism and sarcasm. A part of her knew that at some level she could be ridiculed for her sappy hormonal reaction to the situation and his corny declaration. But a larger part of her really liked this guy. She felt it too, not just in her mind but in her chest and stomach. There was no irony, no need to analyze the situation or define her own place in it. This person was who she really was, a woman in love. Roger's former student, colleague, lover, confidant, and now wife. Whatever future generations might say about her life and work, her lack of accomplishments, her lousy diner, her extra weight, her grey hair, this woman was the sum total of her identity. She hugged Roger closely on the bridge, kissed him firmly and deeply, full on the lips.

"Ah-hem," a hiker from across the bridge cleared his throat. Roger and June broke their embrace with slight embarrassment. On the far side an elderly gentleman was waiting to cross. In one hand he held a gnarled wooden cane covered from handle to tip with medallions of famous hiking destinations. In the other hand he held the wrinkled hand of a woman who could only have been his wife of many decades. She glanced away downstream to a patch of brilliant blue columbines, unable to hide the crimson blush on her cheeks. Roger and June broke their clutch and skipped to the far side to let the elderly couple have the bridge. The couple stepped gingerly onto the planks, the woman went first reaching back to the man's hand for support and him clutching his cane with equal care. Roger and June watched the crossing, half fearing they'd have to rescue the old couple from the rapids downstream. At precisely the point they'd interrupted Roger and June, the old woman paused, turned to her man, and planted on him a kiss no less passionate than if it were their wedding night. Now it was Roger and June's turn to blush. The couple finished with a prolonged gaze into each other's eye, seemingly oblivious to their audience. They continued gingerly to the other side, turned to give Roger and June a wave and went off down the trail.

"Why don't you take the lead," Roger said and June headed up the trail past the bridge. The forest started to thin out, the trees getting smaller until soon they barely reached to waist-high. Dozens of hikers passed them now going in the other direction. Each hiker they encountered incited a riot of discussion. June commented on their equipment or lack thereof. Some folks gave a hello or just a nod, while others wouldn't even make eye contact. A few couples would be talking only to stop when they came within earshot as if their conversation was so private that even a snippet of it shouldn't be heard by other hikers. They'd resume their train of thought only after passing down the trail and out of earshot again. Roger reasoned they were just being polite, like fellow riders on an elevator. There were serious outdoorsmen with full beards and all the gear, wide-brimmed hats down to thick-soled boots and hiking poles. An occasional family would pass wearing nothing but tennis shoes, no water in sight. Apparently they hadn't seen the sign about entering the Park prepared for every emergency.

 The weather remained clear with only a few puffy white clouds in the otherwise deep blue sky. They could see all the way out to the plains and the city of Boulder. To the west their view was blocked by the massive east face of Long's Peak and its attendant neighboring mountains, both over 13,000 feet and challenging destinations in their own right. After a few more switchbacks they came to a fork in the trail and took the southern path leading to Chasm Lake. The opposing crowds thinned out as did the flora. The dwarf trees gave way to low bushes which surrendered in turn to a low mat of tundra. Every few hundred yards they could hear water rushing under the rocks of the trail. A glance up the shoulder of Mt. Lady Washington would reveal an occasional snowfield, the most likely source of the trickle. Those trickles of water gathered in a chain of large ponds at the floor of the canyon and gave perspective to the massive north face of Mt. Meeker. The trail narrowed to a single-file track with a steep drop off to the south. The path remained flat for ½ a mile. They could see the narrow brown stripe in the distance. It curved slightly south and then descended to come level with the uppermost of the ponds. It didn't take much imagination to envision a time lapse film of the unfolding geology. While difficult to comprehend a sheet of ice several miles thick, there was a vestigial glacier at the head of the canyon drooping over a saddle on the horizon. June paused on the narrow track and blocked Roger's way. Inspired by the view she demanded, "Kiss me or you can't get by."

"Hmm. Let me think about it," Roger said.

"Come on, you know I'm a great kisser. It's a small penalty to pay for staring at my rear end for the last two miles."

"That's not the issue." Roger crossed his arms, then put a hand to his chin as if he was deep in thought with a long division math problem. "Noone here is doubting your technique. I'm debating whether or not to risk that beef jerky flavor again."

"I kind of like it. Do we always have to taste like toothpaste before we can swap some spit?"

"That's a moot point."

"No, it's not." Now it was June's turn to carry on the charade. She put both hands on her hips and started tapping her foot. She looked up directly into Roger's eyes and tried not to laugh. "There's nothing to discuss. You can't argue for an opinion. You either like the beef or you don't. Now plant one on me," and she closed her eyes and puckered her lips. Roger side-stepped her with a do-si-do square dancing move and jogged off down the trail. June turned to chase him down but was unable to make up any ground. Roger gained speed where the trail descended after a hundred yards then disappeared around a curve in the trail, blocked by a massive boulder. When June caught up to him, she saw instantly his reason for stopping. Roger stood there with his mouth open, as much in awe of the scene as to catch his breath. An acre of blue columbines was scattered on the side of a gently sloping cliff. Cascades of water were trickling over the ridge from some unseen source. Behind the ridge rose the imposing east face of Long's Peak. Roger took June's hand and they stood there a full 5 minutes catching their breath and marveling at the scene.

"I'll give you that kiss now," Roger said.

"You owe me two for skipping the last toll booth." Roger paid his debt and they turned to continue up the trail around the cascades.

"Hey, wait a minute," Roger said. He turned his back to June. "Reach in my pack for the camera." June gave a pout and said she forgot to pack it. "No problem, get out my phone and I'll snap a photo with that."

"Uh, yea, about that," said June. "I left it in the RV. I wanted you all to myself on this hike."

"What if Emma calls? I want to know how she's doing."

"Use your head, Roger. She's not going to get any better cell reception where she is than you are here. We'll check in after the hike, I promise. Now concentrate on either kissing me or stepping over these rocks."

The trail disappeared into a slope of randomly stacked stones of various sizes, from toaster and microwave on up to mobile home. They picked their way through and over them, each hiker thinking they'd gone the best way. Roger stepped onto a boulder the size of the RV and nearly lost his balance when it teetered a foot to port side before settling. June heard the massive boulder knock and looked over to see the wide-eyed look on Roger's face. He broke out in a nervous laugh. "Whoa. Check it out." Roger took a step to starboard and the massive boulder rocked in the other direction. "Maybe we should hold hands for extra balance the rest of the way."

"Yeah, not a bad idea. Now I see why those hard-core hikers have the poles," June said and joined him on the boulder. They hopped off together and up the remainder of the slope, assisting each other over the more dicey gaps. Over one slot they couldn't see to the bottom between the stones. Roger found a small pebble and dropped it in. They counted to 3 before hearing the sound of it hitting the bottom. They gave each other a look with eyebrows raised.

Another dozen hops and jumps and the slope tapered at the final ridge. Roger skipped up first then turned to pull up June. They were struck by a cold breeze that had previously been blocked by the talus. The unexpected drop in temperature sent them for the shelter of a nearby boulder and into their packs for more layers. Properly clothed against the wind they were able to walk more comfortably down the scree to the edge of the lake and enjoy the view. About two acres in size, Chasm Lake seemed larger than it would have appeared to be from the map. Roger said it seemed so large that the sheer wall of the Diamond was rendered less impressively than he thought it would be. "See those climbers?" June said and pointed to a spot ½ way up the face.

"No. Where?" Roger bent over to sight down her arm like a telescope. "Whoa," Roger said. "Now I get it. I'm gonna sit down." He was feeling a touch of vertigo but it was also a good idea to get out of some of the wind. They rummaged through the packs for the snacks that June had prepared. Roger found a flat boulder to lean against for back support. June sat in front of him and they held each other with hands and arms crossed in front to keep warm. Clouds spilled over the summit of Long's Peak from the west and evaporated as they made their way over the canyon. Though it was only mid-afternoon, the clouds began to thicken and darken and the sun lowered behind the rocky shoulder of the summit. Not wanting to test the double dangers of lightning and hail, June and Roger collected their things and headed to the safety of lower altitude.

"Hard to believe we've got two months and twenty more Parks to visit, huh?" June said. Roger smiled, picking his way over the boulders holding June's hand.

"True, but let's not rush out yet. I've done enough driving for one day. We'll check out the west side of the Park tomorrow. Maybe have some Italian in town tonight. I read about a place that's supposed to have a killer Alfredo."

"Twist my arm, Air Freshener."

Out of the wind and back in the sunshine they managed to work up a sweat again, so peeled off some layers. June remarked that it always seems shorter going back, not just because of the downhill direction. It wasn't long before they were at the bridge, through the Goblins Forest and back at the trailhead. They signed out of the logbook and compared their time to some others who'd been to Chasm Lake. Not bad for a couple of middle-aged bookworms from New Mexico. June fished the RV keys out of her pack and opened the door for Roger. They threw the backpacks onto the bench seat of the dining table and got into the cab, June taking her turn at the wheel. Roger opened the glove box and examined his phone. "See? Emma called," Roger said and clicked on a folder to check for messages. When he found none and was unable to call he instructed June to drive to town where he might be able to get a signal. "Maybe there's a tower somewhere near civilization." A quick check of the map showed the road to the city was also the quickest way over Trail Ridge Road to the west side of the park. As they approached the town of Estes Park, Roger's phone lit up with a call from Emma. He held it out to June as if to prove his point that he should have been carrying it all along. "Dad? Can you hear me?"

"Yea, but we're on some winding roads here and we might lose you," Roger said. Then to June, "Let's pull over so I don't lose Emma." June pulled into the lot of a supermarket, for ease of parking the RV and assuming the reception would be adequate. When Roger gave her a thumbs up she cut the engine, took off her seatbelt and turned to face him on the bench.

"That's better. Sorry I didn't leave a message or text earlier, but I wanted to tell you directly. I'm engaged!" Emma screamed into the phone so loudly that June could hear it as well.

"What?" said Roger. "You've only been there a week and you tell me you're getting married?"

"I met him last year during my student teaching," she said, her voice more in control. Roger looked over to June who just shrugged in response. "I didn't think much of it, like maybe one of those summer romance kind of things, you know? Anyway, he was part of the reason I wanted to come back this year, to see if we'd have the same feelings." Emma went on to explain how they met at the school and shared some teaching duties. With the steady academic schedule and his presence on most of the charitable weekend projects, they spent at least part of every day together. "He's so interesting, you've got to meet him and his dad before the wedding."

"What? Wait, you're going too fast here. Do you realize we're up in Colorado and headed to Canada? And what makes him so interesting? You know I don't like you using that word," Roger said into the phone.

"Good, that means you've got your passports with you, right?" Emma said. June nodded and pointed to the glove box. Roger confirmed it to Emma.

"Does this fella have a name?" June said. Roger nodded and repeated the question.

"Well for starters, have you ever met someone who didn't know their own birth date? His name is Ramon, he's somewhere in his late twenties, he doesn't know exactly, and yes, he's Mexican, from Mazatlan. His dad was a fisherman, but the commercial side of things sort of dried up years ago. Now he takes out tourists for deep sea fishing. Even though he's from the coast, Ramon says he doesn't like the water, so when he was old enough, he moved inland and started work with the school. But get this, he's got blonde hair. Weird, huh?"

Roger had an idea but couldn't bring himself to ask right away. First he had to test something. "Emma, this fella you've never mentioned before, the guy with a first name starting with R, like all my characters, he isn't some sort of practical joke you're playing on us to make us change our plans, is he? A little white lie who happens to be away on business when we get there, but by then it's too late so we just end up spending the summer with you in Mexico?"

"Dad, don't be silly. I'm not like that. You know." She was right. They'd always been frank with each other. It would be unlike her to make up such a story. If she'd wanted them to visit over the summer, she would have said so, then arranged to meet them somewhere on the coast. Emma had her father's pragmatism in full measure. Still, he tried to trip her up by asking a detail to see if she paused.

"What color are his eyes?" said Roger.

"Well, it's funny you should ask," Emma said. Roger could tell from her tone she wasn't just stalling to think up a fib. "That's another thing that's so inter…er, unique about him. He's got a blue one and a brown one."

Roger dropped the phone to his lap and looked to June with his mouth open. His brain quickly added up the details. Ramon was from Mazatlan, in his late twenties, with a fisherman for a dad, blonde hair and odd eye coloration. Emma knew about RJ in broad strokes, but couldn't have been aware of that physical feature. Roger kept a few pictures around the house when Emma was an infant, but since most were taken by Roger and included Sharon, he'd long ago stored them away. That particular detail had never come up, even during years of bedtime stories and father-daughter talks. There was no way she could have known.

"Dad? Dad? Are you still there?" Emma's faint voice shouted from the overturned phone. Roger picked it up, put it to his ear and collected his thoughts.

"Yes, Emma. I'm here. We're on our way. We've got a lot to talk about before the ceremony. I trust this won't be at some bingo hall with caterers." Emma confirmed his assumption. This wedding was to be a native village ceremony with regional quirks and rituals. No, she wouldn't be registered for gifts at the local department stores. Most likely it would involve donations of livestock, not kitchen cutlery. "I'll hang up now and call you when we get closer to the border. You can let me know what the father of the bride is supposed to do." Roger closed the phone and turned to June. "We'll have to postpone the Anniversary Trip, we're heading to Durango."

"What? Is Emma okay? Why Durango? Are we flying?"

"Not that Durango. The one in Mexico," Roger said. He opened the atlas to the mileage page and traced his finger down I-25 to El Paso, then on into Mexico, to Durango and over to Mazatlan. "We've got about 1,500 miles to go. I'll tell you everything on the way." June put her seatbelt back on, turned the key, put the RV in gear and pulled out of the parking lot. They drove back down Highway 7 in silence. June had no idea the conflicting thoughts and emotions crashing around in Roger's brain. He was staring straight out the windshield but not seeing the road. His rational brain knew better than to think RJ could still be alive. At the same instant his optimism held out hope against all odds that he could see his long lost son in less than two days. Either way, if his daughter found him worthy to marry, what did it matter? He must be a special man and that fact alone was worth postponing their trip to meet him.

June was sure Roger would work through whatever was on his mind and share it when the time was right. This much she had learned from their years together, even from the time before they were married. His process might be painstakingly slow at times, but the results were worth the wait. Finally he spoke and she was able to exhale. "Speaking of flying, how come the windows on airplanes never line up with the seats?" Roger said. "One seat, one window. How complicated is that?"

"And how come they're the size of a dessert plate?" June said. "The pilot gets a picture window sturdy enough to face a 500-mile per hour wind. We poor suckers in the back get neck pain and half a view of the wing." June reached one hand across the bench seat and wiggled her fingers in the air. Roger took her hand and smiled back at her.